"You planned to steal my son!"

Before Mack could respond, Claire continued. "Don't deny that the purpose of your lawyer's visit was to get me to agree to have Danny's name changed to McMollere. The man rattled on and on about the wonderful heritage Danny has here at Sugarland, about how as Carter's son, it's rightfully his. All I have to do is sign on the dotted line and presto! Danny's a McMollere and everything's just peachy keen."

Mack was shaking his head long before she finished. But she paid no attention to him.

"I'll be out of here just as soon as possible. And I'll be taking my son with me. My son, Daniel *Woodson*."

Mack took a deep breath, obviously coming to a decision. "The problem with Danny's name was going to resolve itself," he said. "At least, that's what I was hoping."

"How?"

"I was thinking that you'd change Danny's name to McMollere—if that was your name, too."

Claire's heart was suddenly in her throat.

"I'm talking...*marriage*, Claire."

ABOUT THE AUTHOR

RITA Award winner Karen Young needs no introduction to Superromance readers. This talented author has published eleven books for the line. *Sugar Baby* is set in Louisiana, where, until very recently, Karen and her husband lived. The couple has now moved to Jackson, Mississippi, which means Karen—a native Mississippian—has come home. An added bonus is that they're close to their daughter and her family, including three grandchildren.

Be sure to watch for upcoming titles by Karen Young. This Christmas she appears in Harlequin's Christmas anthology (*Merry Christmas, Baby!*) with a short story entitled "It Takes a Miracle." Then, early in 1998, her first mainstream novel will be published under the MIRA imprint.

Books by Karen Young

HARLEQUIN SUPERROMANCE

Don't miss any of our special offers. Write to us at the following address for information on our newest releases.

Harlequin Reader Service
U.S.: 3010 Walden Ave., P.O. Box 1325, Buffalo, NY 14269
Canadian: P.O. Box 609, Fort Erie, Ont. L2A 5X3

Karen Young

SUGAR BABY

Harlequin Books

TORONTO • NEW YORK • LONDON
AMSTERDAM • PARIS • SYDNEY • HAMBURG
STOCKHOLM • ATHENS • TOKYO • MILAN
MADRID • WARSAW • BUDAPEST • AUCKLAND

To the Ladies of the Club—
the Thibodaux Literary Guild.

Thanks for the memories.

ISBN 0-373-70712-6

SUGAR BABY

Copyright © 1996 by Karen Stone.

SUGAR BABY

CHAPTER ONE

"POLICE...FREEZE! FREEZE!"

Rat-a-tat-a-tat-a-tat-a-tat-a-tat!

"Officer down! We need backup!"

Rat-a-tat-a-tat-a-tat-a-tat-a-tat!

With her face buried in a hand towel, Claire Woodson froze. Oh, great! Just what she needed. Danny was channel surfing with the remote again. Thanks to the hotel's free premium channels, she could just imagine what he was watching. Muttering a word she never got to say out loud, she balled up the towel and tossed it in the sink, then with blood in her eye, she marched out of the bathroom.

Her five-year-old son sat cross-legged in front of the TV, his nose no more than a foot from the screen. "Oh, boy, shoot 'im, shoot 'im."

"Danny! What are you watching?"

His eyes were glued to a scene in which a man lay covered in blood, his body in a grotesque sprawl. "This guy just killed a policeman, Mommy. Bullets were everywhere! It was neat!"

Claire marched over and took the remote. "It isn't neat to kill policemen, Danny."

"But he was really bad!"

"That was make-believe. In real life, policemen are here to help us." She began flicking through the channels. "You know you're not supposed to watch adult

channels. Look, here's something good.'' She stopped
at a cartoon.

Danny crossed his small arms and poked out his bottom lip. ''I don't wanna watch dumb ol' cartoons. Why
won't you let me see anything *I* like? Ryan gets to watch
whatever he wants on TV.''

''Too bad. I don't happen to agree with Ryan's parents.''

''I wanna go home! I don't like it here.'' Scrambling
up from the floor, he stomped across the room to the
French doors.

Join the club.

With a sigh, she let him go out. Their room had a
balcony overlooking a courtyard. He could hardly get
into mischief from the third floor.

She sank onto the bed and willed away the start of a
headache. She was here in LaRue and she would make
the best of it. Hadn't she been making the best of things
for about six years? This situation wouldn't be any different.

Rubbing her temple, she gazed around the room. At
any other time, she might have enjoyed the place John
McMollere had recommended.

Complete with slowly revolving ceiling fans and pa-
trons in rumpled suits and Panama hats, the White Hotel was like something out of a Hemingway novel. Built
in the days of Louisiana's rice and sugarcane barons, it
was garishly grandiose. But just as those were bygone
days, the hotel was past its heyday.

Not that any of this mattered. Claire was in no mood
to appreciate decor. Her thoughts were on the upcoming meeting with her son's grandparents, the Mc-
Molleres. Because of their power and arrogance, they'd

won this round, but she was determined they weren't going to win the war.

They were not going to take Danny away from her.

She glanced at her watch. Three hours before she and Danny had to meet them. Just the thought sent up a flock of butterflies. She touched her stomach, and her troubled gaze strayed to the balcony and Danny. He was usually a happy, good-natured boy, but lately he was picking up on her anxiety. Somehow she was going to have to keep from communicating her distress to him. Closing her eyes, she vowed to do better at keeping her fears to herself.

The telephone rang.

She stared at it, knowing the caller had to be one of the enemy. If not the lawyer, then old Angus McMollere, himself. If not him, then John McMollere, the older son—the one everybody called Mack. He was the one she most hated dealing with. Not that she'd seen him during the negotiations for this visit. They'd communicated only by telephone. Knowing that she was being silly—even childish and cowardly—she allowed the telephone to ring four times before she picked up the receiver. "Hello?"

"Claire Woodson?"

The voice was dark and deep and confident. Not cold, but not friendly either. She recognized it instantly and sighed. John McMollere. Strangely enough, a picture of him flashed vividly in her mind even though she'd only seen him once. Six years ago in Houston on a night that had changed her life forever.

"Claire?" he repeated.

"This is she."

"John McMollere here."

"Yes."

"I expected to hear from you earlier."

"The appointment is for seven. Has that changed?"

"No. Nothing's changed. But a woman and a child traveling alone, I thought—"

"Danny and I are used to traveling alone, Mr. Mc-Mollere."

"Mack."

She murmured something. She wasn't ready for a chummy relationship with any of them.

He waited a beat. "Satisfied with our hotel?"

"It's . . . interesting."

"How's Danny?"

Her gaze went to Danny who was leaning over the balcony railing obviously interested in something going on below. "He's fine. Bored with no one to play with, but he'll be okay."

"He'll like it here at Sugarland. No little kids, of course, but it's a big place. He can explore to his heart's delight. His grandparents can't wait to see him."

Two days. Only two days and we can go home.

She clutched the receiver. "I need directions to get there."

"No need. I'll pick you up."

"*No!* I mean . . . ah, that's not necessary. I'm—"

"I know it's not necessary, Claire," he said patiently. "But you've been on the road most of the day. It's another twenty miles out here with twists and turns you might miss."

"I can follow directions."

"I know this whole thing is stressful for you. It's not exactly easy for us on this end, either."

"What does that have to do with whether or not I drive myself to Sugarland?" she asked. Even to herself she sounded negative and testy. She heard him draw in a deep breath.

"I think we should all try to make this visit a happy one, Claire. For Danny's sake."

She gripped the receiver even tighter. "Where was all this concern for Danny when you people first learned of his existence, Mr. McMollere?" she asked. "Forgive me for being blunt, but I'm here only because a judge ordered it. And we both know he ordered it because of the prestige of the McMolleres. You've got what you wanted—a weekend to meet my son. And contrary to what you might think, I will do everything I can to see that nothing upsets Danny. As his parent—his *only* parent—how could I do otherwise?" Touching her head, she wished for a pill to take away the headache and the weekend. "Maybe that's the one thing you, your parents and I can agree on," she ended in a weary tone.

"Then there's no problem."

"Fine." The man sounded as though he agreed with everything she'd said, which was impossible. "Good. So how about those directions?"

"Are you always this stubborn?"

"The directions, *please.*"

There was a moment when she thought he'd argue, but he made a sound—surely not a chuckle?—then began to rattle off a string of instructions which would get her to Sugarland.

Birthplace of Danny's father.

"Thank you." she said stiffly.

"See you at seven."

Quietly she replaced the receiver. Above her, the ceiling fan sliced slowly through the humid air. After a minute, she looked up and sighed.

Are you satisfied, Carter?

SHE'D MET Carter McMollere when she was a student at
Louisiana State University after her mother died. It was
her second attempt to obtain her degree. An only child
of divorced parents, she never knew her father except
through her mother's bitter memories. Shy, imaginative
and intelligent, she had studied liberal arts at LSU that
first time around, but left before earning her degree to
care for her mother who'd become ill. When her mother
died, Claire reenrolled and like a bird out of a cage, she
wanted to try everything she'd missed.

She'd missed love. Loving. Sharing the singular joy of
passion with a special man. She'd fallen eagerly into
Carter's hands. He'd made her feel special for the first
time in her life. When she was with him, the long years
devoted to caring for her mother seemed part of another lifetime, one she was only too happy to forget.
Carter had painted a glowing picture of their future together, and she had happily pictured a life as his wife.
He'd been vague about his background. She never knew
Sugarland by name. She'd learned later it was one of the
few sizable sugarcane operations remaining in southern
Louisiana. In her naiveté, Claire had believed every
promise Carter made. She'd been heartbroken to learn
that he was a married man, and had broken off with him
that same night.

It was even worse when she discovered that she was
pregnant. Believing Carter had a right to know, she'd
phoned to tell him. He'd immediately urged her to get an
abortion. Painful as it had been to discover that her
lover had a wife, to hear him coolly suggest that she destroy their baby was devastating. Everything in her rejected the idea. She had wept an ocean of tears before
finally deciding that Carter wasn't worth such heartfelt
despair. *He* might casually dismiss the tiny life growing

inside her, but *she* never could. From that moment, the baby was all that mattered. *Her* baby.

The bond that was forged then with her unborn son had sustained her through all the misery and fear of the months that followed. She'd lost her job as a teacher in a small parochial school when her condition became obvious. She'd been forced to leave her friends and relocate to Houston. Her pregnancy had been a difficult one and she'd gone through it alone. But good can come from bad things and Daniel was a constant source of joy to her. And now, with Carter dead, the McMolleres wanted their only grandson.

They weren't going to take her son away from her.

"Mommy, Mommy! Come quick." Danny dashed in from the balcony and grabbed her hand. He began tugging her toward the French doors. "That policeman just killed somebody! Come and see!"

"Danny, don't be ridiculous!" With only a glance at him, she pulled away and headed for her luggage. That's what happened when kids were allowed to watch unlimited violence on TV. Their imaginations went wild.

"Mommy, please, this is not radickalous." He stood before her looking distressed. "Those men were fighting! Honest, they were."

"What men?" She bent to unzip her cosmetics bag.

"Those men outside," Danny repeated impatiently. "The policeman had a gun. He shot somebody. I saw it." He was nodding his head furiously, his eyes round as marbles. "I did, Mommy."

"Policemen don't shoot people in a hotel courtyard, Danny." She found shampoo and body gel and tossed them on the bed. Maybe a cool shower would banish her headache and refresh her. Even though she was meeting the McMolleres under duress, she didn't want to look frazzled.

Danny caught her hand and tugged on it. "Mommy, please come and look. That man fell on the ground, honest. I bet he's hurt really bad. I bet he's *bleeding!*"

"Not now, Danny. Please." She drew her hand away, thinking her first task when she got home would be a phone call to Ryan's parents. Somehow, they would have to keep the children away from the violent TV programs.

"You gotta look, Mommy. What if he comes up here and shoots us, too?"

She chuckled in spite of herself. "Come on, honey. Nobody's going to shoot anybody."

"But he did!" Danny insisted in exasperation.

She ruffled his dark hair. "And you saw it?"

He nodded. "Uh-huh."

"Danny, we're on the third floor."

"But I could see 'em good from where I was standin'. The one who got shot had a T-shirt like mine—you know—my Olympics T-shirt. And he had a ponytail."

"A ponytail?" Claire repeated.

"Yes, like Jason," Danny replied, referring to the college student who serviced the pool at their condo.

Claire hesitated. Danny seemed so certain. "And where were these people?"

"Way over by the bushes." He pointed as if she could see from inside the room. "I had to lean real far out."

She frowned at him. "Not on the balcony railing, I hope."

"It's okay, Mommy," he said confidently. "It has these places you can put your feet. Don't worry, I was careful."

Claire marched over to the balcony to see for herself. Her heart dropped. The ornate wrought-iron did indeed have places a small foot could wedge into. Standing there, Danny was raised beyond a safe level. He could have plunged three floors!

She turned and pulled him into her arms. "Danny, you mustn't ever do such a thing again! The railing is old. It isn't meant to be climbed on. What if you'd fallen?"

He looked crestfallen. "I wasn't gonna fall, Mommy," he muttered. "I was just lookin' at those men. They were actin' really bad, just like on TV. They were hollerin' and all!"

She shook her head helplessly. Obviously she was not going to convince Danny that he'd been imagining things. "You think you saw a policeman shoot somebody?"

He nodded with new life. "I did! Honest!" He caught her hand again and began tugging her along. "Right over there on the path."

Claire let him lead her to the balcony. She could see a large rubber plant flourishing in the lee between the main wing of the hotel and the covered walkway leading to the pool. It was almost directly beneath their room. To one side was a space obviously designated for housekeeping. The lush vegetation probably obscured the flagstone pathway from ground level, but the view was good from this spot three floors above.

There was nothing there.

"I don't see anything, honey."

Beside her, Danny put his foot into the wrought-iron toeholds, ready to climb. "Danny!" She grabbed him and set him firmly back on the floor. "What did I just say?"

"I was gonna show you where."

"There's nothing there, Danny. Even if the men were standing where you say they were, I don't think a gunshot would go unnoticed."

"Maybe nobody heard it but me."

She put a hand on his shoulder. "How could that be, honey? Guns make a big noise when they're fired."

He stared at his feet. "You think I made it up."

"Well..." With a finger beneath his chin, she tilted his small face up.

"I betcha Ryan would believe me if I told him."

She sighed. "I believe you think you saw something." She paused a minute. "What made you say he was a policeman? Was he in uniform?"

"No, but I saw a badge. On his belt. We had some policemen visit us at school and they said not all cops have a uniform, but all cops have a badge."

To humor him, she asked, "Where did the gun come from if he wasn't in uniform?"

His face screwed up in thought. "I don't know. I just saw it when he held it in his hand."

"What did the other man do?"

"He just fell over."

"And then what?"

"I don't know. That's when I ran inside to tell you."

She studied him intently for a minute. "Okay, champ. Here's what we'll do. I'm going to call the desk and ask about this. If something like that actually happened, they would know about it. Okay?"

"Okay, Mommy." He drew a big breath and went over to the bedside table, planting himself firmly by the phone. Claire sighed again. No getting around it, she was going to have to call.

Two minutes later she hung up feeling chastened. Her questions had been greeted with patient good humor by the desk clerk. A shooting? At the White Hotel? Ha-ha. By LaRue's finest? No, ma'am, hardly. Somebody was surely having a joke at her expense, she was told. This was just lovely, she decided, kicking off her shoes. For the rest of her stay at the precious White, she would be known as that paranoid woman in three-twelve. Grumbling, she headed into the bathroom. That shower seemed more appealing with each passing minute.

"WHAT CAN WE DO NOW, Mommy?" Danny asked the instant she reappeared. She was somewhat refreshed, but even a cool shower didn't wash away the Louisiana humidity. Nor did it do much for her headache.

"We can both get dressed, Danny," she told him, glancing at the clock. "We've got to be ready to leave in a little while."

"If I hurry, can we go down to the place where I saw the guy fall and see if there's blood?"

She rolled her eyes. "No, absolutely not."

"Aw, Mommy..."

"Tell you what," she said. "We have about two hours before it's time to meet those people for our visit. I saw a Star-Mart as we drove into town. Want to pop in and check out their toy department?" It was blatant bribery, but she would resume being a principled parent later.

LaRue was a small town, but Star-Mart looked as large as any in Houston. Claire cruised the parking lot twice before settling for a space the length of a football field from the entrance. "The exercise is good for me," she muttered, grabbing Danny's suspenders before he could dash too far ahead of her. For a second, her irritation faded. With his red suspenders, he looked so cute in khaki shorts and navy polo shirt.

"I need a Power Rangers gun, Mommy!"

"So you can shoot somebody? Not today, buddy-boy."

"Awww."

At the entrance, they followed behind a young mother with an infant and a little boy who looked about Danny's age. Danny and the boy sized each other up solemnly. Over their heads, both Claire and the mother smiled.

Inside, Danny scoped out the store with practiced skill, then headed like a homing pigeon for the toys. Behind her, the young mother fastened her infant into the shopping cart while her son darted away in the same direction as Danny. His mother gave an exasperated sound, then laughed as she and Claire again made eye contact.

"We're headed for toys," Claire said with a shrug.

"It looks like we are, too," the woman said, still smiling.

The store was busy. Although school wasn't scheduled to begin for almost a month, supplies were already fully stocked and kids in LaRue were shopping with the same enthusiasm as those in Houston.

As usual when Danny was faced with an excess of choices, he couldn't make a decision. He picked up and rejected no less than a dozen items when Claire finally lost patience. With her head throbbing, she glanced at her watch.

"We have to get on the road if we're going to be on time for our visit to Sugarland. Five minutes," she told him, ignoring his injured expression. "And then we're out of here. I mean it, Danny."

The other boy ran up to Danny. "There's some neat stuff on the next aisle. I found this!" He held up a weapon that might very well be used by real power rangers in the next century. Danny sent her a pleading look and she nodded. "Go take a look, but don't wander beyond the next aisle. I'm going to pick out an electronic game. They're on sale."

"Okay!"

The games were good for a five-year-old confined in a car for a long, boring trip. Unfortunately, it appeared that every other parent in LaRue had had the same idea. The sale table was a jumble of plastic cases. She started looking, thumbing through the leftovers, aware only vaguely of the kids and parents sifting through the merchandise along with her. A couple of minutes later, the young mother appeared with disposable diapers and a few other articles in her cart.

"Have you seen Jeremy?" she asked anxiously.

"Your little boy?" Claire glanced at the intersection and a display of no less than a hundred Mickey Mouse lunch boxes. "He was just here with Danny." She walked a few steps and looked into the next aisle. Both boys were gone.

A child screamed suddenly. Her heart plunged to her feet at the sound.

Danny!

And like any mother, her first thought was for her child. For a second, she was frozen as the piercing, shrill shrieks ricocheted through the huge store.

It was Danny!

All the blood drained from her body, leaving her sucked empty of everything except a desperate need to find him. Galvanized by fear, Claire darted frantically into the next aisle. Then the next, pulled along by the sound of his shrieks as surely as if she were connected to him by electric wire.

And then his screams ceased and there was only the murmurings of the crowd, the isolated whimpering of a baby. But no Danny.

He wasn't anywhere she looked. Suddenly she was in Shoes. People were murmuring, looking concerned, checking for their own young ones. Still no sign of Danny. Somewhere nearby, she heard the young mother calling for Jeremy.

"Danny!" she cried desperately. "Where are you?"

Utterly panicked now, she dashed across the main traffic lane into Electronics and there he was.

"Mommy!" He ran up to her and threw his arms around her, holding on with all his might. She dropped her purse and swept him up. He was trembling. For a minute, she wasn't sure she could stay upright.

Danny leaned back, looking her in the eye. "It was the bad policeman, Mommy! He tried to get me to go with him, but I wouldn't."

"Oh, Danny..." She closed her eyes, swallowing the fear that was lodged in her throat.

"I screamed. Just like you tol' me if a stranger wants to do bad stuff."

"Yes, yes..." She realized she was rocking back and forth, but his small sturdy body just felt so good right now.

"Is everything all right here, ma'am?" A man touched her elbow and she nearly jumped out of her skin.

"Oh! What? I—I'm not sure." She drew a deep breath. "Someone just approached my son."

"It was the bad policeman," Danny said eagerly. Now that the danger was past, he was wiggling to get down.

"Policeman?" the man repeated.

What should she do? Could Danny really have witnessed something in the hotel courtyard? Something that was bad enough to force the "policeman" to follow them here.

Oh, God.

"Ma'am? Nobody noticed a policeman." He wore the familiar Star-Mart name tag and was handing Claire's purse to her. Then he looked at Danny. "Can you describe him, son?"

Danny took a breath. "He was *big!* He was pulling me real hard, tryin' to make me go with him. He had a gun!"

The employee managed to hide the quirk of his mouth. "A gun, you say?"

"Uh-huh. I mean, yes, sir."

"A gun right here in the store?"

"Are you sure, Danny?" Claire gave him a stern look.

"Not here. I mean he had a gun at the hotel, not here."

Claire caught his hand and squeezed it meaningfully. "I'm sorry about this, Mr.... Taylor?" she said, reading the man's name tag.

"Yes, ma'am. I'm the assistant manager."

Assistant manager. She tried to think. Oh, God, she was so scared. "Um, yes. Mr. Taylor, my son says somebody—a man—tried to approach him, but apparently he's gone now."

"He can't have gone far," Taylor said firmly. "I'll just call security and—"

"No."

"Pardon me?"

She managed a weak smile. "We've caused enough commotion this afternoon, Mr. Taylor. I'm not sure what happened, but . . ." She shrugged. "I just realized that we're late for an appointment. Come on, Danny."

"But Mommy—"

"Come *on,* Danny."

"Are you sure, ma'am?" Taylor trailed after her. "If something actually did happen, we really should let the police—"

"No, no. It's okay. It's fine."

They were hurrying past the checkouts when somebody called Danny's name.

"Hey, Jeremy," Danny said, waving at his new friend. He tugged at Claire's hand. "It's Jeremy, Mommy. Now you'll believe me, 'cause he was there and he saw that man try to get me!"

She gave Jeremy's mother a harassed look. "Did Jeremy see what happened?"

The young woman nodded. "He said a man tried to take your little boy out of the store." She pulled Jeremy a little closer. "I can't believe something like that happened in full view of dozens of people. What's going on?"

"I don't know." Biting her lip, Claire studied the sidewalks and parking area. She shivered, feeling unseen eyes.

"Have you called the police?" the woman asked.

"No. I—"

"Surely you're going to report what happened?"

Should she? Or should she take Danny and go while she could? "I'm not sure," she said.

The woman lifted the infant from the cart carrier. "Look, my husband is an auxiliary policeman. I can call him and—"

And what if he's a friend of the "bad policeman?" The crazy thought darted through Claire's mind. Crazy or not, she could not take the chance. "Thanks," she said, summoning a smile, "but we're late for an appointment, as it is. I'll take care of it later."

"Well, if you're sure." Nudging her son, the young mother hoisted the baby onto her shoulder and stepped off the curb, heading for her car.

"Where's our 'pointment, Mommy?" Danny asked, squinting up at her in the sun.

"At the McMolleres, honey."

"Is it time?"

"Not quite."

Claire gazed uneasily at the cars and people milling around in the parking lot. What next? She couldn't go back to the hotel. Not yet. Not until she knew for certain that he wouldn't be waiting for them. Whoever he was.

What was she going to do?

"What's wrong, Mommy? Did you forget where we parked?"

Her gaze went to the car parked at the most distant edge of the lot. It was nearing dinnertime and some of the crowd was clearing out. Walking to her vehicle was a chance she didn't want to take. What if he was waiting nearby? He knew her car, but she didn't know his.

She looked around, terror welling up inside her. Her eyes fell on a pair of pay phones just outside the store entrance. She walked over and deposited a coin.

"Whatcha' doin', Mommy? Who you callin'?"

"Your uncle Mack, sweetheart."

Danny's eyes got big. "Really?"

"Yes. He wanted to drive us to Sugarland. Now's his chance to do just that."

CHAPTER TWO

EVEN BEFORE Mack pulled into Star-Mart's crowded parking lot, he was scanning the store entrance for a glimpse of Claire Woodson, but there was no tall redhead with a little boy anywhere he looked. He followed behind a slow-moving Suburban, his thumbs drumming with impatience on the wheel, his blue eyes sharp beneath the brim of his Stetson. Where was she?

He'd hung up after her S.O.S. totally baffled him. Why had she changed her mind? Why did she now want him to pick her up, when not an hour before she'd acted as though riding with him was second only to a touch of ptomaine? He'd been left with the definite feeling he wouldn't hear from her again until she arrived at Sugarland with Danny. Had he only imagined a hint of panic in her voice?

Pulling the Jeep Cherokee to a stop at the front door, he scrutinized every departing customer, but still no Claire. Hell, he might not even recognize her. It had been five . . . no, more like six years since he'd seen her and then it had been for only a few minutes. But as much as he'd resisted it all these years, the picture he had of her was pretty clear in his mind. And God knows, he had resisted it.

A small boy darted through the automatic doors and behind him was a woman in a long denim dress. Mack knew her instantly. Six years, and not much had changed, he thought, feeling a little kick in his gut. She was a tad slimmer. And maybe slightly taller than he recalled. Her hairstyle was different, too. Pulled back tight like that, she must be trying to look like a librarian, he decided. But its rich auburn color was exactly as he remembered, as was the disconcertingly candid look of her wide gray eyes as she stared right at him.

There was no warmth in that look.

She hurriedly opened the back door of the Jeep Cherokee before he could get out and hustled the boy inside. Mack beat her to the passenger side only because his legs were six inches longer than hers. Hers, however, were extremely interesting from what he could see when she stepped to get into his Jeep. They were long and shapely. God, yes, he remembered Claire Woodson.

He also remembered what she'd done. She'd wrecked his brother's marriage. She was heartless and selfish. She had spent the last two years throwing up every obstacle possible to keep Carter's son from knowing his grandparents.

Beautiful she might be, but he wasn't going to be taken in the way Carter was.

He waited for her to tuck the tail of her dress inside, then closed the door and walked around to the driver's side. He drove away from the entrance before glancing over at her. "I wasn't sure you'd recognize me."

She wasn't looking at him; instead, she seemed to be studying the people in the parking lot as he drove through. "I recognized you."

Her interest in the pedestrians puzzled him. "You find something especially interesting about the folks shopping at Star-Mart?"

"What?" She spared him a glance. "Oh, no, not really."

"You're looking for someone in particular?"

"Someone, yes," she murmured, her eyes busy again.

She was acting nothing like he'd expected. Where was the hostility that was so palpable in every telephone encounter they'd had since he had made that initial call over a year ago? Her eyes were darting everywhere. She seemed distracted, even fearful. She was pale. But that might be natural in a redhead.

"What's this all about, Claire?"

"It's going to sound like something out of a movie when I tell you..." She turned to see that Danny was safely belted in before settling back herself. She took a deep breath. "I'm afraid that Danny and I may have stumbled into a nightmare."

"If this is about the weekend with my parents, you're overreacting, Claire. They're going to do everything they know to make you and Danny feel welcome. They don't want to alienate you, they just want to get to know Danny. And you."

She was shaking her head as he finished, rubbing her temples. "It's not that. At least, right now it's not that." She glanced over her shoulder once more. Danny was scrutinizing the town of LaRue with the intensity of any child in a new place. "It's something a lot worse. Danny thinks he witnessed—" She shook her head. "This is going to sound so crazy!"

"Just say it and let me decide what's crazy."

"He was on the balcony of the hotel while I was talking to you on the phone and he claims he saw a man shoot somebody."

He stared at her. "You're kidding."

She dropped her head against the back of the seat wearily. "Don't I wish."

"He saw a man get shot?"

"He says he did."

"Kids say things." He looked in the back seat where Danny sat with his nose practically pressed against the side window. "He's an only child. They say lonely kids have big imaginations."

She was again rubbing her temple. "Being an 'only' doesn't necessarily make him a 'lonely only.' And he does have a vivid imagination, but this time I think he actually witnessed what he says he did."

Mack snorted. "A murder at the White Hotel?"

"Yes."

"You called security, I assume."

"I called the front desk after Danny kept insisting that he wasn't making up the story."

"And they said?"

"Pretty much what you just said, 'Murder at the White Hotel? No way, lady.'"

"Nobody believes me," Danny piped up from the back seat.

"I do now, honey," Claire said, reaching back and giving his knee a pat. She turned, looking at Mack. "We called you because someone tried to grab him in the store a few minutes ago. We were afraid to get back in the car in case the man was watching us."

Mack stood on the brakes, swearing, and stopped at the curb with a jerk. He turned in his seat, one arm draped over the wheel. "You're telling me somebody actually tried to snatch Danny in front of all the customers?"

"That's right."

"So where is this guy? What happened to him?"

"No one knows. He just disappeared."

"If he was ever there."

"Danny says he was there. He screamed. Everybody in the whole place heard him and—"

"And nobody in the place saw this mean ol' molester?" Mack said sarcastically.

Claire breathed in deeply. "That's right, Mr. Mc-Mollere."

"Jeremy saw him," Danny said, ever helpful.

"Jeremy." Mack met the boy's eyes in the mirror.

"My new friend."

"You've already made a friend in LaRue?"

"Uh-huh. At Star-Mart."

"And he saw the bad guy, too?"

"He sure did!"

"Where were you two when this happened?"

"We were in the Nintendo stuff."

Mack glanced at Claire. "Without your mom?"

Danny seemed to sense sticky territory ahead. "Jeremy said it was okay," he said cautiously. "Our moms were just a coupla aisles over."

"Are you quite finished?" Claire demanded, giving Mack an icy look.

He was shaking his head. "Why didn't you just call the cops?"

"Danny says the killer *is* a cop."

Mack glanced at Danny before bearing down on Claire again. "How could the killer be a cop?" He bumped his hand against his forehead. "How could there even be a killer? The hotel would surely have found a body." He paused to add, "They did actually take a look, didn't they?"

"I assume so," Claire said. "The desk clerk certainly stated in no uncertain terms that there hadn't been a murder on the premises. Then, before we left, we saw security guards milling around the housekeeping area."

"Is that where the incident happened?" Mack asked Danny.

"Yes, sir."

Mack forced himself to ease up. "Are you sure about this, Dan?"

"Yes, sir." The kid met his gaze with the same candid quality his mother employed. For the first time, Mack allowed himself to study Carter's son. There wasn't much resemblance that he could see. Carter's face had been fuller, his mouth smaller. Carter's hair had been sort of chestnut. Danny's face was narrow. And he had black hair, like Mack's own. And his mouth...it was like his mother's—full and made for smiling. Although neither of them had favored him with a smile since getting into the Jeep.

No surprise there. He hadn't exactly been the doting uncle to Carter's son, nor had he been particularly warm to the boy's mother. Carter's former lover.

"So, tell me about the guy who approached you in the store. What did he look like?"

"He was tall!" Danny cried, eager to cooperate.

"He says that every time he's asked to describe him," Claire said.

"He was real mean!"

"That, too," she said dryly.

"He has something funny on his hand."

Claire's and Mack's eyes met. "Like what, a tattoo?" Mack asked.

"No..." He screwed up his face, thinking hard. "You know...like a..."

"Like a scar?" Claire suggested.

"Yeah." He nodded vigorously.

"You never mentioned that before, Danny," she said.

"I just 'membered it. I saw it when he touched me in the store."

"Can you tell us anything about how the scar looked?"

Danny looked at his mother. "I don't know, it was like when you hurt yourself and it gets all better."

"It's okay, son," Claire said, giving him a smile. "You're a good detective, isn't he, Uncle Mack?"

"You bet. Just one more thing, Danny. Where on his hand was it?"

"Here." He stuck out his fist, palm down.

"What did he say when he came up to you?"

"He tried to talk me into coming with him. He said we'd go get a treat at McDonald's, but my mommy always says don't go anywhere with strangers, so when he started sorta making me walk beside him, that's when I started yellin' my head off." He settled back. "It worked, too."

Mack smiled. "You did the right thing, hotshot."

"Ryan's dad calls him hotshot," Danny said.

"Is that right?"

"Uh-huh. Do you have any kids?"

"One," he said, shooting a quick look in Claire's direction.

"Is it a boy or a girl?"

"A girl."

"Oh."

He saw more questions in the boy's eyes and was relieved when Claire spoke.

"Now you know why we didn't feel safe returning to the hotel." At his nod, she touched her hair, smoothing a few wisps that had worked free. "What do you suggest now? Should we drive back to Houston tonight or wait until tomorrow? I thought perhaps you could accompany us to the hotel, help us get our things into my car and then follow us onto the interstate for a few miles, perhaps all the way to Beaumont."

"And then what?"

"Well, we'd be able to tell if we were being followed on the highway, don't you think?"

"Maybe. And if you were, what would you do?"

"Well, I've got a cellular phone."

"And you'll whip it out and call 911 to come and rescue you. And while you're waiting, the bad guy is . . . where? Doing what?"

She shrugged. "So what do you suggest?"

With a sigh, he rubbed the side of his neck. "This is a hell of a mess."

"It wasn't my idea to come here at all, Mr. McMollere," she said coldly. "And I certainly hadn't planned on my son's witnessing a murder."

"*If* that's true," he said, "then you've got exactly one option, the way I see it."

"I can hardly wait to hear it." She looked out her side.

"You can't go back to Houston tonight or tomorrow. If things are as you say, this guy knows you, knows Danny, knows your car. If he's in law enforcement, he has access to records. Finding you in Houston will be a piece of cake." Glancing at Danny who was once again taking in the sights from the back passenger window, he lowered his voice. "If this actually happened, you're both in jeopardy, you and Danny. You won't be safe until this whole thing is cleared up."

"Gosh, I feel a hundred percent better."

He blew out an impatient breath. "Don't you see what I'm getting at?"

She turned to look at him. "I see that you're trying to scare the daylights out of me. Why? Do you get a kick out of scaring single moms and five-year-olds?"

"I'm sorry." He took off his hat and rubbed a hand over his hair. Glancing at Claire, he saw that she'd put a hand on her throat. God, she was a beautiful woman, he thought, watching the beat of her pulse above her fingers. Even with that severe hairstyle and a minimum of makeup, there was no hiding the perfection of her face. He could almost understand why Carter had lost his head over her. Watching her mouth tremble, he reminded himself that she had willingly seduced a married man and selfishly wrecked a marriage without any thought of the hurt it would cause others.

But she was in deep trouble now *if* the kid had really seen a murder.

"What can I do?" she whispered.

"There's only one thing to do." His tone was brisk, businesslike. Be damned if he would fall for that soft, bruised look in her eyes. Reaching for the ignition keys, he started the Jeep. "You'll have to go to Sugarland."

"No."

He could see it on her face. Sugarland was the last place in the world she wanted to go to for protection. "Then you tell me where I can drop you," he retorted.

When she didn't—couldn't—find anything to say, he grunted something rude, rammed the Jeep in gear and took off.

Claire sat silently gazing at the town as John Mc-Mollere—equally silent—drove. How ironic, she thought, that the safest place for Carter's son was in the bosom of his father's family. The family who had rejected him outright from the moment they had learned of her pregnancy. For Danny's sake, she would have to put that painful memory behind her.

Suddenly they turned off LaRue's main street and she gave in to curiosity and stole a look at the man beside her. She wished she hadn't argued with him. For her, it had been a no-win situation, but her pride had pushed her to challenge the man. He was right, of course. If she had to turn to others to help her protect her son, the McMolleres were surely the logical choice. And John McMollere—Mack—seemed tailor-made for the job. Even though she knew he disapproved of her, there was something about Mack that gave her a feeling of security. Still, she couldn't just let him call the shots without at least letting him realize she was going along with his plan against her will. He didn't have to know how relieved she was to have his help.

As they cruised a secondary street, she thought about what she knew about Carter's older brother. Precious little, she concluded. He was a Vietnam veteran who'd flown helicopters during the war. In fact, it was Mack who'd taught Carter how to fly. She studied his hands on the wheel—hard, work-toughened hands—and then his face. He was less handsome, although his face was a good one, she decided, noting the strong jaw and firm chin. With those sunglasses concealing his eyes—lazer-blue if she remembered right—it was hard to tell what he might be thinking, but she'd bet he wasn't a man to advertise his feelings, anyway. She tried to remember what Carter had told her about his brother, but realized the information was vague in her memory. There'd been grudging admiration, she recalled that, and jealousy. Knowing what she now knew about Carter, she could well imagine that his weaker character had been swallowed up in this man's quiet strength. He was nothing

like Carter. One look at John McMollere and you sensed
the difference in the brothers.

If only he wasn't a McMollere.

A truck lumbered out from a side street forcing Mack
to swerve and hit the brakes. He swore, then cast a wry
look first back at Danny, then at Claire.

"Sorry, not used to kids," he muttered, slowing to
turn between two brick pillars. Claire said nothing,
merely looked around with curiosity. Were they nearing
Sugarland? Wasn't the McMollere homeplace much
farther out of town?

"I need to make a stop," he told her. "My daughter's here visiting a friend. I have to pick her up."

Before she could reply, he pulled into a driveway and
stopped. The house was all brick, large and luxurious
with numerous windows. Off to one side, a magnificent
oak tree dripped Spanish moss. Some distance back,
along the crape-myrtle–studded driveway, was a de-
tached three-car garage. Two teenage girls stood at the
porch railing. Near them, a boy leaned against a square
column. Claire judged him to be slightly older than the
girls. The kids had obviously been expecting Mack since
one of the girls straightened abruptly and started toward the Jeep.

She was there almost before Mack was out. Mid-
teens, Claire guessed. Standard shorts and T-shirt, expensive watch and sandals. This was obviously his
daughter. She had the same near-black hair and distinc-
tive blue eyes. Although right now she was too tall, all
arms and legs and too thin, one day all those characteristics would be assets and she would be drop-dead beautiful. Claire wondered about his wife. Ex-wife?

"You said you'd be here at five," the girl said with undisguised hostility. She jerked open the door to climb inside, but Mack stopped her.

"Just a minute, Michelle."

"What?" She looked straight ahead, her face sullen.

"I told you to stay away from Jake Reynolds. He's bad news."

"This is Ann-Marie's house. I don't have any control over who comes and goes here."

"You've been here all day. When did Jake get here?"

She shrugged. "I don't remember."

"You know the rules, Michelle."

She tossed her dark hair. "You have too many rules."

"I have a right as your father to set boundaries. That's your problem, Michelle, you've never had any rules."

She turned then, her eyes shooting blue fire. "We're gonna start in on my mother now? How bad she is? What a loser she is, right?"

He sighed. "This isn't about your mother, Michelle." He glanced in the Jeep and caught the expression in Claire's eyes. "We'll discuss it later. This isn't the time or place."

With a huffing sound, the teenager climbed into the back seat next to Danny. "Don't blame me. *I* didn't bring it up."

Mack got in behind the wheel, but didn't start up. He turned to introduce Claire and Danny, but his daughter interrupted him.

"You must be the scarlet woman," she said, looking at Claire.

"Michelle!" Mack thundered. "Apologize...*now!*"

Instead of apologizing, Michelle muttered the S-word.

Danny looked intrigued. "Mommy says when you say nasty words it's only because you can't think of better ones."

Michelle gave him a contemptuous look. "You must be Carter's brat. But now that I look a little closer, you could be Mack's. You look more like him than Carter and, after all, he's been loose and fancy-free for twelve years."

"Michelle, I'm warning you...that's enough! And don't call me Mack."

"You're definitely a McMollere, though. Don't worry."

"Am I going to have to stop this car and gag you?" Mack demanded through his teeth.

"I don't think I'm a brat," Danny said, picking up on the only thing he understood in what Michelle had said. "Ryan's a brat. Everybody says so."

"Who's Ryan, your brother?" The girl glanced at Claire. "There's more where he came from?"

"Excuse me." Claire spoke quietly, turning in her seat to give the girl a telling look. "None of this conversation is appropriate. If you have any other observations along these lines, please save them for a time when Danny isn't present."

"I couldn't have said it better," Mack said with a scowl. "We're waiting for an apology, Michelle."

She rolled her eyes. "Sorry."

"What are you trying to do?" Mack said. "Embarrass both of us in front of these people?"

"You're half right...*Daddy*." She said this last with scorn.

"Meaning you only want to embarrass me." For a long moment, he simply looked at his daughter. Claire sensed his anger and frustration. His bewilderment. She wondered what had caused so much hostility between father and daughter. Mack turned to Claire. "Sorry about this. You've guessed that this is my daughter, Michelle. I apologize for her manners. I wish I could say that it won't happen again, but since you work in the library at a high school you know that no one can predict the behavior of a teenager."

"It's okay."

"No, it's not okay."

"I can do my own apologizing, thanks," Michelle said.

He took off his sunglasses and with his thumb and forefinger rubbed his eyes wearily. Behind him, his daughter sat staring stonily out the window. The silence in the Jeep stretched uncomfortably.

Danny had watched and listened with fascination. His eyes were big now as he looked at Michelle. "You're in trouble."

His whisper carried easily to the adults in the front seat. Their eyes met. And for a second, Claire almost forgot where she was. Who he was. They were simply two single parents, each struggling with the problems of trying to rear children.

He leaned forward then and started the car and the spell was broken.

WHEN THEY TURNED OFF the highway about twenty minutes later, Mack told her that they were on Mc-Mollere land—over two thousand acres of flat, treeless bottomland planted exclusively in sugarcane. Fields and more fields of the green plants had reached a height exceeding eight feet in the August sun. The crop was nearing maturity, he explained. Then in the fall, in a flurry of activity, it would be cut, the strappy growth burned off, loaded on large trucks and hauled to the processing plants. Also owned by the McMolleres.

"What are those things?" Danny asked, pointing to mechanical beasts moving slowly up and down in various spots throughout the fields, like pecking birds.

"Oil pumps," Mack explained. "There's oil beneath the surface of the cane fields."

"That's how you get it out of the ground?" Danny was spellbound.

"That's right, hotshot."

Oil wells and sugarcane. Black and white gold. Claire sat stunned, taking it all in. The McMolleres' wealth was more extensive than she'd realized. As was their power. She fought the fear rising in her chest.

"Is it okay to call you Uncle Mack?" Danny asked suddenly.

"That sounds fine to me," Mack said, ignoring the snicker from Michelle.

"Did you like my dad? He was Carter McMollere."

Claire met Mack's startled glance. Why was he so surprised? she wondered. Did he expect her to bring Danny to meet Carter's family and not explain to the child just who Carter McMollere was? Did they think Danny had reached age five without asking who his father was and why that man wasn't a part of their lives?

"Yes, I liked him. He was my brother," Mack said.

"Did you play with him?"

Enough, thought Claire. "Danny, let's save this conversation for later, okay?"

"When, Mommy?"

"Just later, sweetie." To her relief, Mack turned the car into a narrow lane. Finally.

Michelle had the door open almost before the Jeep stopped. "Well, here it is, kid," she said, giving Danny a hand as he scrambled out after her. "Your heritage. Take a look."

"What's a heritage?" Danny asked, squinting in the sun at the imposing residence.

"Ask your mommy," Michelle said, throwing a hostile look in Claire's direction. "I'll bet she has the answer to that one."

"Michelle. Go to your room." Mack's expression was fierce. The girl shrugged and turned, heading for the front door.

Claire was used to teenage behavior. Before she took the job as a librarian, Claire had been an English teacher and had experienced her share of impudence and sheer bad manners from teenagers. She had found that such behavior often came from a deep well of hurt in a child. What, she wondered, was causing this girl such pain?

But there was no time to ponder the problem. As Michelle entered the house, two people came out. Claire reached for Danny, pulling him protectively against her, then turned to face Angus and Wyona McMollere, her son's grandparents.

Later she realized that Mack was the force that had eased those first awkward moments. He had introduced his mother first. Wyona McMollere was tiny, no more than five feet tall. Her skin was fair and unlined, her hair delicately blond. Her hand trembled as she touched Danny's hair, then his cheek. Claire guessed the woman to be about sixty, but her vague and distracted manner made her seem older.

"Mama, meet Claire Woodson," Mack said. "Claire, my mother, Wyona."

"Hello, Mrs. McMollere."

The woman extended her hand. "How do you do?" she said, obviously striving to be polite. "I thought you would be younger."

"Because I was a student when I met Carter?" Claire asked.

"Well, yes."

"My mother was ill, so I had to delay getting my degree," Claire explained, guessing from the woman's surprised expression that she hadn't expected Claire to have enough character to care for a sick mother. "I'm thirty-four."

"Claire, this is Danny's grandfather, Angus McMollere," Mack said. "Dad, Claire Woodson."

She recalled that Angus had suffered a stroke right after Carter's death. Age and illness had apparently taken a toll, because the stern and uncompromising tyrant that Carter had described hardly fit the slightly stooped, fragile-looking man before her. But his eyes—so like Mack's and Danny's—were still fiercely blue.

She shook his hand. "Mr. McMollere."

"Well, the boy certainly has the best of both of you," he declared, studying Danny's face.

"You mean, Carter and me?" Claire smiled coolly. "Is that a compliment?"

"My grandson's a good-looking boy," the old man blustered.

She gave Danny's shoulder an affectionate squeeze. "I think so, too."

"Michelle thinks he looks like me." Everybody stared at Mack in surprise.

"Don't be ridiculous," his mother said, finding her voice first.

"That was a joke, Mama."

Claire felt a hand beneath her elbow and realized it belonged to Mack. She had a wild impulse to turn around and run from these people who represented anything but safety to her and Danny. But Mack was urging her across the threshold, and she had no choice but to keep going. Behind her, the door closed.

"Welcome to Sugarland," he said.

CHAPTER THREE

WYONA LED everyone through the house to a bright sun room. Claire sat where Wyona indicated, then patted the spot beside her for Danny. There hadn't been time to get more than a glimpse of the house, but Claire had an impression of high ceilings, wooden floors, spaciousness and traditional decor. Still, it appeared dated, not in the sense of out-of-fashion furnishings—costly antiques were everywhere—but it had an air of benign neglect.

Claire envied Danny as he looked around, openly curious. She'd have to keep her own curiosity to herself, at least for now. Angus and Wyona took seats opposite her. Mack stood watching, his back to the windows.

"We've been looking forward to this day a long time, Danny," Angus said in his blustery way. "How do you like your daddy's house?"

Danny's eyes got round. "Did my daddy live here?"

"He sure did." Angus pointed up. "He was born right upstairs, in the same bedroom as me."

"Wow." Danny stared at the ceiling as though he could look right through it. "I was born in a hospital."

"Yes, well . . ." Angus cleared his throat.

"I'm five," Danny informed him proudly. "It's only a month until I start kindergarten, but I can already read some 'cause my mommy's a liberrian. She used to be a teacher, but not anymore."

"That's quite a speech," the old man said.

Mack smiled. "Danny's quite a boy."

"I have to be," Danny said, obviously considering that an odd remark. " 'Cause I can't be a girl."

As everyone laughed, Michelle suddenly appeared at the door. "That's the only reason you're here, Danny. Because you aren't a girl." There was a bitter twist to her smile.

Mack moved toward her, frowning. With a sinking feeling, Claire realized he was going to scold his daughter and provoke another confrontation. The man's parenting skills definitely needed work.

"Danny and I were just getting acquainted with his grandparents, Michelle," she said, patting a place on the other side of her. "Come and join us."

Michelle hesitated, meeting Claire's gaze with suspicion. But then she walked over and sat down. "So, how's it going? Is the little heir measuring up to true McMollere standards?"

"Isn't it a bit early to tell?" Claire said, smiling.

"Not really. He's male, he's healthy, he's in."

"I don't understand you, dear." Wyona looked dismayed.

"That girl needs a lesson in manners," Angus said, glaring at Mack.

"I like her," Danny said, leaning forward to look at Michelle. Suddenly, the teenager's eyes filled with tears.

She dashed them away with some embarrassment. "Just what I need, a little twerp to fight my battles. Too bad you aren't gonna be here but a weekend, kid. We might become buddies."

"I think we're staying longer than that," Danny said.

"What's this?" Angus straightened a little, looking at Mack.

"Danny witnessed an incident at the hotel this afternoon," he said, glancing at Claire. "While Claire was talking on the phone with me, he says he saw a man shoot somebody."

There was shocked silence and then everybody tried to speak at once. Mack held up a hand. "There's a problem. Nobody else saw anything. The hotel claims it couldn't have happened, but when Claire and Danny went to Star-Mart later, somebody—a stranger—approached Danny and tried to force him out of the store."

"My God!" Angus said softly.

"Oh...oh," Wyona murmured, touching her cheek.

"Jeezum!" Michelle said.

Mack crossed his arms over his chest. "So until we can be certain Danny's imagination hasn't run amok, it would appear that the safest place for Claire and Danny right now is here at Sugarland."

CLAIRE ESCAPED after the first flurry of questions to take Danny to the bathroom. She needed a moment to get her bearings. It was suddenly so overwhelming. Here she was in Carter's house, with Carter's parents, *dependent* on the McMolleres because of a fluke—a criminal act that had thrown her child's life in jeopardy. She felt as if she were caught in a tidal wave with no more control over her destiny than a sand castle at high tide.

Beside her, Danny was looking wide-eyed at everything. "I like it here, Mommy."

"It's a nice house."

"I like Michelle."

"She's nice, too." She turned a corner, but could see nothing that looked like a bathroom.

"And I like Uncle Mack."

"Uh-huh."

"Did my real daddy look like him?"

Claire sighed inwardly. From the time he'd been old enough to realize that most kids had a father, Danny had been curious about his own. She hated questions about Carter, but she tried not to let Danny know that.

Danny tugged on her dress. "You didn't answer me, Mommy."

"No, they really don't look that much alike, Danny." And I hope there's even less resemblance in their character, she thought.

"Oh." Danny's small shoulders sagged.

She reached out and ruffled his hair. "Cheer up. I think you look a lot like your grandpa McMollere. That's okay, isn't it?"

"I guess so." He wrinkled his nose. "But he's really old, isn't he?"

"I suppose, but he's been sick. Maybe that's why he seems old."

"He talks sorta loud, too."

"Maybe he can't hear as well as he used to."

"But I can," Danny said logically. "He doesn't have to yell."

"Uh-uh." Where was the bathroom, for heaven's sake?

Danny looked up into her face. "What should I call him and my grandmother?"

She had no idea. "Maybe you can ask them that when we get back to the living room."

"My grandmother's funny."

"How do you mean?"

"I don't think she likes me."

Claire stopped and put her hands on his shoulders. "Yes, she does, Danny. She and your grandfather wanted this visit more than anything in the world be-

cause they wanted to get to know you. That's because
they love you. Your daddy was their son and because of
him, you're special to them. That includes your grandmother.''

He gazed at her steadily from eyes so unmistakably
like his uncle's and grandfather's. ''Are you sure,
Mommy?''

With her forefinger, she solemnly drew an X on her
chest. ''Cross my heart.''

''And Michelle likes me, too?''

''That's right.''

''Uncle Mack, too?''

''You got it.''

He smiled. ''Okay. 'Cause I like them and I think I'm
gonna visit Sugarland for the next zillion years.''

Claire rolled her eyes. ''Here's the bathroom.''

''Good. I have to go really bad.''

But he balked at the door. ''Mommy, you don't have
to go in here with me.''

''Okay, honey.''

That wasn't good enough. With his hand on the
doorknob, he gave her a stubborn look. ''You can go
back to the grown-ups, Mommy.''

Terrific.

As she headed down the hall, she could hear Mack's
calm, measured replies to his parents. Fifteen minutes in
the house with them and Claire could tell that John
McMollere, not Angus, was the glue holding the family
together. It was odd that he seemed so inept in dealing
with his daughter.

She turned one of the numerous corners and nearly
bumped into Michelle.

''So what is it, a blessing or a curse?'' the girl asked.

Claire gave her an exasperated look. "Do you make it a habit to sneak up on people?"

"I could have clomped up wearing combat boots and you wouldn't have heard me. You were a thousand miles away."

"No, I *wish* I was a thousand miles away."

Michelle grinned. "Now, *that* I can sympathize with."

"Is that why you're so deliberately rude every chance you get? Especially to your father?"

She shrugged. "I guess so."

"It's juvenile, Michelle. Think of another way if you want people to respect you."

"I don't give a damn if they respect me."

"How about loving you? How do you feel about that?"

She made a bitter sound. "That's hopeless. Not from them. Never."

"I'm sure your father loves you," Claire said quietly.

"Oh, yeah? You've known him exactly…what? Half a day? And you can tell he loves me? Shows what you know."

Claire sighed. "What did you mean just now—is what a blessing or a curse?"

"Being here at Sugarland."

"I'm reserving judgment."

Just then, Danny ran up to them. "I 'membered to wash my hands."

"Good boy." She gave him a smile.

"Back to the lion's den," Michelle quipped.

Claire grimaced. She'd wondered what was causing the girl such pain and now she knew. The question was: why did Michelle think her father didn't love her?

IT WAS MUCH LATER that night when Mack left the house and headed for the sheriff's office in Abadieville, sixty miles north of LaRue in another parish. He wasn't quite convinced that Danny had seen a man murdered, let alone that it was by a rogue cop, but to be on the safe side, he'd avoided taking his concerns to the local sheriff. Wayne Pagett, the sheriff in Abadieville, was a longtime friend, a man he knew he could trust.

The incident in Star-Mart could have been coincidental. However, in Mack's experience, coincidences were as rare as white alligators. Claire clearly believed her son, otherwise nothing could have induced her to accept the hospitality of the McMolleres at Sugarland. He had to hand it to her for dealing with an awkward situation gracefully. He couldn't imagine his ex-wife managing half as well in a similar situation. In the first place, Liz was incapable of putting her child's welfare above her own. Michelle's unhappiness was proof of that.

He rubbed a hand over his face. He didn't want to think about his problems with his teenage daughter tonight.

At the courthouse, he pulled into a parking space reserved for a deputy sheriff and stopped the Jeep. He got out, stretching to ease the stiffness from his thigh. He was hardly ever aware of the old 'Nam injury except when rain threatened. He viewed the sky with a frown, guessing that it would storm within the hour.

He slammed the door and clamped his hat on his head, then took the courthouse steps two at a time. Not much activity in Abadieville this time of night, he noted, but he bet he'd find Wayne Pagett still in his office.

"Yo, Jerry. How's it going?" He waved at a deputy manning the front desk, then caught a glimpse of Wayne through the glass door of the office. If the sheriff hadn't been in, Mack would have had no hesitation in driving out to Wayne's house. God knows he'd spent enough time there when he was growing up. Mike, Wayne's oldest son, had been his best friend throughout high school. Mack couldn't count the lectures he'd received from this man. Sometimes Wayne Pagett had seemed more like a father to him than Angus McMollere. Sometimes Mack had wished he'd been Wayne's son.

He paused before knocking. Wayne spent most of his time now in his office. Mike had told Mack that after his wife died, his dad didn't have much incentive to go home. With his kids grown, Mike living in Houston, and Kayla in Orlando, the big house was too empty. Wayne had even taken to bringing his big yellow Lab, Barney, into the office with him. It was the dog who spotted Mack first.

In the quiet of the courthouse, Barney's bark sounded like the boom of a cannon as Mack pushed open the door. Wayne's head came up and instantly his frown turned into pleasure. "Mack! Son of a gun, this is a surprise." He got up, sending his chair crashing back against the wall, and leaned over his desk, his hand outstretched. "Of all the folks I expected to walk in here tonight, you're the last. How are you, boy?"

Mack shook the man's hand. At his feet, Barney was wagging his tail in joyful recognition. "I'm doing fine, Wayne. How about yourself?"

"Good...good. Yeah, I'm doing all right." He sat again, then reached into his shirt pocket and extracted a cigar. "Have a seat. I'd offer you one of these, but I know you hate 'em. How's Angus? Last I heard, he was up and about, ornery as ever."

"He's doing okay." Mack rubbed Barney's ears, smiling as the Lab licked his hand, then he settled back.

"A little shaky on his feet, but if he follows the doctor's orders, he manages just fine."

"I can imagine how eager he is to follow doctor's orders," Wayne said dryly.

Mack grinned. "His health was affected by his stroke, his personality wasn't."

Wayne grunted, nodding his head. "And your mama. How's Wyona?"

"Same as ever."

"Give them both my best." He paused to light the cigar, then surveyed Mack through the smoky haze. "It's a little late for a social visit, isn't it, boy?"

Mack leaned forward in the chair, lifting his ankle to rest on his knee. "We've got a couple of visitors at Sugarland."

"Oh?"

"Carter's son, Danny, and the little boy's mother."

"Well, well. So Martin Thibodaux finally came through for you. Last I heard, he was trying every legal trick in the book to try and arrange a visit, but the woman was hanging tough."

"Who told you that?"

"Oh, I've got my sources, don't you know."

Mack knew he wouldn't get a name from Wayne, so there was no sense pushing it, but he wondered if Martin Thibodaux, who'd been Angus's lawyer for more than thirty years, realized that sensitive information about one of his most influential clients was being leaked.

"Her name's Claire Woodson," he said.

"I know her name." Seeing Mack's frown, Wayne went on, "Miriam met her once. It was at an education conference in Baton Rouge about six months before I lost her. Sort of a coincidence, you might say, seeing as there was a connection between Miriam and the Mc-Molleres." He paused to take a puff of his cigar. "Anyway, she came away from the conference, Miriam, I mean, with a good impression of Claire Woodson. Naturally, Miriam knew how Angus and Wyona resented being kept from knowing their grandson, and that they had no positive feelings about Miss Woodson. Miriam expected somebody harder, more...ah, flamboyant, I suppose, but Miss Woodson was very nice. In fact, Miriam mentioned that she acted in every way a lady, positively straitlaced, she said."

"She's a redhead," Mack said abruptly, then shifted uncomfortably at Wayne's laugh.

"You don't say."

"Yeah, she doesn't look anything like I expected."

"You mean in all this time you never had a look at the woman you were fighting for custody of Carter's child?"

"Just once. And it was years ago when she and Carter were having the affair." Wayne's attitude made him feel defensive, as if his parents' long, hard-fought legal battle was in some way unjust. "My folks weren't fighting for custody of the boy. They were just trying to assert their natural right to see Danny occasionally, to arrange a visit to Sugarland once in a while. As the boy's grandparents, don't they deserve that?"

"Well, it sounds reasonable," Wayne said, leaning back until he was nearly horizontal in his chair. Smoke curled lazily from his cigar. "And Miriam told me that Miss Woodson seemed like a reasonable young woman, very sensible. Makes you wonder why she fought access so hard."

It was something Mack had wondered about, too. He wished he had an answer. "She's not exactly what I expected."

"You're probably not what she expected," Wayne said, smiling faintly.

"How do you mean?"

"She probably thinks that since you're Carter's brother you share other characteristics." He reached over and gently rubbed the ashes from the end of his cigar. "Nothing could be further from the truth, as anybody who knows you could tell her."

"Wayne—"

"Aw, now, don't go getting that look on your face. I'm not saying anything bad about your brother, 'specially now he's gone and can't defend himself." He hunched a little closer to his desk, looking Mack directly in the eye. "Let me give you some advice, Mack. Don't assume things are as they seem with Claire Woodson. I know you've got a lot on you, son. You're on the board of that oil company now, you're the biggest sugarcane farmer in four parishes, you're struggling to learn to be a parent to your little girl. The two of you hardly know each other at all after all these years Liz kept her from you. And now you've got Claire and her little boy and her feud with your folks dumped in your lap. Angus can't help much, he's sick and your mama...well, your mama is hardly the lady she was before Carter died in that airplane crash." He put his cigar in an ashtray that was an open alligator's mouth, and shoved it aside. "But you need to wait a while before judging Claire. See if you think she's the kind of woman who'd arbitrarily deny decent grandparents the right to have a relationship with their only grandson. And if the answer's yes, then take a minute to ask yourself why in the world she would feel that way."

At Mack's feet, Barney whined, his soft brown eyes full of concern. Mack chuckled softly, shaking his head.

"You're making me feel about ten years old, Wayne. How do you do it?"

"Comes with age, son. You get old as me, you get to say whatever you please, even if it's none of your damn business." He eyed Mack over his bifocals. "So, how long is Miss Woodson's visit?"

Mack drew in a deep breath. "Longer than she counted on. That's why I drove over here tonight to see you, Wayne. She's having to stay at Sugarland whether she likes it or not because the boy claims he saw a man murdered this afternoon at the White Hotel."

"What the hell!" Wayne wasn't shocked often. "You're gonna have to explain that in a little more detail, son."

Mack gave him the whole story, including his own doubts. Unlike Mack, Wayne was inclined to accept Danny's account of what he saw. When he repeated the incident at Star-Mart, the sheriff frowned ferociously.

"You say Miss Woodson believes the boy saw what he claims to have seen?" he asked.

"Yeah. She said she had doubts at first because they'd been watching something on TV that had a lot of violence, and she'd made Danny turn it off and watch cartoons instead."

"Sounds to me like she's a conscientious mama as well as a sensible person," Wayne remarked.

Mack grunted. "Whatever. But the hotel found no signs of a struggle or blood or anything that lent any credence to what Danny said."

"A mother usually knows her child, Mack."

"Yeah. That's why I drove over here. I don't know what you can do without stirring up a hornet's nest, but I'd appreciate your looking into this," Mack told him. "As you guessed, I'm going to be busy at Sugarland.

I've got an office in Lafayette, but since Dad's heart attack and especially now that Michelle is with me, I've been trying to manage at home." He stood up, frowning at the window where lightning flashed intermittently through the ancient oak trees on the side of the courthouse. "It's too risky leaving her alone to do much investigating on my own."

"Who, Michelle?"

"No, Claire." Bumping his hat restlessly against his right thigh, he missed Wayne's sharp look. "She wanted to drive back to Houston, can you believe that? I told her no way. A woman alone, some nut out there looking for her, she needs a keeper, for God's sake."

"It's a nasty job, but I guess somebody's got to do it."

"You can't be too careful," Mack said, ignoring the taunt. He settled his hat on his head. "As you pointed out, I have a family responsibility here, Wayne. This is Carter's son, the only other grandchild my folks are likely to have."

"I don't know as I'd say that, not just yet," Wayne drawled, rising from his chair. "You've still got a few good years. What are you now, Mack, thirty-nine, forty?"

"Forty-two last month, Wayne," Mack said dryly. "And I don't plan on producing any other heirs. For that, a man needs a wife, and I don't intend making that mistake again."

Wayne shook his head. "That Liz sure did a number on you, didn't she?"

"It wasn't just Liz," Mack said, wincing as a crash of thunder shook the windowpanes. "We never should have married in the first place. I knew she was out of her element when I brought her to Sugarland. She was a city girl. She was miserable from day one."

Wayne gave a snort. "What about her vows? A woman's supposed to stick with her man."

"It was thirteen years ago, Wayne," Mack said. He took no offense at his friend's frankness, possibly because Liz's desertion no longer hurt the way it once had. "It's in the past."

"Not the way I see it." Wayne clamped his cigar in his mouth. "What with her dumping little Michelle on you after poisoning her against her Louisiana relatives, including you." He fumbled around, moving things on his desk top, looking for a match. "The woman's a piece of work, that's what she is."

"She's a little spoiled," Mack agreed, heading for the door. "But she's Victor DeBartolo's problem now, not mine."

Wayne squinted at Mack through a fresh cloud of smoke. "He's still in Washington, I guess."

"You know as well as I do where Vic is. You know everything else."

"Good place for him." Wayne reached for his suit coat and shrugged into it. "Her, too."

Mack laughed. "Next time Liz calls, I'll be sure and mention you send your regards."

They went out together, both chuckling.

At the door, Mack stopped. "One thing you can do for me now, Wayne. I need to get Claire's luggage, but it's probably best for somebody besides me to pick it up. If the boy did actually witness something and somebody's watching the room, I wouldn't want them to make the connection that Claire and the boy are at Sugarland."

Wayne turned to the deputy. "Jerry, call Al and tell him to pick up Claire Woodson's things at the White Hotel, then tell him Mack will meet him at Melrose

Crossing in about thirty minutes to take 'em off his hands. Tell him to give no information to the hotel.'' He looked at Mack. ''Thirty minutes ought to do it, huh?''

''It should. Thanks, Wayne.''

''No problem.''

They were walking through the office, when another mighty clap of thunder shook the place. At the door, Wayne clapped him on the shoulder. ''My Miriam was a redhead, did you know that?''

Mack clamped his hat on his head, getting ready to make a run for it. ''I don't remember her hair ever being anything but snow-white.''

''Yeah. Turned that way nearly overnight. She wasn't a day over forty... She always blamed it on you and Mike.''

It was still raining, but Mack was smiling as he dashed for his Jeep.

HE DROVE through a steady downpour all the way to Sugarland. Just as Wayne ordered, one of his men was waiting at Melrose Crossing with Claire's luggage. Not much to it, he thought as he stored a suitcase and an overnight case in the back of the Jeep. If the visit lasted more than a week, she'd probably need to get a few more things.

He tried to convince himself he didn't care whether she was there a week or a day.

As he turned in the curved driveway, the Jeep's headlights swept over the house. Except for the garage area, which was separate from the main house, the whole place was dark. He stopped the car and got out, heading around to the tailgate. As he pulled it open, he glanced up at the second-story bedroom where Claire and the boy were staying. That, too, was dark. Apparently she wasn't losing any sleep worrying about her situation. He slammed the tailgate and started up the steps.

"Is that my luggage?"

Startled at the sound of her voice, he almost dropped the bags.

"Sorry, I guess you didn't see me."

"What are you doing out here?" he said. "This is a hell of an electrical storm. You could be struck by lightning."

"I couldn't sleep. And storms have never made me nervous." She took the overnight case, leaving the larger piece for him to carry. "Thanks for picking this up."

He didn't waste any time getting the door open and urging her inside. There was just enough light to reveal what she was wearing. And how she looked. A big T-shirt and shorts. In the denim dress today, he'd guessed that her legs were fantastic. He'd been right. The only wrong note was her hair. He wondered what it would be like not tied back. Earlier her hair had been pulled back and pinned in some severe-looking twist. Now it was braided, starting at the crown of her head. He imagined her red hair all loose and flowing. He could almost feel his fingers sift through it. He could almost see it spread out and—

He caught himself up abruptly. What the hell was he doing fantasizing about this woman? He cleared his throat. "I see that you found something to wear."

"Michelle generously offered this workout set." She pulled at the T-shirt, trying to stretch the garment to midthigh. "One size fits all. I was glad for the clothes, but I'll feel more comfortable in my own things."

"They couldn't look any better on you."

She was instantly on guard. Like a doe caught in headlights.

"I'll just take this on up to my room," she said, slipping past him to hurry up the stairs.

Watching her escape—there was no other word for it—he wished he could take back the remark, but the words had been out before he could stop them. Why was she so skittish?

Frowning, he climbed the stairs himself, but at a pace that gave him time to contemplate the contrasts and complexities of Claire Woodson. There was a remoteness about her that didn't fit the way he'd thought of her for years. He recalled that night in Houston when she'd been with Carter. Mack remembered her smiling, almost sparkling with emotion as she clung to Carter on the dance floor. And then Carter had spotted him, had made the introductions reluctantly.

The picture of Claire Woodson as she'd been that night had stayed with Mack. As for this woman with the severe hairdo, the disconcertingly direct gaze, the calm grace and quiet manner, she did not fit that other picture. Just who was the real Claire Woodson?

CHAPTER FOUR

THE CONTINUING DRONE of a small plane pulled Claire out of a deep sleep. Her subconscious had been aware of the sound for some time, long enough to pierce her defenses and trigger a dream. She was in a small plane with Carter at the controls. He was talking to her, smiling, gesturing with eager, almost manic, enthusiasm. He didn't seem worried that he was flying the plane recklessly, zipping up and down, buzzing landmarks, going into a tailspin that brought her heart into her mouth. The controls on the instrument panel were going haywire. Trapped and terrified, Claire cried out at him to be careful, but he laughed at her. When she couldn't reason with him, she opened the door to get out of the plane. She looked down in panic on an ocean of green sugarcane undulating in a summer breeze as the plane spiraled to the ground.

She awoke with a start.

To escape the nightmare, she wanted to spring out of bed, but her body felt heavy, weighted down by fear coursing through paralyzed limbs. Even her mind functioned sluggishly. She studied her surroundings in growing confusion. Where was she? The bedroom in her Houston condo had no floral wallpaper, no slowly revolving ceiling fan. Her bed had no tall cherry-wood foot posts.

And then she remembered. She was at Sugarland. Of course. With the McMolleres.

She rose on one elbow and rubbed a hand over her face. It had been such a long night. For hours her mind had been in turmoil. No relaxation techniques had worked. The last time she'd looked at the clock, it had been after four. It was now only a few minutes before six.

Slipping out of bed, she pulled on a robe and headed for the bathroom, which lay between the large guest suite Wyona had placed her in and a smaller bedroom the right size for a child. Unsurprisingly, considering the bizarre day he'd had, Danny had not been eager to stay in his room alone. It had been Michelle who'd persuaded him. Angry, hurting, rebellious Michelle. Claire wasn't sure what the girl had promised him, but whatever it was, Danny had finally settled down. Claire had been grateful. Once again, she'd found herself wondering what was wrong between Michelle and Mack. Almost instinctively she wanted to reach out to the teenager, but she reminded herself that Michelle's problems weren't her concern. She couldn't afford to get embroiled in this family's affairs. Claire was here only because of the threat to Danny. Her son—not Mack's troubled daughter—was the one who mattered right now.

In the bathroom, she realized that the sound of the small plane had not let up. Through the window, she watched the craft swoop low, spewing out a cloud of pesticide, the fuselage almost brushing the tops of the waving sugarcane. Barely dawn and a pilot was already crop-dusting. She rubbed her forehead, groaning at the early hours that farmers kept. Still, Danny would be interested, she thought, making a mental note to ask Mack to tell him about growing and processing sugar before it appeared on the table in tiny white granules to sweeten his cereal.

She went to check on him and found his bed empty. For a second, she stared around blankly. His pajamas were discarded beside a chair and his sneakers were gone. How could he have left without her hearing a sound? Her heart stumbled, but she told herself not to panic. Drawing the belt tight on her robe, she hurried into the hall. The house was eerily silent in the way houses are before their occupants rise. There was no sign of Danny or anybody else.

Fighting panic, she went to the banister of the winding staircase and leaned over it. "Danny," she called, trying to keep her voice under control. "Danny, where are you?"

No answer. She whirled, about to go back to her room and get dressed. She could hardly search the place in her nightgown and robe. Behind her a door opened.

"What's wrong? What's the matter?" Wyona McMollere came out of a bedroom, her fair hair frizzed around her head and her eyeglasses cocked as though she'd donned them in a hurry.

"I'm looking for my son, Mrs. McMollere," Claire said. "I'm sorry if I disturbed you."

"At this hour?" the woman asked, glancing around as though expecting Danny to materialize out of nowhere. "Where is he?"

"I don't know." In a nervous gesture, Claire caught up her long hair as she tried to think. "He's not in his room and his sneakers are gone."

Angus McMollere shuffled up behind Wyona, leaning on his cane. "What's all the ruckus?" he demanded, his scowl directed at Claire.

"My son isn't in his room," Claire said. "I need to find him."

"I'm sure he's fine," Wyona said.

"Of course, he's fine," Angus snapped. "Why wouldn't he be?"

"Then where is he?" Claire cried, her heart starting to pound in panic. "It's not even six o'clock in the morning!"

"Hear now, girl," Angus said, shuffling toward her with his cane. "Just hold on. He's around somewhere. Let's see what Mack thinks."

"Danny knows not to go anywhere with strangers," Claire said.

"What strangers would you be referring to?" Angus demanded, his frown fierce. "There're no strangers in this house, at least none who'd lure off a five-year-old."

"Everyone here is a stranger to Danny," she said tightly, anxiety making her blunt.

"And who's fault is that!" Angus retorted with a thump of his cane.

"Maybe he's just exploring the house," Wyona offered helpfully. "Little boys are like that."

"Danny wouldn't explore anything without asking me first."

"He's a McMollere," Angus argued. "They don't always do what their mamas say."

Disobedience was hardly something to be proud of, Claire thought with disgust. Before she said something she would regret, she turned to go, then halted at the sound of someone entering the front door downstairs. Wyona released a small relieved sigh. "Oh, oh, thank goodness, Mack's here."

Mack? He wasn't in his bedroom sleeping?

All eyes were on him as he came up the curved staircase. His gaze went first to Claire. "What's wrong?"

"Have you seen Danny?"

"Danny?" His blank look said everything.

"He's gone!"

Wyona touched Angus's arm. "Maybe Michelle—"

Mack walked over to them, frowning. "Gone where? What's going on here?"

"He's not in his bed," Claire said. "I checked on him a few minutes ago. He's not in the house. I should have let him sleep with me. He wanted to, but I thought—"

"Hey, take it easy." Mack caught her hand and stopped her, gave it a little squeeze. "Wherever he is, he's fine. He's around somewhere. This is a big house."

She pulled her hand away. "He's not in the house. He would have heard me calling and said something."

"Maybe the crop duster woke him up," Mack suggested. "He probably snuck out to investigate."

"Not without asking me," she repeated stubbornly.

"Well, he sure can't have been kidnapped right under our noses, if that's what you're afraid of," Mack observed.

"That's exactly what I'm afraid of," Claire said curtly, wrapping her arms around her waist. "With everything that happened yesterday, I should have kept him in the room with me. Until we know why that man was killed, Danny shouldn't be out of my sight."

"We don't know yet that a man *was* killed," Mack reminded her.

"*You* may not know it, but *I* do!"

"Okay, have it your way," Mack said, more to calm her, she guessed, than because he actually agreed with her. "But let's see if anybody outside the house has seen him before we panic, okay?"

"I was just about to do that," Claire said. She was trembling, an inch away from falling apart and more relieved to see Mack than she cared to admit.

"I'll get Cleo to make a thorough search downstairs. She might have seen something."

"Cleo?"

"The housekeeper," he said. "You met her last night."

"Oh. Oh, yes." Distracted, she pushed her hands through her hair, only then recalling that it was loose and uncombed and that she must look like something the cat dragged in.

"You might want to change into something else."

Something in his tone intensified her embarrassment. She didn't reply, but turned and hurried down the hall to do just that.

FOR A BEAT OR TWO, Mack stood watching her go. Fresh out of bed in a panic, she'd not taken time to pull her hair back. It was as he'd remembered—a rich auburn with fiery streaks. He was torn between feeling sympathy for her as a scared mother whose kid was probably off exploring interesting new territory, and losing himself in a sexual fantasy over the look of her, all dewy-eyed and sleep-soft. It was no wonder she wore that tight bun and those longish dresses that didn't touch her anywhere except her shoulders. To leave them off was to allow people to see her as she really was: her breasts rounded and lush, her waist small enough to span with his hands, a soft shape he itched to hold.

Was she simply putting on an act for her visit to Danny's relatives? Possibly she thought that if she looked prim and proper enough, she would fool them all into thinking she *was* prim and proper. Not likely, since

Miriam Pagett had been taken in, too, according to Wayne. And that was well over two years ago when Claire couldn't have known she would be compelled to visit Carter's folks.

Whatever the answer was, he didn't have time to figure it out now. Claire's concern for Danny was genuine. And he hadn't just been blowing smoke when he'd told her the boy was safe so long as he was on Sugarland grounds. So where was he? In the car yesterday, everything Danny saw had fascinated him. Like any child might, he'd probably popped out of bed at the crack of dawn and decided to do a little sight-seeing on his own.

Not that Claire was in any frame of mind to accept that, Mack thought, bumping his Stetson against his thigh as he turned to go back downstairs. The problem with these city folks was that they overreacted to everything. It came from being penned up in climate-controlled condos, or barricaded behind the locked gates of some planned community where they didn't know anybody but the manager. They forgot what it was like to live a regular life. Not that things were all that regular around here since yesterday. In all fairness, he had to admit that.

Claire was scared to death. He was surprised to find that he didn't like the idea of her worrying unnecessarily. She'd already gotten more than she'd bargained for in her visit to Sugarland. Quickly putting on his hat, he headed for the front door.

Claire was right behind him. "Michelle's not in her room," she said, tucking in the tails of a plain white shirt. Her hair, he noted, was again slicked back and anchored at her nape with an elastic ring.

"Well, they're together, you can count on it."

"How can you know that!" she cried. "I've been here less than a day, but it's long enough to show me that Michelle isn't a typical teenager. She could be anywhere and you wouldn't know it, what with the relationship you two share. She could be at her friend's house where we picked her up yesterday. She sure wouldn't take Danny with her if I'm right."

"You're wrong."

"About your relationship or the other?"

"The other," he said, his reply clipped. He didn't intend to discuss Michelle with her. "Michelle might well sashay off to her friend's house without asking, but not at this hour. She's at the barn."

"The barn?"

"With the horses. It's the only thing she likes about Sugarland."

"You have horses?"

"Yeah, we have horses. We've got a lot of land, you might have noticed that," he reminded her dryly. "Horses get around in a cane field much better than Jeeps."

"Yes, but..." They were outdoors now and she could see beyond the immediate grounds—which were landscaped and meticulously maintained—to the acres and acres of sugarcane. "I just didn't think."

He headed for his Jeep, and she followed, huffing a little in an effort to keep up with him. He slowed down. He wasn't used to a woman tagging along, but from the little he knew about Claire Woodson, he suspected wild horses couldn't keep her from accompanying him on his search for her little boy.

"The barn's over there." He pointed east.

She looked, and sure enough, over the waving sugarcane she saw a barn compound. "Don't you ever get tired of nothing but sugarcane?'' she grumbled when she'd climbed into the Jeep.

"It's cut by the end of the year and then there's open space as far as the eye can see."

"Oh."

"Until the cane is up again."

She buckled up like a diligent schoolmarm and, hiding a smile, he backed out of the driveway and started to drive the Jeep in the direction of the barn. Catching sight of her worried expression, he said, "Don't worry, they'll be there."

They were. As soon as they reached the compound, they spotted Michelle astride her favorite mare in the corral behind the barn and Danny perched on the fence watching every move she made. The child turned at the sound of the Jeep and began to scramble down to run and meet them.

"Mommy, Mommy, they've got horses! Real horses. Michelle says I can learn to ride. I already touched Cherry. That's her name. She's a mare. That's what you call a lady horse. Mommy, this is a neat place. I'm having fun!"

Mack felt a pang in his middle as he watched Claire sweep up the little boy and helplessly bury her face in his neck. She didn't say anything.

Danny tolerated the emotional display briefly and then squirmed to get down. "Mommy, did you hear me?" he insisted, dragging her by the hand toward the fence. "Michelle is gonna teach me to ride. They have a pony just for me! His name's Bucko. I bet I can do it, too."

"Hi!" Michelle called, flashing a smile incredibly like her father's. With an expert hand, she guided the prancing mare up to the fence. "Danny and I've been out forever. Is it time for breakfast? We're both starved.''

"You may not get any breakfast," Mack told her sternly. "Or lunch or dinner."

She rolled her eyes. "What now, for Pete's sake! I haven't done anything to get in trouble for yet. It's too early in the morning."

Claire caught Mack's eye. Now that her fear for Danny's safety was passing, fury was overtaking it. "I'll handle this," she told him.

"What's wrong, Mommy?" Danny asked, squinting up at her.

"Yeah, what's up?" Michelle looked curiously from one to the other.

"You took my son out of the house without asking my permission, Michelle," Claire said, her voice shaking. "Can you imagine how I felt when I woke up and he was gone? I was scared to death."

"Geez, I'm sorry." Michelle dismounted with easy grace. Keeping the reins in her hand, she bent down to get through the rails. "I guess I didn't think. I go riding every morning, anybody around here'll tell you that. Today was no different, except—"

"You didn't think?"

"No, I—"

"I've only been here half a day, as you reminded me yesterday, but it's long enough to know that other people's feelings don't seem to matter much to you, Michelle."

Michelle glanced uncertainly at Mack.

"Just a minute, Claire," he said.

But Claire's wrath was still focused on Michelle. "You had no right to take my son without asking!" With Danny's back pressed against her thighs, she crossed shaking hands over his chest. "It's bad enough we have no choice except to be here, but for you to think so little of my peace of mind that you'd whisk Danny off and leave me to wonder and worry and imagine all sorts of horrible possibilities is just too much!" She drew in a deep breath, trembling all over.

"Gosh, I'm really sorry," Michelle repeated, with none of her usual flippancy.

"Was it too much trouble to wake me and ask to take my son?"

Danny caught her hand. "Mommy..."

Claire ignored him. "If I could, I would pack our things and leave here this instant!"

"Mommy—" Danny pulled at her hand.

Claire turned to Mack. "What kind of people are you? Don't you ever think of anybody but yourselves?"

"Just a damn minute, now!" He took a step toward her. "Maybe Michelle was wrong in bringing Danny out without asking, but seems to me you're taking out other frustrations on her. You ask what kind of people we are—no different from most. We're trying to be rational, and that's more than—"

"Rational!" Now that she'd vented her outrage, her other emotions were threatening to overflow. Suddenly she felt close to tears. "F-forcing me to c-come here, d-demanding time with my son when you were perfectly happy to deny his existence before Carter died, then taking advantage of that hideous situation at the hotel." She drew a new breath, blinking fast. "And why did we have to stay there, anyway? We would have been just fine at the Holiday Inn. But no, because you say so, we have to experience the quaint southern thing and check into a hotel right out of a trashy novel..." She looked away, struggling to keep herself together.

"Mommy..." Danny tugged again. "I think you need some time in the quiet corner."

All three looked at Danny, then at each other. Sheepishly. Claire pressed her fingers to her temples, realizing how hysterical she sounded. How *irrational*. Even Danny knew it. Shaking her head, she whispered to no one in particular, "What am I *doing?*"

"Mommy, can I talk now?"

"What, Danny?" she managed to say, breathing in to try to regain her composure.

"You're gonna be mad." Warily, he watched her use both hands to wipe tears from her cheeks.

"Try me anyway, Danny."

"Michelle didn't bring me outside this morning. I came all by myself."

She glanced in disbelief at the barn and then in the direction of the big house. It could hardly be seen from here. "How on earth did you find the barn?"

"I followed the dirt road, you know like in *The Wizard of Oz,* only it's not a yellow brick road here, it's dirt."

There was an uneasy silence. Claire glanced at Michelle, then closed her eyes. "I can't believe this."

"Actually, I suppose I'm to blame," Michelle said, shifting a little as the mare nudged her from behind. "Last night, I promised Danny if he'd go to sleep and not bug you, I'd show him the horses and the pony that was just the right size for him." She shrugged, then with a wry look she reached out and ruffled his hair. "Like I said, I always ride early in the morning. When he appeared, I didn't really think about whether anybody knew where he was. I just assumed you knew." She looked at Claire. "He's safe at Sugarland, whether you know it or not."

Claire chewed on her lower lip, wishing she were anywhere but at this horrible place. "I apologize for losing control," she said stiffly. "I don't usually make such a fool of myself."

Michelle shrugged. "You were scared. It's a mother-thing. Forget it."

Nodding reluctantly, Claire glanced at Mack. Michelle might be willing to forget her outburst, but he wouldn't. Fortunately, she didn't care what he thought.

"Can we look at my pony now?" Danny begged.

She let him pull her toward the barn.

Claire wasn't sure what to expect for the rest of that day, but to her relief, Michelle didn't seem to hold any resentment and had even invited her to come along for Danny's promised pony ride. He'd been enchanted with the pony, of course, and with everything else about Sugarland. In a way, Claire envied his youthful enthusiasm. How nice to be innocent enough to accept at face value this place, this new experience, even these people.

He fell into an exhausted nap after lunch. Claire seized the chance to slip out of the house and spend a few peaceful moments with her own thoughts and—she admitted it—to indulge her curiosity about Sugarland. Behind the house, at the end of a meandering brick walk, she turned a corner and discovered a pond—or maybe it was a small lake. To her delight, situated in the middle of it was a gazebo.

Did everything in this place look like something out of a storybook? she wondered, walking the wooden footbridge that spanned the water. Inside the gazebo, she spent a moment gazing around at the peaceful setting. In one direction, the big house was visible, its frame shimmering in the August heat. To the west was a vast expanse of green sugarcane. Along the perimeter of the field, a dust plume billowed out behind a slow-moving farm vehicle. Beyond that, a lush, dark line of trees marked a bayou.

She sat down on a wrought-iron settee. Only a light breeze stirred the willow trees ringing the pond. Clumps of purple iris at the water's edge attracted butterflies and bees. Leaning her head back, she closed her eyes. All her life she'd been a city dweller, but she had often imagined she would like country living. Pushing aside thoughts of why she was here, she lost herself in the peace and sounds and smells of deep summer.

Something brushed her ankle. Glancing down, she saw that a dragonfly was perched on the end of her sneaker. Gazing at its wide, fragile wings, she thought of her own precarious fate. How could she continue to stay with the McMolleres indefinitely? Where else could she and Danny go to be safe?

"Want some company?"

For a big man, Mack McMollere moved almost silently, she thought. Backlighted by the glare of the sun on the water, he seemed to fill the arched entrance of the small structure. How had he managed to get so close without making a sound? Shrugging wordlessly to let him know she had no objection to his company, she watched him push away from the arch and come inside.

The settee creaked with his weight as he took a seat beside her, shifting until he was wedged between the back and side arm. It gave him a clear view of Claire.

"Didn't take you long to find the choice spot at Sugarland, did it?"

"It's beautiful," she murmured. "I can see why southern Louisiana has inspired so many writers and poets."

"Yeah, mosquitoes, humidity, relentless heat ten months out of the year, and to top it off, alligators. You can't get much more romantic than that."

So he had a sense of humor. Damn. It was hard to hate a man with a sense of humor.

"Just kidding," he said. She didn't look at him, but there was a smile in his voice. "I'll grant you it's a unique spot on the planet and I wouldn't trade it for, say, Houston."

She turned and studied him as he looked out past the pond to the endless stretch of green cane and beyond. For once, he was without his Stetson, but he wore his sunglasses. "Did you always want to be a sugarcane farmer?"

"No, and I didn't always want to be here. I wanted to fly airplanes and see the world."

"I suppose that is more glamorous than farming."

"To an eighteen-year-old, you'd better believe it." Shaking his head, he smiled wryly. "And the good ol' U.S. Army was happy to oblige me. A few missions in Vietnam and I appreciated Louisiana and farming a lot more."

"Carter said you taught him to fly."

"Yeah. He took to it like a duck to water."

"Does that mean he was a good pilot or that he simply had a flair for flying?"

He looked at her. "He could have been a good pilot, but he was too reckless. He took too many chances. When he finally did crash the Cessna, it was a shock, but I'd always been apprehensive when he went up. You know how it is when you worry about something. When it hits, you aren't taken completely by surprise."

"He took me up only once," Claire said, nodding. "It was an exhilarating experience, but not one that I particularly wanted to repeat."

Mack seemed intent on the line of trees in the distance. "Carter lived on exhilarating experiences."

Claire had no doubt he considered her one of Carter's experiences. Let him think what he pleased.

"You know something? You don't look like a librarian."

She knew where such a remark could lead and she wasn't about to bite. If she was going to keep her relationship with these people as distant as she hoped, she couldn't afford to be chummy with this man. She made a point of studying the view from the gazebo. "You know, you're right to call this spot special. Is there anyplace else at Sugarland you'd care to recommend?"

He was not the kind of man you had to hit over the head to make a point. After a moment, he asked, "Does that work often for you?"

"What?" she asked, giving him a puzzled look.

"That tone. Does it make students quake, or quell uprisings in the library?"

"Usually." She started up, but he stopped her with a touch on her arm. One of her eyebrows streaked upward. "What?"

"Don't go. I admit to some curiosity about you, Claire. Surely that's understandable." He glanced at his watch. "I've got to be back at the house for a conference call in a few minutes, then you can have the gazebo all to yourself."

She eased back down reluctantly.

He brought up a knee and locked his fingers around it in a purely masculine pose. Not only was he bigger and more confident than Carter, she thought, he was simply more of a man. "You wouldn't believe the hours I wasted out here when I was a kid. It's a good place for thinking."

"Yes, I felt that when I found it. And I've certainly got a lot to think about," she admitted. "Where to go from here, for starters."

"There's no need to worry about that. You can stay at Sugarland as long as it takes."

She brushed another dragonfly from the arm of the settee. "Hardly."

"Sure you can."

"I have a job, in case you forgot. Responsibilities. A mortgage to pay, a car note. Danny has to be in school the Tuesday after Labor Day. We have a life."

"What if none of this is resolved by Labor Day?"

"What do you think I'm sitting out here worrying about?"

"And I repeat, you don't have to worry. You'll be safe here."

"And if the situation drags on, you'll loan me the money to keep my condo out of foreclosure and my car from being repossessed?"

He nodded. "Absolutely."

That's all she needed—to get so beholden to the McMolleres that she'd never get them out of her life again. "Thanks, but I'll manage," she said dryly. "Somehow."

"I don't mean to pry into your personal life, but do you have any family? I know your mother died, but what about your father?"

"My parents were divorced when I was very young. I never even knew him."

"What about aunts and uncles?"

"What is this, research for the family tree?" she asked, suddenly realizing what he was doing. "Or ammunition for the custody battle?"

"It's neither," he said. "What if, God forbid, something should happen to you? We know very little about you, Claire. You don't meet people very often who don't have a relative in the world."

"I do have a relative. I have Danny."

"Ah, yes. Danny." He'd shifted a little on the seat beside her. Now his ankle was crossed over his knee. "My brother's heir."

"If that's a dig about Carter's will," she snapped, "you're way off base. I didn't know anything about it until Martin Thibodaux contacted me." She ignored his snort of disbelief. "And even if I had, it would have made no difference. Carter was Danny's biological father and nothing more."

"Excuse me, but that seems a pretty heartless attitude on your part."

"Heartless?" She turned to face him and got a start when she met his incredible blue eyes head-on. He'd taken off the sunglasses and anchored them by one template in the front of his denim shirt. "Try this for heartless, Mr. McMollere. Carter rejected Danny from the moment I told him I was pregnant. He wanted me to get an abortion. When I refused, he let me know in no uncertain terms that he wouldn't be 'blackmailed' into paying for a kid who could never have a place in his life. Then suddenly he appears out of the blue expecting to step into my life—or Danny's life—as casually as he'd opted out of it three years earlier."

"I'm not making excuses for him, but if you're the mistress of a married man, you have to expect these complications."

She jumped up, stung by the ugly label. "I was *not* the mistress of a married man, for your information. I'm no home wrecker, in spite of what you think. I had no idea when I met Carter that he was married. He wore no ring and he denied having any serious relationship until he met me."

Her laugh was a travesty. "And I believed him, can you imagine anyone being so naive? I believed him when he said we'd be getting married, too. I believed him when he said he'd take me to Louisiana, although he made sure he gave me precious little information about where that was in Louisiana. And his parents. Oh, yes, his parents would love me, he said. Then I believed him when he said I couldn't meet them right away because it was the height of the cutting season, but we'd go later. At Christmastime."

She walked to the edge of the gazebo and stared across the willowy pond to the picturesque dwelling in the distance. Then, drawing in an unsteady breath, she turned, leaning against the lattice wall. "But by Christmas, I was pregnant and alone. We'd run into *you,* big brother, at that party in Houston and the cat was out of the bag when you mentioned his wife in front of me. You can imagine how chagrined Carter was." She laughed bitterly again. "But I bet you can't imagine how I felt."

Mack got up and took a step toward her. She rushed on before he spoke. "If you must know, your brother was a pretty spoiled and selfish person. Only someone as naive and inexperienced as I was would have been taken in. Carter didn't love me, he never did. And he certainly didn't love Danny. Oh, he wanted him when he realized Danny might be the only child he'd ever have. Only then did he decide to acknowledge his son." The look she gave Mack was full of disgust. "Danny was almost three years old when that finally happened. Three years!"

Mack reached to touch her.

She put out a hand, shaking her head. "Stop. I didn't mean...I don't want to talk about this right now. To tell the truth, I don't want to talk about Carter ever. I have enough problems, as it is." She looked up, lifting her chin. "Seems every time I get mixed up with you McMolleres, my life takes a bad turn."

Mack crammed his hands deep in his pockets, scowling. "I don't think we can be blamed for the predicament you're in right now." Maybe he sounded a little too emphatic, but, damn it!, she'd caught him off guard with that sob story.

"I wouldn't be in this predicament if I hadn't been dragged here to make this visit! You can hardly deny that."

"Agreed. But now you're here and I don't see you have any choice but to wait it out, at least for a few more days." He rammed his sunglasses back on.

She was looking at him intently. "Then you do believe there's been a murder."

"I didn't say that. But I'm not willing to take any chances with Danny's safety."

"Well, that's something."

Mack watched her put both hands up to check her hair, still smooth at the temples in spite of the heat. Beneath the neat French braid, a few rebellious curls escaped. She found them, tucked them away.

"Talking about Danny, I need to go check on him," she murmured, slipping outside before he had a chance to stop her.

Mack watched her hurry across the footbridge and then break into a graceful jog on the path back to the house. Even though her white blouse was tailored and prim and her khaki shorts were anything but provocative, it was impossible for a woman who looked like Claire to hide her feminine assets. Remembering how she'd looked that morning when she'd rushed out of her bedroom all sleep-tousled and drop-dead sexy, Mack admitted that her efforts to play down her beauty only enhanced her appeal for him.

But then, he'd always chosen the wrong kind of woman.

CHAPTER FIVE

MICHELLE SLIPPED into her chair at dinner that night just as everyone else was finishing up. "So-o-o-o, has the dead body turned up yet?"

Danny, who was busy mixing carrots and mashed potatoes on his plate, looked up with interest.

"Michelle!" Mack glared at her across the table.

"Oops." She put both hands to her cheeks and looked comically apologetic. "Just wondering."

"You're late," Mack said sternly. "We're almost finished. Where have you been?"

"Oh, around. Actually, I drove into town and checked out a few videos for the little buckeroo here." She winked at Danny across the table. "I figured he'd be bored."

"Thank you, Michelle," Claire said, touched by the fact the girl had gone out of her way to do something nice for Danny.

Claire had not looked forward to the evening meal. She was still stinging from her conversation with Mack in the gazebo and braced herself for questions from Angus and Wyona about her relationship with Carter. So far there had been no awkward moments. Possibly because there'd been no time. Danny had been bursting with news of his first pony ride and his first ride on a tractor, courtesy of Mack. The man kept surprising her.

Having a five-year-old underfoot would hardly make his job easier.

"I want to talk to you after dinner, Michelle," Mack said.

Michelle said nothing, simply lifting her shoulder in a so-what-else-is-new shrug.

"Did you get something good, Michelle?" Danny asked.

"*Pulp Fiction,*" Michelle said, plucking a roll from a tray in front of her. "You'll love it, Danny-boy."

"Michelle!" Mack roared.

Claire met his eyes. "She's kidding, Mack." He looked discomfited. Where was the sense of humor he'd displayed in the gazebo? she wondered. Why did it disappear when it came to dealing with his daughter?

"Did you get *The Lion King* and *Aladdin?*" Danny asked eagerly. "I've watched them a thousand times at home."

"I got 'em, sugar baby."

"Sugar baby?" Claire repeated faintly, meeting Mack's eyes fleetingly.

"That's what she calls me, Mommy," Danny said proudly. "'Cause I'm the sugar baby at Sugarland!"

"Not the only one," Claire said with a warm glance at Michelle. "Michelle's a sugar baby, too."

"You've got to be the only person who thinks so," Michelle said, her roll forgotten.

Claire gave Mack a telling look, but he didn't seem to notice. Was the man brain-dead on the subject of his daughter?

The conversation now did not include Danny. He steered it back. "Michelle promised we'd watch videos, Mommy. When we were at the barn."

"Did you thank her?" Claire prodded him with a look.

"Thanks, Michelle." He grinned at her.

"Did you tell them about riding Bucko?" Michelle asked, buttering her roll.

"Yeah, I told 'em. And today I learned how to put on a saddle, huh, Michelle?" He munched on the last of his dinner roll. "Michelle said I could ride Bucko every morning."

"Don't talk with your mouth full, Danny."

He swallowed a big lump. "But I can't leave the house without telling Mommy first, huh, Michelle?"

"Yep. That's the rule, sugar baby."

"And I rode in the tractor with Uncle Mack and he said I could do a line and I did, all by myself."

"A row," Mack corrected, a smile in his voice.

"A row. And I helped him finish that field. It was fun." He looked at Claire. "Did you know tractors have a radio, Mommy? Just like our car."

"I didn't know that," she murmured.

"Can I go watch a video now?"

"Eat a few more carrots, Danny."

"Carter always hated carrots," Wyona said, gazing beyond Danny as if peeking into the past. "I never made him eat them."

"Mommy—" Danny was eager to seize any excuse.

"Don't even ask," she said.

"Wow," Michelle breathed. "How are you with broccoli and peas?"

"Unyielding," Claire answered.

"Too much discipline makes a child timid," Wyona said.

"And too little spoils him rotten," Mack said.

While Claire stared at Mack, Angus waded in. "You can never start training a boy too soon. Trouble starts when you slack off." He waggled his fork in Michelle's direction. "We've got a good example here. Ran wild all over Washington, D.C., Michelle did. Now, if she'd been a boy—"

"I guess it's too late for a sex change," Michelle said.

"Michelle—" Mack sounded exasperated.

"Can I go watch a video now?" Danny begged. "I ate these dumb old carrots."

Claire saw that he'd taken a few bites, but obsessing over Danny's diet would only add to the turmoil at the table. "All right."

As he scrambled out of his chair, she rose to follow, intending to help with the VCR. Michelle popped to her feet. "I'll set it up for him." As Claire hesitated, she added, "It's okay. I know the system." She glanced around the table. "I'll hardly be missed here."

"Well..." Claire didn't want to reject Michelle's offer. She felt she still needed to make amends for the things she'd said that morning. But once Danny was gone, she'd be wide open to an interrogation. So long as he'd been at the table, they'd all been careful about what they said.

"I'll help," Mack said, standing up. "Stay, Claire. Finish your coffee."

She was even more nervous at being left alone with the elder McMolleres without Mack. This whole situation was enough to send her around the bend.

Mack put a hand on Danny's shoulder and the boy smiled blissfully up at him. Another complication. After that tractor ride, Mack had assumed all the qualities of a hero in Danny's eyes. He looked so remarkably right walking between Mack and Michelle. The family resemblance was almost uncanny. Claire wanted to spring up and snatch her son back.

I'm overreacting again. They aren't kidnapping Danny. They're just taking him into the next room to watch TV.

Sinking back into her chair, she forced her uneasiness aside. Danny was fitting in almost too well here. The problem was, where did she fit in?

"My Carter was such a beautiful boy," Wyona said, her pale blue eyes soft with memory.

"That he was, Mama." Angus dipped into his banana pudding. "A pistol, he was, too. Never knew what he'd be up to next."

Wyona frowned, twiddling with the ornate silver beside her plate. "But his eyes were nothing like Danny's. Carter's eyes were green, as green as grass."

"You can never tell about genes," Claire murmured.

"I always thought Carter's son would look just like him." She seemed bewildered that it wasn't true.

"Are you disappointed?" Claire asked coolly.

"Now, Mama. Claire'll be taking offense." His dessert finished, Angus reached for the brandy that Cleo had placed at his elbow and poured it into his coffee. "Why, we love that boy of Carter's. Naturally. He's a McMollere, isn't he." The last was not a question.

Claire murmured a reply. She could guess how they felt about her. She was definitely not a McMollere.

Wyona set her cup carefully on its saucer. "Of course, these types of... ah, relationships make things so... difficult from a grandparent's point of view."

What could she say to that? Claire thought, sipping her coffee. Carter's parents couldn't be blamed for their son's lies. Still, it was hard for her to forgive their heartless attitude when they had learned about Danny.

"Of course, we would have liked a relationship with Danny from the beginning," Wyona said. In her fretful way, Wyona was as persistent as a bulldog.

Claire stared at her. "You would have had no relationship ever if I'd had the abortion," she said bluntly.

"Abortion?" Wyona's eyes were wide with shock. "Surely you never considered such a thing."

"No, I never did. But Carter told me that was what his family wanted me to do, Mrs. McMollere."

Angus put his cup down with a clatter. "Now wait just a minute here, missy! You can't go accusing us of wanting to destroy our son's baby."

"We loved Carter," Wyona said in a wounded tone. "We would have welcomed his baby. You owe us an apology!"

Claire got to her feet, but before she could say the words trembling on her tongue, Mack came into the room.

"What's going on here?"

"I need to check on Danny," Claire said, attempting to brush past him.

"Wait a minute." He caught her by the hand. "I heard the tail end of that conversation. Don't run off until you tell everybody what you told me this afternoon."

Claire pulled her hand from his. "Why should I? What's past is past. I don't need to subject myself to a grilling about my personal life. We all know I'm only here because of Danny."

"Claire, come on. Sit back down." He pulled her chair out at the table and touched her—just barely—at the small of her back. "For Danny's sake, tell them what you said about not knowing that Carter was a married man."

"What's all this?" Angus sat forward suddenly, almost knocking his water goblet off the table.

Claire hesitated, sinking onto her chair. Maybe Mack was right. There would never be any affection for her in this house, but if she were going to be here with these people for God knows how long, there should at least be some honesty between them. And maybe some plain speaking, as well.

Drawing a deep breath, she looked at Carter's parents. "I don't know what Carter told you about me, if anything, and at this point it doesn't make much difference." Realizing that her hands were trembling, she took them off the table and laced them tightly in her lap. "He didn't tell me much about you, just that you lived in Louisiana in an area noted for raising sugarcane. I didn't know anything about Sugarland, nor did I guess the extent of your wealth." When Angus started to speak, Mack silenced him with a look.

"In hindsight," she went on, "I can see a lot of things that should have clued me in to Carter's true colors, but at the time I was simply dazzled by him. I don't have to tell you how attractive and charming he was. I thought I loved him. He *said* he loved me. We were going to be married." She laughed bitterly. "The night I learned he already had a wife, I broke off the . . . affair, but when I discovered I was pregnant a month later, I felt he should know, not because I wanted him to divorce his wife and marry me—I already knew I didn't want him anymore—but I felt he should know he was going to be a father."

"You wanted money," Angus said gruffly.

"I wanted nothing from Carter McMollere," she said.

Wyona made a protesting sound. "My Carter wouldn't—"

"Mama, let her finish," Mack said quietly.

"He urged me to get an abortion," Claire said. "I refused. He said you—his parents—were on record as wanting nothing to do with my bastard. You agreed with him that I should terminate the pregnancy."

Wyona held her clasped hands beneath her chin. "These are blasphemous things to be saying," she whispered.

Claire gave her a sympathetic look. "I didn't ask Carter to help with medical bills, but he let me know that I alone would be responsible for any expenses that came from having the baby. I didn't hear from him again until a few months before the plane crash that killed him. He rang my doorbell one night. Danny was barely three years old. He said Renee had left him, that she was infertile because of endometriosis. He had suddenly realized that Danny might be the only child he would ever have."

"And you turned him away!" Wyona said tearfully. "How could you do that?"

"I asked for time to think about it," Claire said calmly. "I wasn't sure that having Carter for a father was any better than not having one at all."

Angus muttered and fiddled with his napkin, frowning ferociously.

"He died before I decided one way or the other," Claire said.

Mack was studying her silently. "And what do you think your decision would have been?"

"I don't know."

"But why have you been so cruel in keeping Danny away from us?" Wyona sounded genuinely bewildered.

Claire looked at her. "Do you think if you'd been in my place, you would want a relationship with people who'd judged you so harshly without ever having met you? My only contact with anyone besides Carter was that brief encounter with Mack in Houston." Claire felt his gaze, but kept her eyes on Wyona. "He'd made it clear what he thought of me."

"You're saying you read my mind that night?" Mack said.

"A person wouldn't have to be a psychic to read your expression when we were introduced."

She was relieved when Michelle strolled into the dining room. "Is Danny still watching television?"

"If he is, he's doing it with his eyes closed."

"He's asleep?"

"He lasted about eight minutes." She took her seat, surveying the faces around the table with interest. "Uh-oh! What'd I miss? Something heavy's going down, right?"

"Nothing that concerns you." Mack reached for the brandy decanter.

"Is it the murder?" Her blue eyes lit up.

"No, it's not the murder," he said.

"Shoot." She piled a huge salad onto her plate. "Let's talk about it anyway."

"Don't push me tonight, Michelle," Mack warned.

"Wait, wait. I've been thinking," the teenager said. "Listen to this. Has anybody considered the fact that the victim might not have been killed? That he might've just been wounded? That he's probably had to get treatment? Which would force him to see a doctor."

"That's assuming there was a victim." Mack poured himself a stiff brandy. "The word of a five-year-old isn't much to go on."

"There was a shooting." Claire's tone was firm.

Mack looked at her. "I've arranged for someone to keep watch at the hospital and private clinics in the area."

"Cool, Dad." For once, Michelle looked at him with approval.

Claire frowned. "How did you manage that without compromising our safety?"

"Let's just say I managed it."

Michelle eyed them both with interest. "Friends in high places, huh, Dad?"

"I managed it," he repeated.

"What if the killer has the same friends?" Claire wanted to know.

"I don't think so."

Claire chewed uneasily on her lip. "Well, if you think—"

"Trust me."

She had the oddest desire to do just that.

AFTER AN IRRITATING search, Mack finally located Michelle on the front porch. Sprawled on the swing with one leg draped over the side, she was totally absorbed in the music coming through a headset, unaware of him until he was close enough to touch her.

"Oh. Hey." She looked up at him with a puzzled expression. "What's up?"

He had put off a confrontation until after dinner so that he and his daughter could have it out—yet again— without advertising to the world what a hopeless failure he was as a father.

"Where were you this afternoon, Michelle?"

"I told you. I drove into LaRue to get some videos for Danny." She removed the headset.

"Before that."

She flicked the off-switch. "There's nothing to do around here, so I took Cherry out after lunch. I guess I sort of lost track of time."

"I've asked you to tell somebody when you leave the house. And especially if you're on horseback. Something could happen to your mount. You'd be stranded God knows where."

"Nothing happened, and I didn't get stranded."

Mack sighed. "I know. Because you weren't riding at all, were you, Michelle?"

"Meaning what, Dad?" She spoke with heavy sarcasm.

"You rode Cherry out to the bayou to meet Jake Reynolds. The two of you rode off together in his car."

"What if I did?"

She said it defiantly, but her voice was a little unsteady. Maybe she wasn't as tough as she talked, Mack thought. "Then you deliberately disobeyed me. I told you I didn't want you seeing Jake. Take it from me, he's no good for you."

"Why? Because his family doesn't belong to the country club?"

He sighed. "No, Michelle, because Wayne Pagett arrested him last year in Abadie Parish for stealing merchandise from the store where he worked."

"He didn't steal that stuff! It was the guy who worked there before him. Jake was innocent."

Mack shook his head. Trying to convince her that Jake was bad news was a waste of time. Hell, his bad-boy image was probably half his appeal. Mack gazed beyond her, gathering his thoughts. He hadn't forgotten how it felt to have a crush at age fifteen. "Michelle, I wonder if you realize the trouble you can get into if you're not careful. A boy like Jake—"

"You mean I could get pregnant?"

"No! I mean you could get hurt." He gave her a sharp look. "You aren't . . . ah, you haven't . . ."

"We're not having sex, Dad." The sarcasm was heavy again. "And thanks for your concern."

God, how did other single fathers handle moments like this? "Michelle, I know you want to have the freedom to choose your own friends, but—"

"Jeez, he's finally catching on."

"But I'm telling you for your own good—keep away from Jake Reynolds. He'll only cause you trouble. He's too old for you. Believe me, he was *born* older than you."

"You're wrong! You don't know anything about Jake. He's nice. He doesn't say mean things about you like you do about him."

He could believe that. Jake was too smart to bad-mouth a girl's father until he got what he wanted. Mack's stomach roiled at that thought. He was definitely not ready to deal with this. He and Michelle still had so much to learn about each other. "I'm telling you, Michelle, if I catch you seeing him again—"

"What'll happen? You'll beat me?"

He pushed a hand through his hair and searched for some way to say what had to be said. "I'll have to come down hard on you, honey." Hell, he didn't *want* to threaten her, but how else to steer her away from certain danger?

"You already come down hard on me," she argued, facing away from him again. "I don't get to do anything. I have the strictest rules of all my friends. Everyone has more freedom than me."

"I can't help how other people raise their kids, Michelle. I do what I think best for your own good."

Her head whipped around. "My own good! It's funny you didn't think about what's good for me before now. You didn't even know I existed until my mother packed me off down here."

He rubbed the back of his neck wearily. "Let's not get into that one tonight, Michelle."

"Oh, excuse me. We're having a talk about my rules, my behavior, my life, but we're not supposed to mention how it is that I'm even down here in Louisiana in the first place." She turned from him. "Well, don't worry, I won't put you on the spot, *Daddy*. I guess we both know it's not because you wanted me."

Lord. His hand went out as if to touch her, but then fell to his side. He wished she was Danny's age so he could just sweep her up and hold her, tell her how much he regretted all the years she'd been apart from him. It hadn't been because he didn't want her, but because Liz...

But hell, how could a father say something as ugly as that? He was having difficulty enough trying to find common ground so they could somehow connect. Trashing Liz was definitely not the way to go.

Michelle sprang up and went to the porch railing. "If I can't see Jake, then what am I supposed to do around here? I have to practically punch a time clock, as it is, otherwise you're out in that stupid Jeep hunting me down and dragging me back to this...this...overgrown swamp in the back of beyond."

He recognized her mother's description of Sugarland. "Is that what you really think?"

"Well, it's true, isn't it?"

"For some, maybe. I know Liz never liked living here."

"Well, now I know why. This place is nowhere!"

He looked out at the vast sweep of cane fields set against a brilliant orange evening sky. Directly in his line of vision was a two-hundred-year-old live oak, its trunk too wide for five men with outstretched arms to span. The limbs, sixty feet across, dripped Spanish moss. In the distance was the pond with its willows and purple iris. Five generations of his family had lived and died on this land. Thanks to Liz, his angry, hurting daughter felt no connection with any of it. He fought the sting of old resentments. Old frustrations. How had he allowed this to happen?

"Michelle, I know you don't understand, but I—"

"Okay, all right, I know this song. Mention my mother and you want to change the subject, or better yet, just decide everything's been said that needs to be said and time's up, you're outta here and off the hook."

"That's not true, honey."

Her eyes glistened with tears. "Well, that's the way it seems to me. I guess I have to do what you say because you're the big man around here and everybody jumps when you say the word, but your fatherly interest seems to be coming a little late. If you really cared about me, you wouldn't have dumped me when I was three years old."

"I didn't dump you, Michelle. Your mother and I got a divorce when you were three. She got custody and moved with you and her new husband hundreds of miles from here. There's no way I could pack up Sugarland and take it to Washington, D.C."

"Right. No way. Hey, no problem, there aren't many parents around who'll go the whole nine yards for their kid like Claire Woodson."

Mack wanted to roar a denial. No one could twist his heart like Michelle. He drew a deep breath, his anger at

Liz heavy in his chest. Had his ex-wife destroyed any chance of his ever getting close to Michelle? "This isn't getting us anywhere, little girl." He ignored her huff at the endearment. "We're way off the subject and the reason why I wanted to talk to you. You might not like it, but I don't want you sneaking off to meet Jake Reynolds. Can I have your promise on that?"

For a long moment, he thought she might tell him to go to hell. What would he do then? How would he handle a challenge to his authority as her father, when he hadn't been much of a father to her in the last twelve years?

"Do I have a choice?" Without looking at him, she picked up the headset and walked past him to go inside.

CHAPTER SIX

CLAIRE AVOIDED a collision with Michelle by quickly sidestepping as the girl rushed through the front door, brushing at the sheen of tears in her eyes. Before Claire could ask what was wrong, the teenager was halfway up the stairs. No need to ask. Only one person seemed to be able to make Michelle cry. Claire stepped out onto the porch and, sure enough, there he was.

If Mack heard her, he gave no sign. He faced the horizon, as rigid as the big white column beside him. Softly closing the door behind her, she sighed and went across the porch to the swing, then sat down. With a little push, she sent the swing into motion.

"Admiring the sunset?" she asked.

"Yeah." He did not move.

It was a spectacular sight, a brilliant red sky that darkened to crimson, but she didn't believe he was thinking about the beauty before him. She chanted quietly, " 'Red sky at night, sailor's delight, red sky at morning, sailor take warning.' "

"I was in the army, not the navy," he growled.

She couldn't see his face, but she could make out the line of his jaw. It could have been carved out of swamp cypress, it was so hard. She shrugged. "Just making conversation."

Waiting a few seconds, she added, "Which is probably the last thing you're interested in, but I've got a couple of questions about something you said at dinner. Then I'll leave you to your brooding.''

He made a grumpy sound, then turned to look at her. "Was I brooding?"

"It looked that way...but of course I could be wrong."

As their eyes met, she felt a quick connection, something that altered her heart's rhythm for a beat or two. She could not be attracted to this man—to Carter's brother. It was the last thing she needed. Only a fool would be drawn into something so wildly impossible.

"What kind of questions?"

"What? Oh, the point Michelle made. If a man survived a gunshot, where would he go if he needed medical attention?"

Mack leaned against the column and crossed his legs at the ankles. "It depends." At her frown, he added, "If he had nothing to hide, he'd go to a hospital."

"Nothing to hide?"

"If it was a drug deal gone wrong or something along that line, he would probably try to avoid questions."

"How would he do that?"

"Your guess is as good as mine. It's pretty hard to keep a serious injury a secret...unless you're in a major city with connections to the underworld."

"New Orleans, for instance?"

"Yeah, and we're only a couple of hours away. If the victim is in a hospital or has visited a reputable physician, he'll be easy to find. Gunshot wounds have to be reported. If for some reason he needs to lie low, my source will probably come up dry."

"Who is your source?"

"A man I'd trust with my life."

"Just one man?"

"Yeah."

She could tell from his expression that he wasn't going to name names. Besides, what would a name mean to her, anyway? Everyone here was a stranger.

"Good." She tucked a stray wisp of hair back into her bun. Unaware of his eyes following the gesture, she continued. "Meantime, I suppose Danny and I are stuck here."

"Yeah, but don't worry, we have running water, plenty to eat and air-conditioning."

"I'm sorry." She touched her mouth. "That sounded rude. I'm thankful Danny's safe, even if I don't sound like it."

"I know it's hard for you." Mack pushed away from the column, walked to the swing and sat down. The smell of the outdoors still clung to him. Mixed with the faint hint of his after-shave, the scent was more than a little appealing.

"If we weren't here, I shudder to think about our options," she murmured.

"Forget it. You *are* here."

She accepted that with a nod. Later she would try to figure out why she was willing to trust this man, when his brother had been anything but trustworthy. He shifted, bringing his arm up to rest on the back of the swing. Suddenly she was intensely aware of him, his size, the breadth of his shoulders, the power of his thighs, the only part of him she could decently examine without turning and looking him over. Because she wanted to do just that, she felt a rush of heat, a definite sexual response that confused her. Frightened her.

She studied her hands, aware now that he was watching her. Then, as if he'd pulled a string and turned her to face him, she found herself staring at him. Eyes so dark they were the color of a midnight sky. Features defined with harsh lines and sharp angles. A mouth unsmiling, but with a soft sensuality that made her heart do another little tap dance.

"I've been wondering about something," Mack said, his low tone shivering over her skin. She didn't reply—couldn't!—but her eyes followed his hand as it moved toward her. He caught the unruly wisp of hair that wouldn't stay put and rubbed it between his fingers. "Why do you keep your hair bound up so tight?"

While she was thinking what to say, he went on, "And why do you wear those prissy blouses and baggy shorts? It doesn't hide the fact that you're a beautiful woman."

"I'm not beautiful." That wasn't what she'd meant to say at all. She'd meant to say, *Keep your hands to yourself. Don't speak to me like that. Just because I was your brother's lover doesn't give you the right to come on to me.*

Mack didn't plan it, but somehow his hand was on the comb holding her hair in that awful bun. In one twist, he had it out and her hair spilled onto her shoulders. "Oh, yes, you're beautiful, all right. It's no wonder Carter lost his mind."

He wished the words back the instant they were out. She caught her hair in one hand and moved out of his reach. "Your brother didn't lose his mind, Mack. He was bored in his marriage and he decided to have a little fling. Or if he was momentarily crazed with passion for me, he certainly got over it fast when he realized his family knew what he was up to."

"Not his family. Only me."

He could feel her outrage. And now that he knew her better, he knew she had every right to be outraged with Carter—hell, with the whole McMollere clan.

She wasn't done. "When Carter realized he might have to suffer a few uncomfortable consequences—like a baby—he certainly didn't seem like a besotted lover."

"No, once he knew about the baby, he did what he always did when he found himself in hot water. He looked for the easiest, quickest way out."

She glanced at him in surprise. "That's exactly what happened." She put out her hand. "Now, I'll take my comb, if you don't mind."

He held up the hair fastener.

"Thanks." She took it and with a deft move or two, wound her hair into the tight coil he hated, and secured it with the comb. Without another word, she stood up and went inside, closing the door softly behind her.

He sat there for a moment. Her perfume lingered. Something so light and flowery and feminine that it was almost not there. Liz had always worn heavy, expensive-smelling stuff. Nothing like Claire's fragrance. *Liz* was nothing like Claire. He turned his gaze to the horizon again and for a long time was lost in thought.

It was dark when he finally got up and went inside.

FOUR LONG DAYS PASSED. Claire was used to a busy schedule, up early with precious little time to while away doing nothing. At Sugarland, the high point of her day was midmorning when the newspaper arrived. But so far, no murder had been reported. No dead body had been discovered. No person had gone missing. She began to wonder how long she would have to keep her life on hold. Even though the McMolleres wanted to get to know Danny, she was certain they hadn't bargained on having to put up with her, too, especially after hearing the details of her affair with Carter.

She stood at the kitchen window, her eyes following a plume of dust boiling up behind a farm vehicle in the distance. The McMolleres were scrupulously correct in their Southern hospitality. They'd repeatedly urged her to treat their house as her own, and she had to admit that if she had to go into exile anywhere, Sugarland was a lovely place to do it.

She watched the farm vehicle stop, and smiled when she saw Mack get out and then turn to help Danny scramble down. "Riding shotgun" with Mack again, she thought, and her smile faded. Her son was in heaven. He rode Bucko every morning with Michelle and then, when he could wangle it, dogged every footstep Mack made in his rounds of the place. Danny was dazzled by his uncle. It wasn't new or unusual behavior to Claire. With few adult males in his life, he was always on the lookout for a father figure.

Claire was troubled as she reached for lemons and sugar to make herself a cool drink. Danny had adjusted to life at Sugarland as if he'd been born here. Another concern. The longer they stayed, the greater Danny's disappointment when they had to leave.

But as soon as it was safe, she vowed, they would leave. Neither of them belonged here, no matter how beguiling life at Sugarland might seem.

She took a tray with the pitcher of lemonade and headed for the sun room, grabbing a paperback and the Baton Rouge newspaper on the way. In the mornings, the sun room had the best view. And the most privacy.

With the toe of her sneaker, she managed to work the door open, then backed in, carrying the tray carefully, mindful of the glossy white floor. She didn't realize the room was occupied until she heard Michelle apparently talking on the phone.

"But, Mom, you promised I could come and visit before school starts and that's the Monday after Labor Day."

As Claire turned around, the door clicked shut. She made a face. Too late to leave without letting Michelle know she'd intruded, although the girl's back was to Claire. She was sitting on the floor, hugging a cushion, the fingers of one hand spread wide on the crown of her dark head. She still wore the jeans and T-shirt that she rode in every day, but she sounded far different from the sassy teen that Claire had come to know.

"A cruise!" Michelle's tone was full of dismay. "But you already went to Florida. Why—" She broke off, waited a few seconds. "I know it was in February," Michelle said plaintively. "I know it's cold in Washington in the winter. I know you and Vic have to grab time for yourselves when the House is in recess, but, Mom, you *promised!*"

Claire looked around for a place to set the tray down and get out. She had no desire to eavesdrop on such a personal exchange.

Michelle's voice was now low and trembling. "Listen, Mom, I know I acted real . . . difficult before and that's why you made me come here, but I'll try not to bug you so much if you'll just—" Her voice caught in a sob. "No, Mom. Please. *Pleeeze.*"

Claire walked over to the glass patio table and put the tray down. If Michelle noticed her, she gave no sign. Claire turned and headed for the door.

Michelle was crying openly now. "I know why, Mom. You don't have to make up lies. You don't want me with you. You never did want me, not really. I'm in the way and I embarrass you, isn't that what you're always saying? Well, Daddy doesn't want me either. He hardly ever says anything to me and when he does it's to criticize me or nag me or threaten me. I hate it here! I hate it in Washington, too! Just tell me this, Mom. Where in the stupid world is there a place for me?"

She slammed down the receiver with a crash, then buried her face in her hands, weeping in great, gulping sobs. At the door, Claire hesitated. The last hurtful words hung in the air. No adult could have a conversation like that with her own mother and walk away unscathed. It was ten times worse for a teenager. With a sigh, she turned around and stepped back into the room, pulling the door closed behind her.

"Michelle . . ."

Her face still buried in her hands, still sobbing, Michelle shook her head. "Go away."

"When I'm sure you're okay."

With a bitter laugh, Michelle looked up at the ceiling. "That might be when I'm about forty." Then she turned to Claire. "Do you think you'll stick around that long?"

Claire smiled. "Maybe not, but I'll probably be here till next week. And I'm a good listener."

"Why would you bother?"

"I heard some of your conversation—I didn't intend to eavesdrop, but I didn't know you were in here when I opened the door. It sounds as though you're homesick."

Michelle looked at her. "Homesick? You've got to be kidding."

"It's nothing to be ashamed of." Claire spread her hands with a wry expression. "I'm pretty homesick myself."

Using both hands, Michelle wiped her tears. "I'm not homesick. I just—"

Claire sat down beside her, crossing her legs, and waited.

Michelle licked at a stray tear slipping down her cheek. "Did you ever wish you'd never been born?"

Claire's heart missed a beat. She had seen too many teenage tragedies in her years as a teacher to brush aside such a remark. "I've been pretty unhappy at times, Michelle. When things are bad, most people look around and wish there was a way to avoid the pain. That's human nature."

Michelle studied her palms. "How about this one—did you ever wish you were born male, not female?"

"Honestly?" Claire smiled. "Not really. Being female has gotten me into trouble once or twice, but I think I prefer being a woman to the alternative."

"No offense, or anything, but one of the reasons everybody's so gaga over Danny is because he's a boy. He can carry on the name and all that stuff."

"Not exactly," Claire said, smiling again. "His name's Danny Woodson, not McMollere."

"They'll fix that."

"We'll see." Claire let it go. Michelle was the wrong person to hear her thoughts on that subject.

Michelle made another distressed sound. "I just can't believe my mother intends to leave me here f-forever."

"Is this a custody thing?" Claire asked, hesitant about making a sticky situation worse.

Michelle raked her fingers through her hair. "I guess it used to be a custody thing. My earliest memories are hearing my mother rant and rave to my stepfather about my dad, about how selfish he was and how he didn't care about her and me. Which was true, because I only ever visited him in the summer and then for only a couple of weeks. If he'd cared about me, wouldn't he come to see me at Christmas or Thanksgiving or something?''

"Did you enjoy those summer visits?"

She looked away thoughtfully. "I guess so. We didn't do much, you know, together. Mostly he left me here with my grandmother because he was outside all day. Farming isn't like an office job. He left early and came home late."

"As he does now."

"Yeah."

Claire resisted the urge to come to Mack's defense. She knew the pitfalls in trusting any McMollere, but there was such an air of...dependability about Mack. No longer than she'd been here, she could see that he was the hub around which everything revolved at Sugarland. No decision was made without running it by Mack first. She had come to respect him, but what did she know of him personally? How could a man like that fail so utterly as a father?

"How is your situation different this summer from all the other summers you've spent at Sugarland?" Claire asked.

"I didn't just ar...rive." She drew out the word, wiping her cheeks with both hands. "My mother dumped me here at the beginning of the spring semester. She said it was because of some things I did, but it's really because she doesn't want me around anymore."

To see her face, Claire reached over and tucked a strand of midnight-dark hair behind the girl's ear. "That's a pretty incredible statement, Michelle. Do you really believe it?"

The teenager toyed with the laces on one sneaker. "I know it. Without me, she and Vic—"

"Your stepfather?"

"Uh-huh. She and Vic are free to do anything, go anywhere on the spur of the moment. When I'm around, there's school and stuff, my friends and all. Having kids around is a real negative for some people."

"It's worth it for most parents."

"Yeah, I've noticed how you are with Danny. You'd do anything for him. Shoot, you'd even move in with people you hate for Danny's sake. People like you can't understand people like my parents."

"Two things, Michelle." Claire touched the girl's chin, forcing Michelle to look her in the eyes. "One, I don't hate the McMolleres. I barely even know them. I'm all Danny has in the world except for them, so I have to be careful that he doesn't get hurt. So I'm wary, I'm concerned. And second, I can't speak for your mother. I know nothing about her, but in the few days I've been around your father, I've seen a man who takes his responsibilities very seriously. And you, as his only child, are the ultimate responsibility. As fathers go, you could do a lot worse."

Michelle stared at her feet. "The only time he ever notices me, it's to yell at me."

It must seem that way, Claire thought with a sigh. The man loved his daughter. She saw it in his eyes. Why couldn't he show it to Michelle?

"If just once he would...would..." She darted a look at Claire before focusing on her feet again. "Maybe give me a hug, or something. Is that too much to ask?"

With a soft murmur, Claire leaned over and stroked the girl's hair. "Or say something like, 'Michelle, I love you'?"

There was a sharp catch in Michelle's voice. "I'll never hear him say that, I bet."

"Oh, I don't know. Stranger things have happened."

They sat for a moment, each with her own thoughts. Then Michelle spoke. "You know something?"

"What?"

"I did it on purpose."

"Did what?" Claire bent to see her face.

"The reason I had to come and live with my dad is because I was at this party with some friends and we decided we wanted some beer and on the way home we were stopped and I had an open container. Me being only fifteen, and all, it was a big deal. Boy, were they mad."

"I can imagine," Claire murmured.

"But it worked. They sent me to my dad, just like I planned all along. But it's turned out to be a real bummer. Except for Jake." She flipped a wing of dark hair over her shoulder, and met Claire's eyes. "I guess it was stupid of me to think my dad and I could finally get to know each other, huh?"

"Again, stranger things have happened. Maybe the two of you just got off on the wrong foot by your mother's suddenly deciding you needed to live here. I assume she told him why."

"She couldn't wait."

"And did you tell him you'd planned the whole thing?"

"No way."

"Then maybe you should."

"And maybe you live in a dreamworld," Michelle said, but she had a thoughtful look on her face as she gazed through the windows. "Speaking of my dad, here he is now."

Claire had spotted the Jeep coming up the driveway, too. She saw Mack get out and walk to the passenger side of the Jeep, then lift Danny up into his arms. Her son was unconscious! Her heart stopped. With a muffled cry, she scrambled up and ran to the sun-room door, fumbling at the old-fashioned catch before bolting into the hall. Mack was already inside the house when she reached the foyer. With Danny cradled on his shoulder, he pushed the door closed with the toe of his boot.

"What happened to Danny?" she cried, rushing over to take him from Mack.

He shifted slightly to hold her off. "Hey, hey, it's okay, he's asleep, that's all."

"Oh, Lord." With a hand on her heart, she went limp, closing her eyes. "You scared me to death."

"Come on," he said, already starting up the stairs. "I'll carry him to his room, since you don't look like you could carry a newborn at the moment. He's dead-weight, out like a light. Too many pony rides and too little sleep."

Reaching the bedroom, he put Danny down on the mattress and waited while Claire removed the boy's sneakers and checked him over.

"What are you looking for? I told you he's fine. He's just pooped out."

"I don't know." The motherly inspection over, she stepped back. Her heart was finally quieting, though her hands weren't yet steady. To hide them, she slipped her fingers inside the back pockets of her jeans. The pose pushed her breasts forward. Because it was hot, her shirt was unbuttoned three from the top, and she realized how she must appear when she saw Mack looking. She felt a flush of heat. At the same time, she caught the musky, male scent of him, fresh in from the fields—sun and sweat and cut grass. Hastily she pulled her hands free and crossed her arms over her midriff, a purely defensive reaction to the look in his eyes. He absolutely did have the bluest eyes she'd ever seen.

Mack didn't know what it was about this woman that she could get to him the way she did. He knew now she didn't do it intentionally. Everything about her was buttoned up tight, as if she was afraid of even looking female. But when she was scared for Danny or flustered over a certain kind of look from him, no amount of buttoning up or tightening down of her assets worked. Didn't she know that?

With his thumb, he pushed his Stetson back slightly. "You need to get a grip, Claire. Otherwise Danny's going to pick up on your panic, and it's not good for a kid to sense turmoil in a parent. Take my word, it'll come out in ways you won't like at all."

She stared at him for a long moment, her red hair for once all squiggly around her temples. Damn, he'd forgotten how downright pretty her face was. How creamy-smooth her skin was. What a kissable mouth she had.

"I can't believe you," she said, blowing a loose strand away from her cheek.

He shifted his weight onto one hip and stuffed his hands in his pockets to keep from touching her to see if she was as soft as she looked. "What can't you believe?"

"You. Telling me how to be a good parent."

"Why not? I'm a parent, too."

"Exactly. And I just spent the last thirty minutes listening to your daughter pour her heart out about the state of affairs between you and her and her mother."

His mellow mood evaporated like mist in the sun. "What has she been saying?"

"She's confused and hurting," she told him. "I overheard her talking to her mother on the phone. Michelle thinks she's a nuisance to you both, that nobody has room in their lives for her, not you or her mother. Kids who feel like that do desperate things sometimes.''

''Desperate? How desperate?''

''Who knows? I'm just telling you what I sensed when we talked. Worse yet, she thinks you don't love her.''

''That's crazy. She's my daughter. Naturally I love her.''

''When did you last give her a hug?''

He clamped a hand behind his neck and frowned.

''When did you last give her a compliment?''

His frown grew darker and he found it hard to meet her eyes.

''When did you last tell her that you love her?''

She'd hit a real nerve there. ''Why don't you mind your own business?''

''Fine. I'll be glad to.'' She started toward the door, taking care not to touch him as she passed. ''And I'll thank you to keep your ideas about how I deal with my son to yourself, as well.''

Mack was right behind her as she stormed out of the room. For some reason, he wasn't ready to let her go. She'd caught him cold about Michelle, but everything she said was true. He'd been worrying about it ever since Michelle got here. In fact, he'd been toying with the idea of getting some advice from Claire. Who better, since she worked with teenagers all day every day? He was about to stop Claire, when Michelle called to him from downstairs.

''Dad, someone's here to see you.''

''Who is it, Michelle?''

''Sheriff Wayne Pagett.''

CHAPTER SEVEN

"THE SHERIFF IS HERE?" Claire looked at Mack, her eyes wide. Fear and uncertainty poured through her.

"He's an old friend." Mack gave her a reassuring touch on the shoulder and headed for the stairs.

"Then he's not here because of Danny and me? Not because of the murder?"

Mack gave her an impatient look. "I don't know why he's here, Claire. I'm on my way down to find out."

"Is he your source?"

He drew a deep breath and looked away briefly. "Yeah, he's my source."

She stared at him angrily. "You told a policeman?"

"I told Wayne Pagett, a trusted friend."

"You know what Danny said, Mack. It was a policeman who shot the man!"

"It wasn't Wayne Pagett."

"What if the culprit is one of his deputies?" She looked around wildly as though the shooter might be lurking nearby. "What have you done?"

He was at the top of the stairs. He stopped and came back to her. "Look, Claire, don't you think you're jumping the gun here? Wayne Pagett isn't just the sheriff, he's an old friend of the family. He could be here on a social call, not official business. Or maybe he's found out something that might be helpful. After all, that's what I asked him to do."

"It's exactly what I asked you not to do. Danny told us the gunman was a policeman."

"And this policeman I would trust with my life."

"It's not your life! It's Danny's!"

He caught her by the shoulders. "Stop it! It's not helpful to go off the deep end before you even know why Wayne is here."

For a few seconds their eyes locked stubbornly. Then the fight seemed to go out of Claire. "I'm coming down with you."

Mack hesitated, then he let her go, and with a resigned look, threw out a hand indicating she could go in front of him.

Fine, she thought, doing just that. Because if he assumed she was going to sit back and play a passive role, he was one hundred and eighty degrees off the mark. Then, halfway down the stairs, she glanced back and caught him watching her, the look in his eye openly sexual. She didn't know why. Surely there was nothing very appealing about her figure in jeans and an overlarge man's shirt.

Still, she was flustered by the time she reached the bottom of the stairs.

A tall, middle-aged man with iron-gray hair stood in the foyer chatting with Michelle. He looked up as she and Mack approached and seemed as interested in Claire as she was in him.

If there was a stereotype for a lawman, then surely this guy filled the bill, she thought. He wore his tan uniform as though it had been tailor-made for him. His hat was tucked beneath his arm, his sunglasses anchored in his shirt pocket. His boots were polished to a fare-thee-well and his weapon was holstered at his waist—a waist surprisingly lean and trim for his years. He had a good face, strong with attractive, carved features.

"Ma'am." He nodded, giving her a shrewd look before speaking to Mack. "Hope I'm not interrupting anything," he said after the two had shaken hands.

"We're glad you came," Mack said. He looked at Michelle. "Would you drive the Jeep down to the pumping station, Michelle? Tell the crew that I'll be awhile up here at the house and that I'll see them when I'm done."

Michelle hesitated, then said, "Okay, Dad. It was nice seeing you, Sheriff."

"You too, honeybun."

"Tell Barney I said hello, okay?"

"You got it, sugar."

Pagett gazed at the door after she left. "Now, there's a darlin' girl, Mack. A little more time at Sugarland and she'll forget D.C.'s on the map."

Mack didn't reply, but drew Claire forward. "This is Claire Woodson, Wayne."

"I guessed that," Wayne said, turning and giving her a warm handshake and a smile. "My wife, Miriam, met you once at a teachers' conference in Baton Rouge, Miss Woodson. She came away a real fan of yours."

"Call me Claire. Please." It was impossible not to respond to his easy charm. "I remember Miriam. She was such a help to me at that conference. It was my first and she was an old hand. In fact, we had lunch together the last day. How is she?"

His expression changed, became somber. "I lost her, I'm afraid, to breast cancer. Two years ago."

"Oh, I'm so sorry. She was a lovely lady."

He nodded. "She was that, for sure."

"Wayne has a grown son and daughter." Mack tried to ease the awkward moment. "Grandchildren, too, a boy and a girl, right, Wayne?"

The sheriff chuckled. "Right, Kayla's kids. But that son of mine..." He shook his head. "He's like you, Mack. Just can't seem to find the right girl."

"What brings you to Sugarland, Wayne?" Mack asked.

"No good news, I'm afraid." The sheriff fumbled in his pocket and pulled out a small spiral-top notebook. "A body was discovered this morning by some company inspectors at a remote petroleum site off Bayou Chene. Been dead four or five days, according to the coroner."

Claire felt a little jolt in her chest.

"How did he die?" Mack was watching the sheriff closely.

"Shot. Single bullet in the chest. Still there, lodged at the spine. Coroner's just guessing about that, of course, although he believes the autopsy'll confirm it."

Claire held her fingers against her mouth. "What...who...?"

"If you're asking whether he's the man your little boy saw at the hotel, it sure seems that way." Pagett tugged at one ear. "The boy's description fits to a tee."

"Oh, God." With her hand stretched out blindly behind her, she found a chair and sank into it. "It's true, then."

"Well, there's no way we can be sure, but if Danny—that's your son's name, right?—if Danny's eyewitness account of the shooting is to be believed, then this is our man. Now it's up to us to figure out what was going on."

Claire was shaking her head helplessly. "Have you identified him? Who was he?"

"Now, that's a shocker, I can tell you." He rubbed a hand over his chin, then looked squarely at Mack. "It's Tim Landry, Mack."

Mack's head came up with a jerk. "Good Lord, Wayne. What the hell's going on here?"

"Beats me."

Claire was looking from one to the other. "Tim Landry? Who is he? Did you know him, Mack?"

"Yeah. He was . . . Carter's friend, his roommate in college. They were close, real close."

"Oh, no." She touched his arm. "I'm sorry."

Mack was frowning in thought. "That's why there was no blood," he murmured.

She didn't understand. "What?"

"The bullet didn't exit. That would explain why there was no blood on the sidewalk."

"He could have fallen on the grass." Wayne slipped the notebook back into his pocket. "First thing the next morning after you described the incident to me, I took a look at the scene. Keeping in mind where the boy was standing, it could be that Tim fell to the grass, not onto concrete."

Mack nodded. "Maybe. But how did the killer get the body away without anybody seeing anything?"

"Somebody did see something," Claire reminded them.

"Yes, ma'am," Wayne said. "And we don't plan to forget that. Which reminds me, the whole thing was pretty reckless, shooting somebody at a hotel when anyone who happened to be looking could see. Then that incident at Star-Mart in a store crowded with shoppers . . ." He was shaking his head. "This guy is either stupid or deranged. Or both."

"Anybody who'd try and kidnap a child is deranged," Claire said with quiet conviction.

"Too bad you didn't file a formal complaint at Star-Mart," Wayne said. "We'd have some kind of file on the guy."

It was a minute before Mack spoke. "I went back that night and talked to Taylor, the assistant manager," he said. "He hadn't dismissed the incident as Claire assumed. In fact, he asked around to see if anybody else had noticed the guy schmoozing up a five-year-old. Like most eyewitness accounts, people contradicted each other. But essentially it's this—we have a six-foot-tall white male in a baseball cap and sunglasses wearing jeans and a sport shirt rather than a T-shirt. Hair color was everything from blond to black. Nobody noticed any scars, tattoos or other peculiar markings. Since he was so average in appearance, it leaves us little to go on."

"I didn't know you'd gone back to Star-Mart," Claire said, realizing suddenly how busy Mack had been on her behalf ever since she'd arrived in LaRue. It felt good, having somebody to care. Maybe a little *too* good.

Wayne was watching her with a half smile. "You could do a lot worse than having Mack in your corner, Claire."

She didn't need *any* man in her corner, especially a McMollere. She'd made that mistake once before. Besides, Mack's first priority wasn't her, it was Danny, his brother's child, his parents' only grandson. So no matter how comforting his support was or how secure it felt, she was on her own, as always. But that was what she wanted, wasn't it? As long as they were looking out for Danny, she could take care of herself. Hadn't she always?

"Who would want to kill Tim Landry?" Mack said suddenly, the words bursting out. "He was nothing like Carter. I never saw him lose his temper. He liked to play the piano more than sports. Carter wanted him to learn to fly, but he was too timid. Froze up every time he tried to land. He was an accountant, for God's sake."

"I understand he was an alcoholic, Mack. Is that right?"

Mack shrugged. "I've heard that, but I can't say for sure."

"Here now, what's going on?" Angus shuffled into the room, taking in the occupants in a single glance. In spite of the pulled muscles in his face, his expression was shrewd. He approached Wayne Pagett, leaning heavily on his cane, but his handshake was firm. "Is this official business, Wayne, or has crime dried up enough in Abadie Parish that you can while away the afternoons drinking coffee and shooting bull?"

Wayne pulled out a cigar. "You don't need to worry about my work habits, Angus. You worry about the sheriff of *your* parish."

"You aren't gonna light that thing, are you?" Angus backed up hastily.

"In front of a man who never appreciated quality and aroma in fine tobacco?" Wayne retorted, clamping the cigar in his mouth unlit. "Hell, no."

"Hmmph." Angus turned his attention to Mack. "Well, y'all gonna tell me what's going on here? I had a stroke, but it didn't scramble my brains, at least, not much. I'm gimped up, not senile."

"You better have a seat, Angus," Wayne said.

The old man's blue eyes got sharper. "Y'all got a lead on that killing my grandson reported?"

"Here, Dad, sit here." Mack pulled up a chair he knew Angus favored.

"Am I gonna need to be sitting for what you're gonna say?"

Wayne took a seat beside Angus. "I'll be honest with you, Angus. It's troubling."

"Let's have it then." Angus seemed more testy than anxious.

"A body has turned up matching the description the boy gave." Wayne eyed the unlit cigar he was rolling between thumb and forefinger. "It's Tim Landry, Angus."

Angus was silent for a moment, his thoughts not revealed on his ravaged face. But Claire sensed that he was deeply moved. The hand holding his cane clenched and he couldn't seem to steady it. After all, Tim Landry had been Carter's boyhood friend. Any reminder of Carter must be painful.

"Godalmighty," he murmured finally. "Jess and Birdie will take it hard."

"I just got back from telling them," Wayne said, nodding gravely. "I guess you'd understand that better than most."

"Hmm, yes . . . yessiree." He studied the head of his cane pensively. The thought came to Claire that he wasn't thinking about Tim's parents. He didn't seem grief-stricken, either. Not exactly. Just what was he feeling?

Angus looked up sharply. "What do you make of it, Wayne? Who'd want to kill Tim? And why?"

"That's what we've been asking ourselves."

"And what's the answer?" Angus turned to Mack. "You got any ideas about this?"

"Not really, Dad. We'll just have to wait until there's more information." He frowned as if a thought struck him. "Who has jurisdiction here, Wayne? Bayou Chene stretches into Larue Parish. Which is it?"

"Abadie. It's mine." He glanced at Claire. "For the time being I don't think I'll mention what Danny saw. He's five years old, a little young to distinguish fact from fantasy. We all know different, but it makes a reasonable argument."

"Thank you," Claire said and felt some of her unease lessen.

"No problem, ma'am." Wayne got to his feet, ready to go. He gave her a nod as he put on his hat. "It's been a pleasure meeting you."

"And you." Claire put out her hand and he took it, smiling.

"You take care of that little boy, now, you hear?"

"I'll do that."

"He's safe as sunshine here at Sugarland."

"I hope so."

"Believe it. I'll look forward to meeting him next time." He waved at Angus. "Don't get up, Angus. Mack'll see me out. Give my best to Miss Wyona."

"You keep me posted," Angus called as they departed. When they were gone, he looked at Claire, who was on the point of leaving, too. "Where are you going, girl?"

"Upstairs. I want to check on Danny."

"He's fine. Didn't you hear Wayne? What could happen to him right here in the house, for God's sake?"

"Was there something you wanted to ask?"

"Here, sit down." He pointed to the chair where Mack had been sitting. She sighed as he pinned her with those blue eyes, so like Danny's. And Mack's. "Did you have any visitors at the hotel before you and the boy checked out on Saturday?"

"Visitors?" She frowned. "No, of course not."

"Nobody called?"

"Only Mack."

"Tim didn't phone you?"

She stared at him in astonishment. "Tim Landry? Certainly not. Until the sheriff said his name, I'd never heard of Tim Landry. Why would you think I might have gotten a call from him?"

"He was Carter's best friend. Didn't Carter ever discuss his friends?"

She leaned back and took a deep breath. "Mr. McMollere, I never met any of Carter's friends. Not Tim Landry or anybody else."

He was nodding. "Well, just asking, you understand. Trying to make sense of this."

"I can certainly understand that. Unfortunately, I can't help."

"You never can tell about these things."

She said nothing.

He looked directly at her. "Bit of a coincidence, eh?"

"I suppose so."

But as she climbed the stairs moments later, she thought it was more a mystery than a coincidence. And one she was going to try to unravel.

"WHAT DO YOU MAKE of it, Wayne?"

The sheriff pulled his sunglasses out of his pocket and put them on, then fumbled around in the same shirt pocket for matches. He spent a few moments lighting up and thinking. "Like I said in the house, Mack. It beats me. I considered drugs or a pissed-off husband or gambling debts. Didn't turn up so much as a delinquent parking ticket when I ran a check on Landry."

"Tim was too straight for anything like that, including parking tickets."

Wayne studied the skyline for a minute. "Speaking of straight..."

"He wasn't gay, Wayne."

"Well, I didn't actually think he was, but in my line of work I've got to consider all the angles."

"He was Carter's roommate at LSU. There's no way my brother wouldn't have known if Tim was gay." Mack rubbed the back of his neck. "And he wouldn't have been tolerant, we both know that."

"Hmm." It was as near an outright agreement as Wayne apparently intended to make. He squinted at the end of his cigar. "Carter and Tim and Glenn Thibodaux were always mixing it up, weren't they?"

"Yeah, the three of them were like musketeers." Mack frowned, thinking back. "Glenn roomed with them, too."

"Think I'll talk to Glenn...see if he's got any ideas."

"Wouldn't hurt," Mack said.

"He's living in Baton Rouge, isn't he?"

"On the governor's staff, I think. Dad mentioned it. Martin's real proud," Mack added, referring to the family lawyer. "I think he's got visions of Glenn as the next attorney general."

Wayne rolled his eyes. "Politics. He'll probably go far."

Crossing his arms over his chest, Mack transferred his weight to one side. "One other thing I wanted to ask you, Wayne."

"Oh?"

"Michelle's seeing a boy named Jake Reynolds. Do you remember arresting him a few months back?"

"Sure. A classic case of being in the right place at the wrong time."

Mack frowned. "How so?"

Wayne pushed his hat back with his thumb. "Well, I was never able to prove anything, but in my gut I don't believe Jake was guilty," he said. "He was hired by Dixie Hardware on the recommendation of an employee who left for a job somewhere out of state. Just a week or so after Jake was hired, they conducted a spot inventory and some expensive stuff was missing from the auto-service department, which is where he was assigned. Wouldn't you know, Jake's vehicle—a pick-up—had new tires, just like some of those reported stolen. Only he claimed he'd bought them in Oklahoma. I checked, and sure enough, his family had just moved here from Oklahoma City, but he couldn't produce the bill of sale. Personally, I think the former employee was the thief, but like I said, I could never prove it. In short, Jake was fired."

"Sounds like a bad break."

"More than bad," Wayne said, resettling his hat. "The family's had a run of bad luck. His mother is trying to raise three kids with no husband. Don't know where he went or why, but she inherited the house in town where they live from a distant relative. Far's I can tell, it's about the only asset they have." He turned his gaze toward the horizon. "She's a fine-looking woman, conscientious. Works for Dr. Shelley as his insurance clerk. Not much income for a family of four."

"As usual, you're pretty well informed."

He drew on his cigar, squinting in the billowing cloud of smoke. "The boy's not bad, not with Helen as his mother."

Mack's eyes narrowed. "I hope you're right."

They stood in silence for a minute, then Wayne opened the door of his vehicle and climbed in, but Mack stopped him before he closed the door.

"Fine-looking, you say?" It wasn't often Wayne Pagett looked disconcerted, but he did now. He recovered quickly, however.

"She's a redhead." With that, he gunned his engine and was down the driveway, leaving Mack grinning.

CLAIRE HEADED for the sun room after checking on Danny, but Wyona stopped her at the foot of the stairs.

"Was that Wayne Pagett who just left?"

"Yes, it was. He came to see Mack."

"What did he want?"

"Ah, I think Mack has more details." Claire peered through the leaded glass, hoping to catch sight of him. She didn't want to be the one to tell Wyona about Tim Landry. The woman was fragile enough where Carter was concerned.

Wyona caught at Claire's shirtsleeve. "Was it about Carter?"

Claire's demeanor softened. "No, Mrs. McMollere, it wasn't about Carter. Look, why don't you come into the sun room and I'll make us something cool to drink? Wow, this has been the warmest August I can remember, don't you agree?"

"What did he want then?"

"Sheriff Pagett?"

She sighed impatiently. "Of course! Isn't that who just left? What did he want? Was it about the murder?" She put a hand to her throat. "It was, wasn't it? Something's happened. Tell me."

"Mrs. McMollere, I don't think—"

Wyona shook her head, losing patience. "Oh, for heaven's sake! Stop trying to put me off, Claire. Was Wayne here about that man Danny saw murdered?"

"Yes, but other than that, there was very little he could tell us." Maybe that would satisfy her.

"Who was it? Do they know that yet?"

"Well . . ."

"Well, what! I declare, it's like pulling teeth getting anything out of you." She looked around. "Where's Angus? *Angus!*"

"He was here a second ago," Claire said. "I think he headed for the kitchen. I'll just check. And," she added brightly, "I'll fix us some fresh ice tea while I'm there."

"Never mind, girl. Who was the victim? Was it anybody we know?"

Claire stopped, suddenly giving in. "It was Tim Landry, Mrs. McMollere."

"Tim," Wyona murmured. Then, shaking her head, "Oh, no. No, it couldn't be. Not Tim. Not Tim, too."

Claire guessed she was linking Tim's death with Carter's, whether the connection was logical or not. "Come on, let's go to the sun room," she said gently. Taking Wyona's arm, she led her away from the foyer and moved down the hall.

"What's this? What's the matter, Mama?"

It was Angus. Thank God, Claire thought. "She knows about Tim Landry, Mr. McMollere," Claire told him. From the look on the old man's face, he would probably have something to say to Claire for telling Wyona, but she'd like to see anybody resist the woman when she made up her mind to something.

"Angus..." Wyona's voice quivered. She reached for her husband's hand, her fingers trembling violently. "Angus, it's happening. Didn't I tell you? I knew it would. They—"

"Hush up, Mama. You're upset. This whole thing is upsetting, no doubt about that. Poor Tim."

"Poor Tim," Wyona repeated, nodding her head pitifully. "You know how worried I've been all these years. I told Carter when they—"

"Wyona!"

Claire blinked at the sharpness of Angus's tone. It was the first time she'd ever heard him call his wife by her given name. Couldn't he see the woman was devastated over this? She had somehow confused Tim's murder with their own tragedy.

"I was just offering to make something to drink," she said to Angus, looking him straight in the eye.

"Eh? What? Oh, yes. Yes, good idea. How about a little taste of my brandy, Mama?"

"Why's Granny crying, Mommy?"

"Danny! You're awake." Claire held out her hand as he came to her. Wonderful timing, she thought, rolling her eyes.

"What's wrong, Granny?" he asked, looking concerned. "Are you having a heart attack?"

Heart attack. Where did he get that? Claire wondered, ruffling his hair. "No, honey, Granny's not having a heart attack. She's just sad over some bad news about an old friend."

"Carter's friend," Wyona said mournfully. "I know who'll be next."

"Mama—" Angus gave her another warning look.

"My daddy?" Danny's eyes went wide, as always, when his father was mentioned.

"That's ancient history, m'boy," Angus said in a hearty tone. "We're just about to have some refreshments. How about a cold drink?"

"Okay! I'll have a root beer. Can I, Mommy?"

Absolutely. Anything to get off the subject of dead men. Glad to leave Angus to deal with Wyona, she turned to go to the kitchen with Danny just as Mack came in the front door. One look was enough to tell him that his mother had heard the news.

"I'm sorry, Mama. I know you always loved Tim."

"He was good," Wyona said softly. "When those boys got in trouble, it was never Tim starting it." Her voice caught. "And now they're both dead."

"How about that brandy?" Angus said, urging Wyona toward the sun room. "You folks take care of the boy's root beer and I'll see to Mama."

Mack frowned, watching them go. "How'd she take it?"

"She was terribly upset," Claire said, still trying to make sense of Wyona's rambling. "She confused Tim's murder with Carter's death."

"She's never been the same since Carter died." He looked down as Danny tugged on his pants leg.

"Will you teach me to fly an airplane, Uncle Mack?"

Mack smiled. "You don't think you'd be scared, hotshot?"

"No way," Danny said.

"Okay, when you're old enough."

"When's that?"

"Twenty-one," Claire said.

"Sixteen," Mack said at the same time.

Their eyes met and they laughed.

Oh, Lord, Claire thought, she was beginning to like him.

CHAPTER EIGHT

"WHERE THE HELL'S my Jeep?"

Mack looked at his watch. Most of the afternoon was shot, what with Wayne's visit, then calming his mother and trying to get a fix on the odd reaction his parents had to Tim Landry's death. He had a crew waiting at that pumping station and now when he finally could get away, he had no transportation.

"You asked Michelle to drive it out to the pumping station," Claire said.

"Yeah, but that was an hour and a half ago." He pushed a frustrated hand through his hair. "How long does it take to drive two miles and say twenty words?"

"She probably just lost track of the time," Claire said. "Fifteen-year-olds have a tendency to do that." She glanced at Danny, who was building something with the plastic cups and plates he'd pulled from Cleo's cupboards, with the housekeeper's permission. "If you want, I'll drive you out to look for her. You have something in the garage I can drive, don't you?"

He was on his feet before she finished. "The Lincoln," he muttered. "A little low-slung for the fields, but it'll get us there."

Leaving Cleo to watch Danny, they went outside to the garage. As usual, when Claire walked beside Mack, she was forced to skip a little to keep up. Without exception, he was the busiest man she'd ever been around. He

was never still. If he wasn't in the fields, he was over-
seeing the crews tending the pumps at the oil wells. Even
at night, he didn't rest. He holed up in his office for at
least a couple of hours when everyone else was sleeping. Why didn't he get a secretary? she wondered. Surely
someone else could handle the paperwork, if nothing
else.

But it wasn't any concern of hers. If he wanted to
work himself into the ground, it was his business. Still,
she couldn't help wondering why nobody seemed to notice that he was overworked. Overburdened. The man
needed a keeper.

Or a wife.

"Where are we going first?" she asked when they were
off the winding lane that led to the house.

"She could be anywhere," he said in a clipped voice.
"Sugarland's acreage isn't all connected. Some state-
owned land separates the east section from the original
property. We'll just have to take it section by section.
She's got some explaining to do, damn it!"

"You're mad at her again," Claire said in a resigned
tone. "Look, Mack, kids do this when they get their
hands on the family wheels."

"What do you bet she's with Jake Reynolds?"

She settled against the door, looking at him. "I don't
know much about Jake Reynolds. Is he all that bad?"

"According to Wayne Pagett, no. He believes Jake
was a victim of circumstances. That he was accused of a
crime he didn't commit."

"The sheriff seems a pretty good judge of character,
at least to me. Men in his profession usually are."

"Not while visions of redheads dance in their heads,"
he muttered.

"What?"

Mack laughed shortly. "Are you ready for this? Somehow or other, Wayne is neck-deep in the affairs of this family."

"Your family? Well, naturally, he cares about—"

"No, not my family. The Reynolds family. He's met the mother, a fine-looking woman, to quote him precisely. She's on her own, struggling to raise three children, Jake being the oldest. The kid needed that job, to hear Wayne tell it, and it was a rotten break that he lost it if he was really innocent."

"You can't disagree with that," Claire murmured. "Or can you?"

"Well . . ."

"Is there something else?"

"Hell, I don't know. I mean, how's a man supposed to handle these things? Michelle's fifteen, just . . . you know, blossoming into . . . womanhood, I guess you'd say. Now, some good-looking, fast-talking teenage Romeo comes along." He shook his head. "No, I'm keeping her under a close watch. Better safe than sorry's my motto."

Claire studied the landscape past his profile. "That's one way to handle it, I guess."

He shot her a look. "But it's wrong from your point of view, is that what you're saying?"

She shrugged. "Forbidden fruit's the sweetest, to quote a very trite, but very true old saying."

"Then what do you suggest, madam librarian?"

She looked hard at him. Sarcasm always got to her. But his mouth was hiked up in a half smile. And his blue eyes were . . . she failed to come up with the word for his eyes. "No suggestion. It's none of my business."

"Go ahead, I'm desperate."

"I'm not so quick to dismiss Sheriff Pagett's assessment of the situation. *And* the family. Whether he's noticed the mother is an attractive woman or not. He's human, after all. But what would happen if Michelle could see Jake more often, if circumstances were such that she wasn't sneaking around, of course. That way, she wouldn't be so tantalized by him being labeled forbidden." She was silent for a moment, then added, "I take it he's still unemployed."

"Yeah." Mack turned into a road that ran alongside a densely wooded bayou. "Wayne said Jake was the chief suspect because he was sporting brand-new tires on his beat-up vehicle and he couldn't prove he'd bought them elsewhere."

"A pickup?"

"Jake's wheels?" He gave her a puzzled look. "I think so."

She pointed. "That pickup?"

He looked. "Well, I'll be go-to-hell." He slapped the steering wheel. "Didn't I tell you?"

Michelle and Jake stood between their respective vehicles, Mack's Jeep and the boy's pickup. They were talking, so deeply absorbed in their conversation that they were not even aware of the big town car until it was almost upon them.

Claire put out a hand and stopped Mack as he got ready to charge out of the car. "Just a minute, Mack. If you aren't careful, you'll drive an even deeper wedge between yourself and Michelle. Have you considered asking her for an explanation before you jump down her throat?"

Half out of the car, he looked back at her. "What explanation can there be? They're together."

Claire muttered something and opened the door on her side.

"What're you doing?" he asked.

"I'm coming with you."

"I don't need any help."

"Consider me an unbiased mediator."

"Unbiased? Hah!" Rolling his eyes, he slammed his car door. The sound was like a shot in the hot afternoon.

Claire caught up with him and lifted her hand to wave at the two teenagers. "Hi, Michelle."

Both kids stared. To give him credit, Jake didn't bolt. He stood his ground, even moved in a protective stance so that he shielded Michelle slightly.

"What is this?" Mack muttered. "Does he think I'm going to beat her or something?"

"Or something," Claire murmured, keeping her expression friendly.

"Hello, Mr. McMollere," Jake said, polite but wary.

"Jake." Mack nodded in the boy's direction, reluctantly impressed. He'd turned strong men inside out with the look he lasered at Jake, but the boy held his ground. Mack then turned his attention to Michelle, who rushed into speech.

"Are you checking up on me, Daddy?" she demanded defiantly.

"Should I?" Mack asked, flicking a glance Jake's way.

"I can explain," she said, tossing her dark hair over one shoulder.

"Okay, let's have it."

She blinked with surprise, but quickly took him at his word. "I delivered the message to the crew at the pumping station, just like you told me to do. Then, when

I was driving back, I must have run over something bad, because I had a flat tire.''

Mack frowned, glancing at the tires on his Jeep. All four were fine.

"Jake already fixed it."

Sure enough, there were marks on the ground near the right front and the Jeep's tailgate was still standing open.

"You're thinking it was awfully convenient that he just happened along," Michelle said.

Mack zapped another glance at Jake, who met the look straight on. The kid had guts. "That thought crossed my mind."

"I called him," she said with less bravado. "On your car phone. I knew you were busy talking with the sheriff and I didn't know any of those men at the work site, so it seemed logical to ask Jake for help. I knew he'd come if I called him."

Beside him, Mack could almost feel Claire urging him to give his daughter the benefit of the doubt. He looked at Jake. "Any trouble with the spare?"

"No, sir. It was in good shape."

"Uh-huh." Mack realized he was nodding.

"She must have rolled over scrap metal," Jake said, "like a blade or something from one of your cane-cutters. It sliced right through the steel belt."

Well. Jake Reynolds obviously knew tires. "You think the tire can be repaired, or will I have to replace it?" Mack asked.

"It's too far gone," Jake said, then added, "but you can check it and decide for yourself."

"I'll take your word." He glanced at Claire. "Claire, this is Jake Reynolds. Jake, Claire Woodson. She's visiting at Sugarland for a while."

"Hello, ma'am," Jake said politely. Clearly, he didn't quite trust Mack's cordiality.

"Hi, Jake. Call me Claire."

"Yes, ma'am. Well..." Jake stepped back. "I'd better be going. I need to pick up my mom at five."

"Jake..."

"Yes, sir?"

"Wayne Pagett says you've had a problem finding a job."

Jake's expression changed, his eyes were guarded. He hitched his chin up a notch. "That's right, but I haven't given up yet. There's something out there. I just have to find it."

"We've got a lot of heavy equipment here at Sugarland. Shorty James, my mechanic, has been with me a long time. He's aging. I've been thinking I need to hire a helper for him, somebody who knows vehicles and isn't afraid of work. Would you be interested?"

Jake couldn't keep the surprise out of his eyes. He cleared his throat, forcing his Adam's apple up and then down. "Are you serious, sir?"

"I'm serious, all right." Mack was careful to keep his own features straight.

"Then yes, sir, I'd be interested."

"Good. You can start tomorrow. Shorty's at work by 7:00 a.m. I know it's early, but farmers start early. Any problem with that?"

"No, sir. I'll be here. Thanks, Mr. McMollere."

"Mack. We're not too formal around here. And don't thank me yet. Wait until you've worked a week or two with Shorty. He didn't get that nickname the way you think. It's his temper. He's got a very short fuse."

Jake grinned. "I'll be careful."

"You'll have to be." Mack put out his hand and they shook. "We'll see you tomorrow."

For the first time since his conversation began with Mack, Jake looked at Michelle. They exchanged a delighted, but mute gaze. "See you later," Michelle said, her eyes as bright as blue stars.

"Okay." He began backing off instead of turning, as if keeping them in sight was insurance that the job offer wouldn't be withdrawn. "Nice meeting you, Miss—uh, Claire."

"Nice meeting you, too, Jake."

They watched silently as he started the pickup and pulled away. Slowly. Mack rubbed his mouth and chin to hide his amusement, then turned just in time to brace himself for Michelle's impulsive leap.

"Oh, Daddy!" She threw her arms around his neck, nearly knocking his hat off. "Thank you, thank you, thank you! That was so cool. Jake'll be the best worker you've ever had. You just wait and see!"

It felt good, getting a heartfelt hug from his daughter. God, how long had it been? Too long. Years. He closed his eyes and savored the feeling. Then, over her dark head, he looked into Claire's eyes and found her watching them. And smiling softly.

See, that wasn't so hard, was it?

It came to him that he wanted to hug her, too.

CLAIRE PUSHED the screen door open and stood looking out at the summer night. Now and then, heat lightning flared briefly in a restless sky. She would welcome a good shower to cool things off. It might erase some of the tension at Sugarland.

She left the porch, lifting her hair to let the breeze cool the back of her neck as she walked, then she let it go.

Unconfined, the wind caught her curls, blowing them everywhere so that she knew she would have the devil of a time untangling her hair when she went back inside. Her dress, long and loose, billowed out and up, revealing a flash of white thighs. But tonight, feeling edgy and unsettled, she really didn't care how she looked. Nobody would see, anyway. It was almost midnight and no one else was awake. Even Mack, always the last to go to bed, had turned in.

But for her, somehow, sleep just wouldn't come.

Her thoughts were too chaotic to let her settle. Too much had happened. Too much was happening. Danny had actually witnessed a murder. The body was now found and he wasn't a stranger, at least not to the McMolleres. The victim was Carter's best friend. To add to that, Claire was perplexed at Wyona's reaction. Wyona had been frightened to learn that the murdered man was Tim Landry. Angus recognized his wife's fear. Claire sensed that the man's attentiveness went beyond a need to comfort her. Angus hadn't wanted her expressing her feelings.

Why?

Claire wandered farther toward the pond. She stopped beneath the sprawling limbs of a huge live oak and stared back at the house. What kind of secrets were hidden inside? Or was her imagination just working overtime? As the wind whipped at her, she turned to look across the pond to the gazebo.

It wasn't only the murder that was keeping her awake tonight. It was far more than that. It was Danny's safety and her own need to accept sanctuary here, of all places. It was Michelle—she was concerned about the teenager in spite of vowing the opposite. And it was Mack.

With a sigh, she left the protection of the tree and started toward the pond. At first, she had simply found Mack an interesting man. Why not? He was oddly complex—an accomplished businessman, a talented manager, an obedient son. But he was an insecure father. It was the last that intrigued her most. Well, not quite. His masculinity certainly appealed to her. She hadn't allowed herself to feel anything like that since her affair with Carter. Which had not been too difficult. She hadn't met anyone who interested her enough to make her want more than friendship. What she was feeling about Mack had nothing to do with friendship and everything to do with sex.

She wanted him.

Just admitting it shook her. She caught her gauzy skirt in one hand and walked in the direction of the footbridge.

Half a dozen steps from the water, she saw movement in the low-hanging willows on the other side. Her heart skittered. She felt so safe at Sugarland that she hadn't worried about wandering the grounds at night. Now she realized how foolish that assumption was. With her skirt in her hand, she was ready to run back to the house, when the shape moved again, and she saw who it was.

"You," she murmured, almost wilting in relief.

"We're going to have to stop meeting like this," Mack said when he reached her. It was too dark to see his expression, but there was a smile in his voice.

She had her hand on her heart. "You gave me such a fright!"

"What's the matter? Couldn't you sleep?"

She looked away, raking at the tangled strands blowing in her face. "Not really."

He was nodding. "Heading for the gazebo?"

Not intentionally, she realized. But that must have been her destination. "Come on, we'll share it." He held up a bottle. "And this."

"What . . . how . . . is that a bottle of wine?"

He lifted his other hand, clinking two glasses together. "And these to go with it."

She gave him a quizzical look.

"I was standing at the window upstairs when I saw you walking out this way. I decided to follow you."

They were two exquisite gold-rimmed crystal stems from a collection in a glass-front hutch in Wyona's formal dining room. She chuckled. "John McMollere, what would your mama say if she knew you were playing with her best crystal?"

"Cheers?" Handing the stems over, he took her arm and urged her up the steps of the footbridge. "After the amount of brandy my mama consumed tonight, she can hardly begrudge us."

Claire didn't know whether she should comment on that. Wyona had indeed been numbed by brandy since the moment she'd learned about Tim Landry.

"No comment?"

"Your mother was upset about Tim Landry."

He paused to let her enter the gazebo in front of him, then they sat on the settee just as they had on that first afternoon. Mack had obviously pulled the cork from the wine bottle before leaving the house. He twisted it free and while she held the glasses, he poured.

"What'll we drink to?" he asked when he'd set the bottle on the floor beside him.

"To finding the man who killed Tim Landry, what else?"

"Yeah." They drank and then settled back. Except for the rustle of leaves and the muted rumble of distant thunder, the August night was unusually quiet. The wind was kicking up more, but neither seemed to notice. Or care.

"It'll rain within the hour," Mack observed quietly.

"Will it matter for the cane?"

"It'll be good for it. But when we start cutting, we like the crop to stay dry."

"I'll bet." She sipped her wine, a mellow-red something-or-other. No connoisseur, she simply enjoyed the rare pleasure.

He refilled his glass and topped off hers. When he leaned back, he was turned slightly, facing her. "I wanted to talk to you, Claire," Mack said huskily. Something in his tone made her go quietly breathless. She drank some more wine. "There's no privacy in the house, day or night, and what I need to say is between us. I don't want Michelle or Danny or my folks interrupting."

She stared at him in silence.

"I want to thank you for what you did today when I went after Michelle. If you hadn't said what you did, I probably would have charged over and chewed her out royally. *Then* she would have told me about the flat tire. It would have been too late. I wouldn't have gotten that hug."

"Maybe not, but she would have been pretty happy anyway once you offered Jake a job."

He was shaking his head. "No, you get the credit for that, too. You planted the seed." He drained his glass and then looked at her. "Did you think it through? Was that what you'd planned when you led me around to the idea?"

"Not exactly, but it seemed logical that you'd have good contacts in LaRue, so if there was nothing at Sugarland, it did occur to me you might help him get something."

He was nodding, half smiling. "Is this the way you manage a bunch of unruly teenagers?"

"I'm a librarian, remember? Not a classroom teacher. And most of the kids who spend time in the library aren't the ones with excess energy and behavior problems."

"Do you think Michelle has behavior problems?"

"No, I don't. I just think she needs reassurance that you truly want her here and that you love her in spite of the fact that you haven't spent much time with her." She finished her wine, then covered the glass when Mack tried to refill it. She wasn't used to alcohol and she could feel it going straight to her head.

"It isn't because I didn't want to have her with me," Mack said. He took her glass and set it on the floor beside his own, then stretched his arms across the back of the settee. "Liz made it so damned difficult. We'd make the arrangements, then she'd cancel at the last moment. Or she would claim that Michelle had commitments to her friends and to miss out on this or that birthday party or whatever just couldn't be. Or Liz would get sick. Or Michelle would get sick. And all the time, Liz was undermining me to Michelle. Suggesting that I didn't want her. That I didn't love her."

Suddenly, he shifted so that he sat forward, bracing his elbows on his knees. "It was an impossible situation. I couldn't win for losing. I didn't know how to combat a propaganda campaign like that without slinging a little mud of my own against Liz. But I'd seen too many kids damaged from infighting between divorced couples. I swore I wouldn't hurt a child of mine that way. And in the end, I wound up losing her."

"I don't think you've lost her, Mack," Claire said gently. "She's old enough to see the truth for herself. I think she's longing to make up for lost time. You just have to give her the chance to get to know you again."

He turned his head to look at her. "Do you think that's really possible?"

"Of course. You're her father." Claire's hair blew wildly in a sudden gust. She caught it, lifted it off her neck, enjoying the cool kiss of the wind. Unaware of the appreciative look in Mack's eye, she went on, "Children want to love their parents. Even kids whose parents have mistreated them look for some way to form a bond. And you have certainly never mistreated Michelle."

She drew in a deep breath, feeling the relaxing effect of the wine. There was a flash of lightning, fairly close, but she dismissed the threat of a thunderstorm. Dropping her hair, she settled against the corner of the settee where she had a good view of John McMollere. "Does anyone call you John?"

He smiled softly. "No. No one."

"Hmm. Well, they should. John suits you."

She was tipsy, Mack thought. He could imagine what she would think tomorrow morning when she realized just how thoroughly she had let her hair down, so to speak.

"Call me John if you want to," he said, still smiling.

"John." She nodded. "It's none of my business, John, but what went wrong with you and Liz?"

"Nothing. Everything." He leaned back, enjoying having someone to confide in. "We never should have married in the first place. She wanted a different kind of life than the one I could offer her at Sugarland. She wanted lights and celebrity and a social pace that was impossible while she was married to me."

"Then why did she marry you? She must have known the kind of man you are."

With his arm across the back of the settee, he toyed with a strand of her hair. "What kind of man am I, Claire?"

"Responsible, dependable, rock-solid."

"I sound boring as hell."

"Depends on a person's point of view." She bent over and found her glass on the floor, then poured it full of wine. With a little toasting gesture in his direction, she took a healthy gulp. "For some women, those traits are sterling."

"Uh-huh."

"Now you take Carter," she said, scowling at the wine in her glass. "Everyone around here seems to think he was everything a McMollere should be. They're always singing his praises."

Fascinated, he watched her with his chin propped in his hand. It felt good to hear her all heated up on his behalf, even if it was the wine speaking. "But not you."

"You can say that again." She ran a hand over her tangled mane to try to subdue it, but just as casually abandoned the effort. "But why? Is it that Carter died young? Because you're much more . . . desirable—from the standpoint of a good son, I mean. You're more intelligent, too. And reliable. They rely on you in a thousand ways around here—incidentally, you need a secretary." She lifted her hair and dropped it again. To Mack, watching, it was an incredibly sexy move. "I'll bet they couldn't rely on Carter that way. And I'll bet you never fooled around when you were married to that woman."

"Liz."

"Whatever." She took a little more wine. "And yet your parents go on and on about Carter. It's Carter this and Carter that. What's the matter with them, anyway?"

He shifted and crossed his arms over his chest—anything to keep from hauling her into his lap and burying his face in that glorious tangle of hair. Less than a week at Sugarland and she saw more than Liz had seen in all the years they were together. If her loyalty to Carter had been half as fierce during their affair, then he could understand all too well his brother's passion for this woman.

She sighed. "It's none of my business, of course."

"No."

"But anybody can see that you belong to this place, body and soul. Just suggesting that you should do something else is ludicrous. Stupid." She frowned, thinking. "What were we talking about that got us on this subject? Oh, yes... Michelle. And how you were going to make her love you."

"Yes."

"It's simple, really." She shrugged. "What's not to love?"

Oh, he was going to pay for this tomorrow. "You think I'm easy to love?"

She looked at him and in a quick flash of lightning, he could see that she realized the intimate turn in the conversation.

She cleared her throat as if to bring a more sober note to the discussion. "Now, back to the two of you—Liz and you, I'm talking about. If you were so incompati-

ble, isn't something like that obvious during courtship?''

''Was it obvious during your courtship with Carter?''

She blinked as if he'd thrown her a curve. ''Do you
think we were incompatible?''

''Hell, yes.''

''Oh. Well, actually, I knew there were . . . differences
in our outlook that needed to be faced, but I was too
busy being a good-time girl.''

He couldn't resist. Reaching out, he touched her hair
again. ''Is this how you look when you're being a good-
time girl?'' He deliberately dropped his voice to a level
of intimacy that made her gray eyes go big and wary.

''I'm never a good-time girl anymore.''

''Why not?''

''It was only an act, anyway. When I accepted the fact
that my mother was gone, I was like a bird out of a cage.
I disregarded all her warnings that men are basically out
for what they can get from women, that you can't trust
them.'' She sighed again. ''So when I met Carter and he
was so charming and so much fun, so attentive,
so . . . so . . .''

''Sexy?'' The conversation wasn't so enjoyable suddenly.

''Not really,'' she said in a thoughtful voice. ''He
simply showed me a world that had always been denied
to me, where there were new and interesting things to do,
where just having fun was okay.'' With a pensive look,
she ran a finger around the rim of her glass. ''The trouble is, there's always a price to be paid for the choices we
make.''

He took her glass, empty now, and set it on the floor.
''You did pay a heavy price, but you have Danny.''

A tiny smile touched her mouth. "Yes, I have Danny."

"You've done a super job as a single mother."

"You think so?"

"Yes."

"I've had too much wine," she said abruptly. Reaching for her hair, she pulled it away from her face, trying to shape it into the usual neat twist.

"Don't. Please." He took her hands and placed them in her lap, then slid his fingers deep into her hair and found it as soft as he'd imagined. "You're beautiful when your hair is flying all over like this, curling around my fingers..." He bent forward a little until he was kissing-close. "Smelling like flowers in the rain."

Her eyes locked with his, wide and dark. "I don't think this is a good idea."

"I even like this thing you're wearing, all soft and flowing, but clinging where it should. It makes me wonder what you're wearing under it."

"Nothing. I mean, it's for lounging." Her voice was breathless. "I shouldn't be wearing the dress outside, but I didn't know—"

"That you'd be taking a midnight stroll?" One hand was still tangled in her hair. The other cupped her cheek and pulled her closer. More than anything in recent memory, he wanted to kiss Claire Woodson. "I'm glad you did. When I saw you from my window, there was no way I could not follow you." He bent to take a kiss.

Her lips were wine-sweet and soft, parting at the first touch of his. God, it was as good as he'd imagined. Better. Her breath caught in a little hitch that was sexy as hell. He moved in before she had a chance to realize what was happening so that he could feel her softness against him, warm and giving, while he plundered the delights of her mouth. It was probably the wine, he decided, falling right down into the tempest with her. But while it was there for the taking, he was damn sure going to take it.

His thought processes stopped there and then, and he was just feeling. Sensing.

She smelled delicious, like flowers and fresh air and woman. She tasted sweet and smoky at the same time. The shape of her curled against him was like no other. He wanted to wrap his arms around her, then lose himself in Claire Woodson.

He groaned with the pleasure of it. He thought she answered, but he was incapable of much beyond the sheer pleasure of the moment. Had she asked, he wasn't sure he could have found the will to let her go. She was his and he was going to have her. Now. Tonight.

The knowledge surged through him, hardening his thighs and pumping blood and lust to his loins.

He moved his hand from her neck down to her breast. Ah, she *was* naked beneath the dress. Instantly he dipped into the scoop neckline and found flesh. Soft, giving flesh. A nipple, pebbled and sensitive. His thumb finessed it, and she shuddered like a candle in the wind.

Lightning flashed in the water surrounding them in the gazebo and a mighty boom thundered in its wake.

That quick, it was over.

With a sharp cry, Claire pulled out of his arms and scrambled up from the settee. Rain had begun, sheets of it sweeping over the surface of the pond. The gazebo offered little shelter from lashing wind that swept rain and debris in its wake and plastered their clothes against them. Claire turned to Mack. Her eyes were dark and wild. Whatever she meant to say was lost in another fierce flash. Thunder boomed again. With her arms wrapped protectively around her middle, she turned from him, obviously weighing her chances of fleeing from the gazebo.

"Don't, Claire. Wait until the rain slacks off."

She hesitated at the opening, looking back at him. "I can't. I have to go."

He moved forward. "No! Wait, it's dangerous. Claire! The lightning..."

She lifted her skirt in one hand and held her hair out of her eyes with the other. And then she ran.

CHAPTER NINE

CLAIRE STARED long and hard at herself in the bathroom mirror the next morning. She should look like hell warmed over, the way she felt, but she didn't. There were no dark circles under her eyes and her skin was dewy-fresh. She didn't even have a headache.

This was a hangover? It had to be. Too much wine last night was the only explanation for the midnight madness in the gazebo. It had to be the wine. Why else had she fallen so easily into the arms of another McMollere male? She buried her face in a thick towel and held it there.

First Carter, now Mack. Oh, but there was something so much more... threatening about her response to Mack. It went deeper, reached a part of her that no man ever had. And if she felt so much with just a kiss, what would happen if he should turn the full force of his masculinity to seducing her?

With a groan, she shut off the water, dried her hands, and began to wind her hair into the familiar severe style. But suddenly, as she was tucking a comb into place, she stopped and impulsively let her mane fall to her shoulders. Using both hands, she shook it loose, then studied the effect of the rich, auburn waves framing her face.

"You're beautiful when your hair is flying all over..."

She closed her eyes against the instant tingling in her belly.

"Curling around my fingers..."

Her breasts throbbed, remembering.

"Like flowers in the rain."

Dear God, he was a thousand times more dangerous than Carter. She lifted her head and gazed into the mirror again. Because she liked him a thousand times better than she liked Carter. Her throat was suddenly thick with tears. She could not afford to fall in love with John McMollere.

Enough. She lifted her arms and quickly shaped her hair into a coil and secured the twist with the combs.

Glancing at the clock, she prayed that Mack would be up and out of the house. He was usually gone by this hour, but last night's weather front still hovered and a drizzling rain persisted. What she wanted most was to hide somewhere in the house and never have to face him again. No, that was a lie. And it was dangerous to lie to herself about her feelings. That led to disaster and she didn't have room in her life for any more disaster.

Downstairs, she followed the sound of voices into the breakfast room. The whole family was at the table, but she was aware only of Mack. He stood up, his incredible blue eyes meeting hers. She saw concern and something else that wasn't so easily read. Could it be that he was as troubled over what had happened last night as she was?

"'Morning," she murmured, feeling heat steal into her cheeks.

"Hello." He waited while she poured herself a cup of coffee. "We were just about to send up a search party."

She tasted her coffee, then looked at him. "I must have overslept." She sounded breathless and... and...*hung over?* That's what he would be thinking and who could blame him? Before she made a complete fool of herself, she slipped into the chair beside Danny.

"Me and Michelle didn't get to ride this morning, Mommy. It's raining."

"I know, honey. Maybe tomorrow."

"I hate this," Michelle grumbled, looking through the rain-streaked bay window.

Danny spooned up oatmeal. "We were gonna go see Jake and now we can't."

"Danny!" Michelle looked pained.

Mack and Claire exchanged a glance.

"Who's Jake?" Angus asked.

"He's Michelle's friend," Danny said helpfully. "He's workin' for Mr. Shorty."

"Shorty needed help," Mack explained to Angus. "Wayne mentioned that Jake was looking for work. He has some experience, so I told him to come in this morning and we'd see how it goes." Michelle was looking at him as if waiting for him to renege. He winked at her. "He comes highly recommended."

Surprise flared in her eyes. She turned eagerly to her grandfather. "He knows everything about cars and stuff, Grandpa."

"Hmmph!" Angus tucked into his pancakes. "He'll need more than vehicle know-how to work with Shorty James. He'll need thick skin."

Danny looked up with interest. "You mean, sorta like alligators, Grandpa?"

"That's right, boy."

"Close enough, hotshot." Mack chuckled. "Now finish up so we can hit the road."

Claire set her cup down. "Where are you going?"

Danny was scrambling out of his chair. "Uncle Mack's gonna let me go with him to check the Big Seven. You know, out on the bayou. We're going in a boat!"

Claire looked at the window in dismay. "In this weather?"

Mack stood, slipping his arms into a rain slicker. "It's only drizzling, Claire. Besides, bayous are sheltered. I'll keep him safe and dry."

"Isn't Big Seven that huge wellhead with all those pumps and compressors and—" she searched for words "—and so forth?"

"That's it."

She was shaking her head. "You can't take him out there. A small boy has no business fooling around at a wellhead. He could fall, or worse. Anything could happen. It's too dangerous."

"I'll keep a close watch on him, Claire," he said quietly.

"Children do the unexpected," she argued, still shaking her head. "Little boys, especially. I just don't think he should go."

"Mommy," Danny said in distress.

"I'm sorry, Danny."

"Pleee-eease, Mommy..."

"No." She gave Mack an indignant look. "You shouldn't have mentioned it without first consulting me."

"You're overreacting again, Claire," he said, his mouth tight. "Do you honestly think I'd take him if I thought there was any chance he'd be hurt?"

"Not purposely, but what do you know about kids?"

"I know enough to safeguard a five-year-old."

"I don't want to argue about this. He stays here and that's the end of it."

"To do what? Cut out paper dolls?"

Claire stood up. They were both on their feet now, so engrossed in the argument that neither noticed the rapt attention on the faces of everyone else at the table.

"This isn't about Danny, is it?" Mack demanded, giving her a shrewd look. "You're ticked off about last night, aren't you?"

"This has nothing to do with last night." But he'd hit a nerve. On some level, Claire realized that she was overreacting and it did have something to do with what had happened between them in the gazebo. Embarrassment and chagrin might be fueling her words, but she was genuinely concerned about her son's safety.

"Hey, wow, listen to yourselves." From across the table, Michelle sounded a calming note. "Danny'll be wondering what's going on."

"Are you mad at Uncle Mack, Mommy?" Danny looked worried.

Claire managed a smile. "No, honey, of course not."

"Then can I go with him to the Big Seven?"

"Oh, Danny..."

Michelle scooted her chair back and stood up. "Tell you what, hotshot, why don't you and I go check the horses at the barn? Even if we don't ride, we have to make sure Cherry and Bucko are fed and watered and they've got fresh hay in their stalls."

"I don't want to," Danny said, crossing his small arms stubbornly.

Michelle sighed. "Well, I guess you don't want to see the surprise in the hayloft, either."

"What is it?"

Michelle squatted in front of him and retied his sneakers. "If I told you, it wouldn't be a surprise, would it?"

"I'll bet it's just some old hay and stuff."

"I'll bet you're wrong. It's something soft and warm and fuzzy."

Curiosity won out. "What's soft and warm and fuzzy?"

"That's for me to know and you to find out."

He looked at his mother. "Can I go with Michelle?"

"Yes." She gave Michelle a grateful look. "He has a rainproof jacket in his room, Michelle."

"Right." She took his hand and headed for the door. "We'll see you folks later."

The minute they were gone, Claire found she was the focus of attention. Angus and Wyona she could ignore, but Mack was something else. By the look on his face, he still had something to say. She didn't think he would say it in front of his parents, but she was taking no chances. She began busily clearing the table. And, mercifully, his beeper went off. He glanced at it, muttered something and reached for his Stetson.

As he shrugged into his rain suit, his blue eyes captured hers. "We're not finished, Claire."

Anything she said would sound wrong, so Claire simply held his gaze wordlessly until he finally shoved his hat on his head and strode out of the room. Only then did she head for the kitchen and Cleo's safe company.

SHE DIDN'T SEE Mack for the rest of the day. As for Angus and Wyona, she could only imagine what they thought about the scene at breakfast. Claire had been a little relieved when Michelle asked to take sandwiches to the barn for her and Danny's lunch. On the other hand, having only herself for company made the day drag. If she was trapped at Sugarland much longer, she was going to have to find something to do with her time.

By midafternoon, when it was still raining and she was getting a little stir-crazy, the phone rang. Her heart did a quick flip when she recognized Mack's voice.

"Claire, meet me in front of the house." His voice was clipped and authoritative. "We're going into town."

She bristled instantly. If he thought he was going to get her into that Jeep alone, he had another think coming. "I don't think so. I—"

"It's Danny."

"What?"

"Before you panic, it's not serious. But he's had a little accident."

Her temper vanished. Fear caught in her throat. "Accident? What...where..."

"The barn. He fell off a ladder. I think his arm's broken."

"Oh, my God! How...what happened?"

"Not now, Claire. We need to get him to the hospital."

Her heart thudding, she gripped the receiver tight. "Where is he?"

"Here in the Jeep with me. I'm using the car phone."

She closed her eyes against quick tears. "Is he in much p-pain?"

Mack's tone softened. "He's tough. And brave. He's okay."

"Are you sure?"

"I splinted it and fixed him up with a sling. He's fine until we get to a doctor."

She made a soft sound, but no words came out.

"Claire?"

"I'm here."

"Can you meet us now?"

She glanced down helplessly at her jeans and sneakers. "Yes, yes, I—"

"Good. Two minutes."

Danny had never been seriously hurt in his life. Fever and a red throat, maybe. *A broken arm!* It was impossible to imagine his small, sturdy bones broken. With an impotent cry, she scrambled up the stairs to get her purse. Her insurance card was inside her wallet. She'd need her checkbook, too, and . . . She stood motionless for a few seconds, considering. Oh, her mind was blank. Whatever else she might need, she would just have to manage without.

Danny, Danny, please be okay. Then, grabbing a jacket, she rushed out of the room.

Wyona was at the bottom of the stairs. "What is it? What's wrong?"

"An accident," Claire said, trying to find the sleeve of her jacket. "Mack just called. We're going to the emergency room."

The woman paled and groped for the banister. "I knew it. I told Angus that it wasn't over yet."

Claire gave her a distracted look before opening the front door. She couldn't cope with Wyona's confused behavior right now. Outside, dull, steady drizzle colored everything a gloomy gray. There was no sign of Mack's Jeep.

Please don't let anything happen to Danny.

Wyona came to stand beside her, gazing out at the rain-soaked landscape. "First Carter, then Tim Landry," she murmured. "And now the other one."

Claire shivered. Was she the only person who realized how truly close to the edge Wyona McMollere was? And where, for God's sake, was Mack?

A horn blew as the Jeep turned off the road and headed up the long driveway to the house. Sighing with relief, she started to dash out into the rain, but Wyona stopped her with an urgent hand on her arm.

"I think you should be careful, Claire. He's out there."

"The man who killed Tim?"

"Yes. And Carter, too."

Claire patted the woman's hand. "Go back inside, Mrs. McMollere. Ask Cleo to make you some tea. We'll be back as soon as we can."

DANNY INSISTED on walking into the emergency room on his own, ignoring Claire's suggestion that Mack carry him. Her suggestion that he use a wheelchair met with the same reaction. The makeshift splint and sling Mack had rigged up obviously relieved much of the boy's pain. Still. She met Mack's eyes indignantly over the head of her son. Danny's little face was so pale and his mouth looked so vulnerable. There were times for stupid male machismo, but this wasn't one of them. Following the two through the automatic doors, Claire decided she was the one who needed a wheelchair.

She still felt shaky when they were finally back in the Jeep heading out of the hospital parking lot. Danny was in the back seat propped on pillows, his arm in a full cast. The break was clean, and according to the doctor, thanks to Mack's quick, skillful splint-and-sling job, setting it had been a piece of cake.

Before pulling out into the traffic, Mack looked at her with concern. "Are you okay?"

Quick tears sprang into her eyes. "Uh-huh. Just . . . used up."

He reached over and squeezed her hand. "He's fine, Claire. Kids are tough."

"I know. And the doctor said he'll be out of the cast in four weeks." She was shaking her head. "It's just that..."

"It hurts to see your child in pain."

She nodded wordlessly, comforted more than she expected by his touch and the warmth of his gaze. She didn't want to admit how glad she was that Mack was with her.

Releasing her, he glanced behind where Danny sat looking out the window. "How you doin' back there, hotshot?"

Groggy from pain medication, Danny's reply was a little slow in coming. "Okay."

"Keep your arm propped on that pillow, son," Mack said. "We're heading home." Clicking on the windshield wipers, he turned left at the traffic light and headed for the road that would take them past LaRue's town square, then onto the parish road to Sugarland.

Slowing at another intersection, he looked at Claire. "Relax, Claire. You heard the doctor, he's going to be okay."

She put a hand to her forehead. "What happened, Mack? Why was he climbing a ladder in the first place?"

"We've got some kittens in the hayloft."

From the back, Danny spoke sleepily. "There's four of them, Mommy. The mama cat borned them right in the hay. Their eyes are just now open."

"Michelle's warm, fuzzy surprise," Claire murmured, nodding.

"I'm afraid so." Mack reached forward and wiped condensation from the windshield. "She feels terrible about this. When I left with Danny, she was sobbing.

She let him play with the kittens this morning, never expecting him to come back later on his own. He was backing down the ladder to refill the mama cat's water bowl when he slipped and fell. It was just a stroke of luck that I happened to be nearby and heard him yell."

"I hollered loud as I could," Danny said around a yawn.

"Scared the hell out of me." Mack chuckled softly.

"Where was Michelle?" Claire asked.

Mack let out a breath. "At the workshop with Jake." He laughed dryly. "Shorty's bitching big-time over having to be their chaperon."

Claire smiled faintly, not surprised that Michelle had managed to figure a way to see Jake. Like her father, the girl was determined and resourceful. One of the reasons—probably the main reason—Mack and Michelle were so often at odds was that they were so much alike.

She leaned her head back against the seat. "Well, I'm just thankful you were on hand when Danny fell . . . and that you knew what to do." She was still shaken over how fast everything had happened. One minute Danny was laughing and healthy, the next he lay broken and hurting. Had the accident been more serious, her whole reason for living could have been snatched from her, that fast.

"It's ironic," she said, her gaze fixed on the swishing wipers. "I refused to let Danny go with you to the well-head this morning and instead he falls and breaks his arm while in the relative safety of the barn playing with kittens." Her laugh was soft and humorless. "Go figure."

"Yeah, I've been thinking along those same lines," he said, adjusting his hat with his thumb. "Whether they're teenagers or little ones, kids are unpredictable. If Danny would crawl up into the hayloft on his own, I break into a sweat thinking of the trouble he could have gotten into out on the bayou if I'd turned my head for a second. Accidents happen. The truth is, I don't know much about raising kids. Just look at my problems with Michelle.''

"You're doing fine with Michelle."

"Yeah. For about two days and counting, thanks to you. So, you were right to object this morning. And I was out of line arguing with you. That crack about paper dolls was stupid."

"As long as we're being honest here, I'll confess that I overreacted," she admitted after glancing to check on Danny. The boy was sleeping soundly.

Mack gave her a quick, shrewd glance. "Any idea why that might be so?"

"After last night? A few. We both know what happened out there was crazy." She became interested in the scenery on her side. "I'm not used to drinking so much, I hope you know that."

"It was the wine, is that what you're saying?"

"I take responsibility for my behavior," she said coolly, "whether I drink too much wine or not."

"I'm glad to hear it."

"I was embarrassed this morning. It made me a little... defensive. I don't think that's so hard to understand."

"It sure as hell is."

That brought her around to stare at him. "What?"

"Why would you be embarrassed? When two people are single and attracted to each other and the opportunity presents itself to do something about it, what's wrong with that?"

"For you and me, it's inappropriate, that's what. Especially for you and me. You're Carter's brother, for heaven's sake! I can't be—I mean, we shouldn't—" She drew in a deep breath. "Can we just drop the subject?"

"Sure, after I say just one more thing."

She looked at him curiously, but he was concentrating on the ebb and flow of traffic. "What?"

"The way I see it, my brother has nothing to do with anything that might happen between you and me." He stopped at a traffic light and looked directly at her. "And I think something is happening between you and me."

Her heart caught in her throat—from surprise or excitement or plain old fear, she wasn't sure. Less than a week ago, she had been a single mother with a little boy, living a relatively unexciting life. Her job was ho-hum, but she could depend on it to put a roof over their heads and food on the table. The trip to Louisiana was supposed to take one weekend only, after which they'd go back to business as usual. What had happened that her life was suddenly turned upside down?

She stared ahead at the tangle of people and cars and activity in the rain and realized they'd reached the town square. The last thing she should be thinking about was John McMollere and the feelings he stirred in her. Had she forgotten why she and Danny were still in Louisiana, threatened by a faceless, nameless killer? If so, this accident was a timely reminder of where her priorities should be.

She rubbed her forehead wearily, wondering how she'd somehow managed to push to the back of her mind the fact that Danny's life was threatened, even for a second. The past hour in the emergency room was only a taste of how it might be if that threat ever became a reality. God knows, she could never survive such a loss.

Suddenly she thought of Wyona McMollere. The woman's persistent references to the past, her confusion, her obsession with the memory of her dead son were tragic. Was that why Wyona seemed a shadow of the person she must have been? Had losing Carter been more than she could bear?

Claire studied the pattern of raindrops on the window. "Your mother said an odd thing as we were leaving."

Mack, trying to cross a lane of traffic, simply grunted.

"She can't seem to separate Tim Landry's murder from Carter's death." Still relaxed in the seat, she turned to look at him. "Was there anything suspicious about the airplane crash that killed Carter?"

Mack flicked a glance to the rearview mirror and saw that Danny still slept. "No. It was pilot error, clear and simple. He went up when he shouldn't have."

Mack paused for a moment, then continued, "When his wife found out that Carter had had an affair, she really took it hard. I think she might have forgiven him for cheating on her, but knowing he had fathered a child by another woman was too much. Being infertile herself, she just couldn't take it. He came home one night and found her gone, no note, nothing."

Traffic stalled suddenly. Mack pulled to a stop behind a minivan. "The weather was rotten, but he took off anyway, heading for Birmingham, where Renee's parents live. His plane went down near Vicksburg in a hailstorm."

"Then your mother's idea that something more sinister was involved is unfounded?"

Mack looked at her. "Who'd have reason to kill Carter?"

She shrugged. "Who'd have reason to kill Tim Landry?"

"The two deaths are unrelated, Claire. Believe it."

She sighed. "Of course. You're right." She looked pensively out at the rainswept street as he started up again. "It's just that your mother seems so—"

She was thrown against her seat belt as Mack slammed on his brakes. She watched, frozen, as a pickup slid sideways through the intersection against the light.

"That idiot!" Mack downshifted, then followed the minivan through the intersection. "What a stupid thing to do, running a red light in a downpour. Some clown must think he leads a charmed life."

"What happened, Uncle Mack?" Danny groggily rubbed his eyes, straining to look outside.

"Just some crazy character driving too fast in the rain, son."

Claire felt her heart give a little bump. It was the second time he'd called Danny "son." Did he realize how Danny hungered to be just that? And how easily his small heart could be broken?

"Lie back again and relax," Mack told Danny. "We'll be out of the traffic soon."

"Okay."

Danny wasn't usually so agreeable, but then it was Mack giving the orders. The man would make a good father, Claire thought wryly. He gave her a questioning look when she chuckled. "It's the pain medication," she told him. "So don't go thinking you've aced the problem of managing a fractious five-year-old so easily."

His expression was pure innocence. "Did I say anything like that?"

"No, but you were thinking it."

He was nodding, his smile crooked. "I see. A mind reader. Well, you—"

"It's him, Mommy! Look, look, it's the bad cop!" Danny was struggling to turn and look through the rear window, but was hampered by his seat belt. "It's him. Turn around, Uncle Mack. Go chase him!"

Claire reached back, catching the cushion before it slid to the floor. "Danny, settle down, you heard the doctor. You're supposed to keep your arm still for a few hours."

Danny was looking behind, literally bouncing with impatience. "It's him, it's him! It's the bad cop."

Claire glanced at Mack, whose gaze was fixed in the rearview mirror. "Which car was it, Danny?" he asked. "The pickup?"

"No, no. It was a car like this one, Uncle Mack."

"A Jeep?"

"I guess."

"A sport vehicle," Mack murmured, scanning the cars behind them.

Claire touched Mack's sleeve nervously. "Do you think he actually saw the guy we're looking for?"

"Why not? It's possible."

"He's medicated within an inch of his life, Mack."

Mack braked at the next street and made a U-turn at the service station on the corner. He pulled back into the traffic and accelerated. "What color was the car, Danny?"

The boy's forehead wrinkled in thought. "Uh, it was sorta dark."

"Dark blue? Dark green? Black?"

"Ummm..." Danny's mouth hiked up. "Black...maybe." He looked distressed. "It was raining, Uncle Mack. I'm not sure."

"Was the cop wearing a uniform?"

"No, he was wearing the same shirt."

"The same shirt?" Claire gave Mack an I-told-you-so look. "How could you know that?"

"It was gray and had all those flaps and stuff on it. Just like he had on that day he shot that other man."

Claire looked back at Danny. "You never mentioned a special shirt, Danny."

He looked crestfallen. "I guess I forgot."

"Of all the—!" Mack bumped the steering wheel in disgust. "I thought I caught a glimpse of the car, but that damn delivery van pulled in front of me and now I can't see anything but his backside."

"You saw the car?"

"I'll never know now." Mack gunned the Jeep, overtaking the van.

Claire's stomach knotted. She'd never expected anything like this. She scanned the side streets as they cruised past. "Danny, are you sure?"

The boy sank back against the seat, his small face set stubbornly. "You never believe anything I say anymore."

"I do believe you, honey," Claire assured him, "but it's raining and it's pretty difficult to recognize people in another car, even when you know them."

"I do know that man," Danny insisted.

Claire reached back and patted his knee, trying not to reveal how shaken she was. Could he possibly have seen the killer? Even scarier, had the killer seen him?

Claire glanced at Mack, who was pulling into another service station to turn around again. "What are we going to do?"

"We're going to head for home." As he waited for a chance to merge into traffic, he reached for his car phone. "I'm calling Wayne Pagett and telling him exactly what Danny said. It's not much to go on, but it's better than nothing. Which is what we've had up to this point." Finding an opportunity, he accelerated into the traffic, then with his thumb punched the numbers on his cellular phone.

Claire settled back, half her mind on what he was telling Wayne Pagett, the other on the sinister presence stalking her and her son. Her mind teemed with questions, but they would have to wait. She didn't want to alarm Danny.

Speeding through town, she studied the faces of the drivers they passed. Who was he? *Where* was he? She clamped her arms around her stomach, feeling as if she were suspended over a dark pit, not knowing when she would suddenly be plunged into the depths.

Mack was still talking to Wayne. She watched his eyes constantly moving, studying the streets, other cars, people. Sensing her scrutiny, he turned and gave her a reassuring look. She felt some of the tension inside her ease. The man had a way of making her feel safe. Secure. If she wasn't careful, she would find herself, like everyone else, depending far too much on John McMollere.

I think something is happening between you and me.

She closed her eyes, feeling the impact of his words again. Relying on him was one thing. How was she going to keep from falling in love with him?

THE RAIN HAD SLACKED OFF by the time they got to Sugarland. Michelle and Jake were waiting out front on the steps. The moment she spotted the Jeep turning in the driveway, Michelle sprang to her feet. Jake rose more slowly, then hung back as she rushed to meet them.

"Claire, how is he?" Before Claire was out, Michelle was opening the back door. "Is he okay? I'm sorry. It's all my fault for not telling him he couldn't go up in the hayloft by himself."

"It's not your fault, Michelle." Claire sprung the catch on Danny's seat belt and helped him out of the Jeep. "He's a little groggy, but just like Humpty-Dumpty, he's all put back together, huh, sweetie?" She fluffed his hair.

"I got a real cast on my arm, Michelle," Danny said, proudly displaying it in the sling. "It's hard and you can write on it, the doctor said."

"Hey, no kidding?" Michelle gave it a gentle tap, her smile a bit unsteady. "You feelin' okay, little buck-eroo?"

"Oh, sure, it doesn't hurt at all now." He seemed struck with a new thought. "Can a person ride a pony if he's got a broken arm?"

Michelle gave him a careful hug. "I don't know, Danny-boy, but we'll check it out in a day or so, after you've gotten used to the cast, okay?"

Danny sighed. "Okay, I guess."

"Hello, Jake." Claire smiled at the tall teenager. "How was the first day on the job?"

"It was good. Real good."

"Shorty treat you right?" Mack asked, coming around to join them.

"Yes, sir."

"Hmm, then he must have turned over a new leaf."

Jake laughed. "I don't know about that, sir. What would you call a new leaf?"

"How many times did he cuss you out?"

Jake was shaking his head, grinning. "Mr. Shorty's still pretty much unchanged, I guess."

Mack gave him a friendly slap on the back. "You'll toughen up." He chuckled ruefully. "You'll have to."

"I'm not worried, sir." Jake turned to Michelle. "Now your dad's back, Mich, I guess I should be shoving off."

Michelle gave him a misty smile. "Thanks for waiting with me, Jake."

"Hey, what're friends for?"

She turned to Mack. "Jake kept me company while I waited to hear about Danny. We stayed right out in plain sight."

Mack nodded, a gleam in his eyes as he looked at Jake, who blushed. To his credit, he did not flinch at Mack's scrutiny.

Danny tugged on Jake's jeans. "Can you sign my cast, Jake?"

"You bet," Jake replied. "But I'll need a pen."

"There's a felt marker inside," Michelle said, taking Danny's hand. "Come on, we'll go get it." Carefully, she helped him climb the steps. At the top, she looked at Jake. "Are you coming, Jake?"

He hesitated, glancing uncertainly at Mack.

"Go ahead, all of you." As they disappeared inside, Mack looked at Claire, rolling his eyes. "First, she's so rebellious she goes out of her way to disobey me. Now, she's too full of parental respect. And Jake's nearly as bad. It makes me crazy. They seemed a lot more normal when they were plotting against me."

"Listen to you." With her hands on her hips, Claire was shaking her head. "Some people are never satisfied."

They were chuckling as they went inside together.

CHAPTER TEN

"ABSOLUTELY NOT. This time, I'm going with you."

Mack clung doggedly to his patience. "There's nothing you can do, Claire. I just want to check with Wayne about what Danny saw this afternoon. While I'm there, I want him to fill me in on the investigation about Tim's death. Don't worry, I'll tell you everything when I get back."

"I'll save you the trouble. I want to hear what Sheriff Pagett has to say for myself, not after it's filtered through you. That's my right. Can't you understand that?"

"I understand it. I just don't agree with it."

Claire glanced upward in frustration. "It's my son who's in jeopardy. I've spent the best part of a week wringing my hands and feeling useless over the situation. It's time I did something."

"You can't do anything! What can a woman do? You—"

"Oh, I get it." Her gray eyes were suddenly narrowed. "This is men's work, right? Never mind that it's my son who's in danger here, I should just stay inside and...and...knit or something."

"Did I say anything like that?" He cursed the fact that he hadn't gotten away before she noticed. With Danny settled and dinner behind them, he'd counted on Claire retreating to her room, as she did most nights. He wanted to talk to Wayne Pagett, but it wasn't the kind of conversation a woman needed to hear.

But then, Claire was nothing like the women in his life. His mother, for instance. A genteel Southern woman, Wyona would have been content to let a man handle something like this. And Liz. God, she would have passed the time talking on the phone, or playing tennis, all the while pretending nothing had happened. Or, better yet, she would have gone shopping in New Orleans. What was it with Claire Woodson?

He raked through his hair with one hand and replaced his hat. "Look, Claire, there's a killer out there and he wants your son. Don't you realize he has to assume you saw him, too? You're in as much danger as Danny, for God's sake! I ought not to have to tell you that."

Her chin came up stubbornly. "I'm not exactly an idiot. I realized that from the start."

"Well, you don't act like it," he growled, rubbing the back of his neck. "Otherwise, you'd accept that you're safer here at Sugarland than gallivanting around the parish inviting disaster."

She dropped her jaw. "Gallivanting? I'll be going straight to the sheriff's office. With you. Then we'll be heading straight home."

He released an irritated sound. "Did you hear a word I said, woman?"

"Don't call me that. It's so condescending."

"Fine with me," he retorted. "It must have been a slip of the tongue. The way you're carrying on sure isn't feminine."

"That sexist remark doesn't even deserve a reply," she said in a dangerously soft tone.

"What is it? No man ever said it straight out before?" His eyes narrowed. "You know the problem with you, lady? You've been wearing the britches too long in your family. With that red hair and that streak of stubbornness a mile wide, you've forgotten what it's like having a man try to take some of the responsibility off your shoulders. You—"

"Responsibility? Oh, excuse me. You're the only one around here who can handle responsibility, right? Well, I've got news for you, mister. I've been taking responsibility for myself and my son since the day he was born—since *before* he was born—and I'm not standing by passively while you 'handle' things." Her breasts were heaving, she was so furious. She turned away, fuming, rubbing her mouth and chin with an unsteady hand. Then she faced him again, her eyes flashing silver fire. "And don't call me lady!"

"Are you two fighting again?" Michelle, coming in to see what the ruckus was about, gave them both an exasperated look.

"No, we're not fighting," Mack said between his teeth.

"You sure could have fooled me." She crossed her arms, studying them both. "I know it's dangerous to take sides here, considering how hot and bothered you both are, but I think you're going to have to let her go with you, Dad. She makes a pretty good case."

He swept the ceiling with his gaze. "What is it with the women in my life?"

"It's 1996, Dad. Claire has a right to make her own decisions, especially about Danny."

"I'm going, Mack." Claire wasn't giving an inch. "If you don't let me drive with you, then I'll simply call a taxi. Or, I'll ask Angus for permission to drive something in the garage. I might get there a few minutes later than you, but I'll be there. Count on it."

Swearing roundly, he jerked open the door. She stepped out. Ramming his Stetson a little harder on his head, he followed her.

Women!

NEITHER ONE OF THEM spoke for the first ten minutes in the Jeep. It was Mack who finally exploded. "Damn it, Claire, are we going to drive all the way to Wayne's office in total silence?"

"I don't know. How far is it?"

He ground his teeth. "That's the trouble with women," he complained to the night sky. "They're always going on about communication, but they've got the market cornered on freezing a person out with silence."

She still said nothing, just sat with her gaze fixed straight ahead. Without even a glance, he knew how she looked. She'd changed into a loose sweater that reached over one of those crinkly, gauzy skirts—the color of sherbet ice cream. She wore sandals, sexy little things that showed her pretty toes. She probably thought because she was well covered that she didn't look as appealing as . . . as ice cream on a hot afternoon.

It was night and it was raining. But it was mid-August. And he was damn sure hot.

He lapsed for a moment into a delicious fantasy, but then his body began responding and so he reluctantly ended it.

He drummed both thumbs on the wheel, then cleared his throat. "Looks to me that what we've got here is a basic difference in philosophy—" he glanced at her from the corner of his eyes "—regarding the role of men and women."

She turned deliberately and looked out of her side.

"Not all women are offended if a man attempts to run a little interference for them," he said.

"I don't see life as a football game."

He rubbed his left hand over his face, then after a second or two, he looked at her. And laughed. It was that, or he was going to stop the Jeep and haul her onto his lap and kiss the daylights out of her. "You're something else, you know that? You look like... like peach ice cream on the outside, but you've got a temper like a little chili pepper."

"Mixing your metaphors," she murmured, but he could see she was struggling not to smile.

"You're the librarian, not me."

"Actually, I'm an English teacher."

"But you prefer being a librarian?"

"No, I prefer teaching English."

"Then why aren't you doing it?"

"I was fired. I couldn't get a reference, which kept me from finding another teaching position."

He frowned. "That's tough."

She was nodding, her face going solemn. "It was. At least, so I thought at the time."

"When was this?"

She sighed. "Oh, Mack, do you really want to know all this?"

"Yeah."

"My first and only teaching position was at an exclusive girls' school near San Antonio. I'd been seeing Carter since the February before I graduated. We were together until... well, you know that part. By Christmas, my pregnancy was obvious. The tolerance of the faculty at St. Mary DeBlanco didn't extend to an unmarried pregnant teacher and so I was terminated. Forthwith.''

Mack felt a flare of raw rage, surprising in its intensity. *Damn you, Carter. Wherever you are, I hope you can hear this.* "It's no wonder you were so determined to stay as far away from us McMolleres as possible," he said quietly.

"I made a mistake assuming everybody in the family was like Carter."

He gave her a quick glance. She might feel favorable toward Michelle or his mother, maybe even Angus, but he bet she didn't include him in that. Not after the brouhaha they'd just had. He groaned inwardly. He'd said she wasn't feminine. He must have been out of his mind. He *was* out of his mind—over her. Had been since... he wasn't sure when he'd begun to change his mind about Claire. Maybe from that first morning when she'd gotten up and found her son missing. He could still see her face. She'd been desperate. Nearly incoherent with fear. Hardly the reaction of a selfish, uncaring home wrecker. No, Carter was the guilty one in that triangle.

"I hope you really mean that," he said softly, signaling a turn onto a gravel road. "Is there any way to fix those records, to purge that termination from your résumé?"

"I don't know, but it doesn't matter very much anymore. At the time, it was pretty urgent that I get something and fast, so I applied at the library. Teachers are usually in demand. If I wanted another teaching position, I could probably get one now. To tell the truth, I'm comfortable enough where I am, I suppose." She looked around with a confused expression. "Where are we? This isn't the way into Abadieville, is it?"

"No, we're going to Wayne's house. I thought we should avoid the office. It's best for you to keep a low profile until this thing is behind us."

"Do you think that might be sometime soon?"

That worried tone was back in her voice and Mack found that he hated it. He pulled up in front of Wayne's house. "That's one of the questions we're going to ask the sheriff."

He got out and waited for her at the front of the Jeep. The problem was going to be solved—and soon—if it meant he had to put on a damn uniform himself.

WAYNE PAGETT hadn't expected Claire, but in the manner of a true Southern gentleman, he refused to get down to business until he'd offered her a choice of coffee or iced tea or lemonade, all of which she politely declined. Standing in the huge family room, he turned to Mack, rubbing his hands together briskly.

"Just name it, Mack," he said, throwing open a small refrigerator behind the bar. "I'm pretty well stocked."

"Beer's good."

Suddenly there was a booming bark from somewhere in the back of the house. Claire blinked and took a small step back against Mack's chest as Barney bounded into the room, heading straight for them.

"Barney!" the sheriff bellowed. The big yellow Lab stopped short, looking so downcast that everyone laughed. Mack gave Claire a reassuring squeeze. It felt too good having her against him. Good ol' Barney. He owed him one after this. "It's okay, Claire. He's not attacking, it's just his way of saying hello. We're old friends."

Setting her aside gently, he went down on his haunches and gave the rapturous Lab a good tussle, winding up almost on his rear when Barney suddenly lunged, planting both paws on Mack's chest. He was trying to get onto his feet, laughing and dusting himself off, when he met Claire's eyes. She was smiling, her mouth soft and so kissable that he had to look away or embarrass them both in front of Wayne.

Shaking his head, Wayne addressed Claire. "The original Barney was crazy over Mack. This one is third generation removed from Barney number one. The boys used to take him everywhere, huntin', fishin', even to school occasionally."

"We took him on a double date once," Mack said, grinning. "But only once. It wasn't the most successful date we ever had."

Claire sank into a big leather chair and Barney immediately went over, tail wagging, and propped his big head on her knee. "Who's we?" she asked, rubbing his soft ears.

"Mike and I. Wayne's oldest son."

"You were good friends?"

"The best of friends. I miss him a lot."

"He's in Houston," Wayne said, coming around from behind the bar. "Works for the petrochemical company that manages the McMolleres oil reserves. Here's your beer, Mack."

Mack took it and drank with gusto. "Mmm, that hits the spot." He sat down on the overstuffed ottoman in front of Claire and gazed around the big, homey room with affection. "I spent many an hour here in this room with Mike. I don't know why Miriam didn't kick us out more than she did."

Wayne's gaze strayed to a family portrait on the wall. "She thought the sun rose and set in her family, that's why." He twisted the cap from his beer bottle, smiling at Claire. "And that included Mack. He was as much a part of our family as—"

"As Barney." Mack grabbed the dog's head between his hands and Barney instantly tried to move into his lap. They both tumbled backward, the dog barking with exuberance, Mack trying to keep his beer from spilling. He knew he was grinning like a kid, but it felt good being here. It felt good having Claire here with him. He got to his feet finally and snapped his fingers to the dog. "Come on, you big mutt. Next thing, you'll be jumping on my lady. You're going outside."

My lady! Claire's heart jumped. It was possessive. It was chauvinistic. But, coming from Mack, it was an endearment that she was helpless to resist.

She watched him heading to the door, the dog trotting happily beside him, and when they were gone, she looked at Wayne and found him studying her. Flustered, she wondered if he guessed her thoughts. To shift his attention, she asked, "Does this happen often?"

"You mean, does Mack visit often?"

"Yes, and does he change so much when he does visit? I've never seen him look so relaxed. Or be so playful. He's so different at Sugarland. It's . . . interesting."

"Interesting, huh?" Now he was openly amused. She felt her face flushing, but forced herself to meet his eyes. "Mack doesn't relax enough." His tone became serious. "I guess coming here reminds him of a time when his life was less complicated. And it's damn complicated now, I don't know whether you're aware of that. He has a bunch of folks pulling at him this way and that. Angus is fading fast, and his mama, well, you've been there long enough to get a pretty good picture of Wyona."

He surveyed his beer thoughtfully. "And if that's not enough, Mack's ex-wife has dumped little Michelle on him after years of doing her best to alienate the two of them. He has all the headaches that come with farming Sugarland, managing the oil and gas leases, plus, he's on the board of the oil company. This is a man up to his rear in alligators most of the time."

"I've noticed that he's expected to shoulder the burdens of everyone in his life."

Wayne set his beer aside and propped an ankle on his knee. "It's the damnedest thing...his brother was never half the man Mack is, but his folks acted just the opposite." Wayne shook his head. "I always wondered at that. They had Mack who was everything a son ought to be, and yet the one they indulged and petted and just about ruined—that's my personal opinion, of course—was Carter." He was shaking his head. "People. Just as you think you've got 'em figured, that's about the time something nutty happens."

"I guess you've seen a lot, as a sheriff, I mean."

"As a sheriff and as a lifetime resident of this community." He jerked his head in the direction of the door. "And there's not a finer man in the community—hell, the whole state—than John McMollere."

They could hear Mack's step on the front porch. Claire smiled. "And you, of course, are strictly an impartial observer."

He got to his feet with a chuckle. "Come on, young lady, let's go get this ugly business over with. I'm old-fashioned, I guess, because it goes against my grain to show you autopsy pictures and talk about murder and such."

"You and Mack," she murmured. "It figures."

"But the world's changed. And we dinosaurs have to change with it or go extinct, I reckon." He opened the door to his office and waited politely for her to enter. "At least, that's what Helen tells me."

"Helen?" That wasn't his daughter's name, Claire thought.

For a second, Wayne's expression was one of chagrin. "Ah, she's a lady friend. Helen Reynolds."

"Lady friend, huh?" Mack reappeared at the door. With a gleam in his eye, he crossed his arms. "That would be Jake's mom, right?"

"That's right."

If looks could wound, Mack would have dropped. Giving Claire a wink, he zinged his old friend again. "A redhead, I think you said?"

Clearly, Wayne had had enough. Fumbling around in his shirt pocket, he found a cigar. After clamping it between his teeth, he sat down behind his desk. Scooting his chair a little closer to his desk, he opened a file. "Now...let's see what we've got here."

After another mischievous look at Claire, Mack disciplined his face and sat on the edge of Wayne's desk. His expression sobered as he bent forward to get a look at the paperwork from the investigation of Tim Landry's death.

"That's the autopsy, right?" he said, recognizing the first form the sheriff picked up. When Carter died, Wayne had been helpful in interpreting the technical jargon used in describing the death. At the time, Mack had been grieving, shocked at the sudden loss of his brother. The details were still sketchy in his mind.

But that had been Carter. Mack felt sad about Tim, but his overwhelming feeling studying this autopsy was curiosity.

"Death was instantaneous, a .38 caliber straight to the heart," Wayne said, shuffling quickly past some official photos of the body at the scene where it was discovered. He sighed as Claire took the liberty of picking one up and studying it. "As you see here," he continued, pointing to a paragraph, "the coroner's unofficial opinion on the morning the body was discovered is confirmed. The bullet did not exit, there was little bleeding, and so forth. These two were standing no more than two feet apart, just as Danny said. Powder burns confirm that."

Mack grunted. "Anything else?"

"Well, he'd been dead about three days, which also confirms preliminary findings." Wayne tucked another color photo out of sight. "Clothing checks with our eyewitness. Hair color, too. And just as Danny said, in a pony tail." Glancing up, he caught Claire's eye. "The boy was far more accurate in his recollection of the crime than about three-quarters of the adult eyewitnesses I usually deal with."

"He watches too much television." Claire spoke evenly, but there was a strained look about her mouth. Mack suspected that the grisly details were getting to her. What they were looking at could turn the stomach of a hardened police officer. He felt an overwhelming urge to shield her, but he dared not say anything. Stubborn as she was, she'd probably give him a piece of her mind right here in front of Wayne.

The sheriff saved him the trouble. Collecting the papers before she could dwell on them, Wayne shuffled them into a neat stack. "I haven't been able to make much progress on this case, I'm sorry to say. But there's one interesting thing—a maid at the White Hotel remembers finding a bloody towel in the laundry cart that was parked in the alcove where Danny said he saw the shooting take place. The cart itself was examined after Tim's body surfaced, and sure enough there was blood on it. I'm having it analyzed to see if it was Landry's, but so far haven't heard anything from the lab.''

Claire looked surprised. "The hotel staff claimed they saw nothing when I asked.''

"They said the same thing when I went there,'' Mack said, scowling.

"Actually, the people you spoke to didn't know anything. This particular maid took sick that afternoon and went home. She was out the whole weekend. Said she didn't think to mention it until we went out there with the forensics people to make another sweep of the scene. That's when the blood on the cart was found.''

"But why on earth wouldn't she report a bloody towel?'' Claire asked.

"To give her the benefit of the doubt,'' the sheriff replied, "she claimed that bloodstained towels are fairly common, and there wasn't an excessive amount on the towel she found. Men nick themselves when shaving, women cut themselves when they shave their legs, kids have scraped knees, that sort of thing.'' He shrugged. "She's right, if you think about it.''

Mack's gaze was thoughtful. "Wayne, going strictly on your instincts, do you think it was Tim who was killed that day?''

Wayne nodded. "I do.''

They sat mulling over what they knew about the case. "Of course, all this really tells us nothing new,'' Claire said finally.

"Except to confirm that Tim was the person Danny saw shot,'' Mack said.

"Provided the blood tests jibe," Wayne said. "He thumbed through the papers and pulled out a yellow legal pad. "Naturally, I did some checking on Landry. He was unmarried, worked out of his house as an accountant. Didn't have a full-time secretary until tax season, starting around the first of the year. So nobody missed him." He was shaking his head. "Kind of sad, if you think about it. A man disappears and nobody notices."

"What about his parents?" Claire asked. "Angus mentioned them."

"Yeah, and what about friends?" Mack asked with a glance at the scribbling on the pad.

Wayne shrugged. "His parents had gone to visit his sister in Texas. As for friends, I talked to Glenn Thibodaux—drove to Baton Rouge to see him. He was shocked. Hadn't seen Tim in a while. They'd drifted apart, he told me. Not surprising, that's how it is with most folks nowadays. Share their whole childhoods, go to grade school together, high school, room together in college, then different careers, interests. Life takes people down different roads."

"It didn't happen with Mike and me."

Wayne smiled faintly. "No, but you and Mike were a lot different from Tim and Glenn."

"And Carter," Claire said.

Both men looked a little startled. It was the sheriff who replied. "Yes, ma'am. You've got that right."

TO MACK'S RELIEF, the ride home was nothing like the trip to Wayne's house. There was silence, yes, but it was comfortable. Soothing. It amazed Mack how he felt in Claire's company. Even considering all the things they found to wrangle over, he liked being with her. It had been that way from that first afternoon, he realized. He admitted something that he would have scoffed at a week ago. He was half in love with Claire Woodson.

Had it happened in just a week, or had Claire been in his mind from the moment Carter had introduced them? Had Mack fought the feeling because he didn't approve of her character? Or because he felt that a woman who fell for a man like Carter would never be interested in a man like him?

It started to rain again and for a while the only sound in the Jeep was the swish of the wipers, the occasional gust of wind and the muted rhythm of soft rock from the CD she'd chosen. The total absence of anybody else on the highway added to the intimacy of the moment. A quick, inner defense flashed in his mind at the word *intimacy,* and some of the calm he was feeling slipped. He didn't know much about true intimacy. It had never been a part of his first marriage.

"I was hoping the sheriff would tell us something more substantial," Claire remarked, gazing at the pattern of raindrops reflected by the headlights.

"We got details," Mack said, relieved to have his thoughts interrupted. "Confirmation of what Danny saw and a lot of dry facts that don't follow any kind of pattern. Certainly nothing that would explain why somebody would want to kill Tim."

"I wish we knew if the shooting was calculated," she said. "I mean, did somebody want him dead for a reason or was it a sudden thing, something done in a fit of anger?"

"A crime of passion?"

"Well, yes."

Mack draped a wrist over the steering wheel before glancing her way. "I'm trying, but frankly I don't see

Tim Landry as a guy with a whole lot of passion in his soul."

"That's another thing," Claire said, frowning. "The evidence has turned up nothing unusual or even interesting in Landry's life. Nobody's that dull and boring."

"He was an accountant, Claire."

She gave him an exasperated look. "And all accountants must be dull and boring? We librarians resent such sweeping clichés."

He gave her a quick grin. "Angling for a compliment, huh?"

"Don't be ridiculous."

He reached over and tugged at a wisp of hair that had escaped from her bun. "You may be a librarian, but take it from me, lady, you aren't dull and boring."

Her hands went instantly to her hairdo, but before she could come up with anything to say to that, he turned into the driveway at Sugarland. The rain was now coming down in torrents. Instead of stopping in front of the house where they would both get drenched climbing the tall steps, he headed for the garage. They'd be dry there waiting out the worst of the storm.

"I've never seen so much rain," Claire said as they got out of the Jeep. "I feel as though I'll never be thoroughly dry again."

He closed his door. "I'll remind you of that in a few days when the temperature is nearly a hundred and you'd kill for a nice soaking rain."

The overhead lights went out automatically, leaving them in virtual darkness. Claire went to the open garage door, as though debating the wisdom of making a dash for the house.

"I wouldn't," Mack said, coming up behind her. Propping one arm above her head, he looked out at the dense rainfall. "This might last a while. There's a small office in the back. Want to wait it out there?"

"I guess we'll have to." She left the doorway and went with him past the car to the back.

"I've got a small bar stocked," he said, opening the door. "Angus can't have the hard stuff anymore, so he sneaks out here every now and then and drinks wine."

"Don't even think it," she muttered as he flipped a switch and gave them a little light.

He chuckled, watching her fiddle with more loose strands trailing on her neck from that silly bun. Did she actually think she was fooling anybody by keeping her hair slicked back like that? Not that tonight it looked anywhere near as prim as she usually favored. The stress of the day had taken a toll. She looked slightly frazzled and very vulnerable. He reached out and gently—not wanting to scare her—pulled the combs out of her hair.

Too late she tried to stop him, but the whole mass instantly tumbled down around her shoulders. She made a little sound, almost a whimper, and it caught somewhere deep in his belly. He took a handful of her hair and rubbed it on his face.

"Ah, sweet Claire, I'm not going to hurt you." He slipped his arms around her waist from behind, burying his nose in her hair, and inhaled deeply. Flowers and freshness and rain-washed air came instantly to mind.

"John..."

It was the damnedest thing. Nobody called him John, yet it sounded so right coming from Claire.

"I can't forget how good it was last night," he murmured, nuzzling the delicate skin beneath her ear, then gently nipping her lobe. His hands moved over her midriff, then down past her waist. She was soft and womanly and giving to his touch.

He pulled her closer, groaning with the feel of her against his arousal. They fitted together so perfectly. Surely he wasn't the only one to feel that way. He wanted to hear her say it, needed to hear her say it.

"Claire..."

"John, I can't..."

Swiping her hair aside with one hand, he kissed her temple, her cheek, the corner of her mouth. "Can't what, sweetheart?" He covered her breasts, wishing the sweater, her bra—all her clothes—to hell and gone.

"I can't think when you—"

"Don't think, Claire. Just feel."

With her hands on his forearms, Claire might have tried getting away—she thought that was in her mind—but he was breathing hotly and insistently in her ear, weakening her resistance. And then he was using his tongue in a way that melted her bones.

"Let me, Claire. It'll be so good..." His mouth skimmed down her neck while his hands went beneath her sweater in search of her breasts. She moaned as he stroked with his fingers, kneading and plucking at tight, sensitive nipples.

Half-dazed, she felt herself swell to his touch, heard her own breathing, let herself go pliant and willing under the magic of his hands. Knees buckling, she groped blindly for his wrists, anything to hang on to, anything to keep the pleasure going.

"John..."

He turned her, and holding her face in his hands, he kissed her eyes and nose. He ran his lips over her cheeks, skating past her mouth down to her throat. "Let me love you, Claire."

Driven by her own need and years of abstinence, she lifted her arms and put them around his neck. Grunting with approval, he gathered her closer. There was no mistaking his erection. He was hard and strong and everything that was female in her urged her to do as he asked. With a shuddering sigh, she lifted her mouth for his kiss.

It was deep, driving and intimate. She held on to his shoulders, lost in a haze of sensation that was wonderfully new. The kiss was blatantly carnal, his taste, his scent, the texture of his skin nearly overwhelming to her senses.

But abruptly he tore his mouth away and, dragging in huge drafts of oxygen, he simply held her. She swayed slightly in his arms, eyes still closed. Her heart was racing, and beneath his soft denim shirt, she could hear the answering thunder of his. Why had he stopped?

"Claire, look at me."

Lashes, heavy and languorous, fluttered open.

"Are you okay with this?"

She blinked, resisting the need to speak. To think. She found it hard to look at him, while everything in her objected to leaving the warmth of his embrace. With a sigh, she leaned her forehead against his chin. "I don't know."

"This has to be something we both want. You talk to me about responsibility...well, this one's your call. I want to make love to you. I have for days. What do you want?"

His words went straight to her heart. Pressed close to him, still captured by the heat and power of his embrace, she knew that all her caution, all her wariness had been in anticipation of this moment. She'd had only one lover and that had been six years ago. Before coming here, she had not even been tempted by another man.

But almost from the first, she had wanted John Mc-Mollere. She might never have another chance.

With her head still bent to his chest, she murmured, "I never expected anything like this to happen."

He gave a short, pained laugh. "That makes two of us."

"This is nothing like when Car—"

"Don't." His arms tightened. "There's nobody else in this room except you and me, Claire."

"But you thought—"

He pulled back, forcing her to meet his eyes. "I had a lot of preconceived ideas about you. They were wrong. I got over them fast."

Maybe so, she thought. But this…if they were to take this step, it would change everything. She wouldn't just be accepting sanctuary at Sugarland. If she went to bed with him, then when all danger was passed and she was forced back into her real life, nothing would be the same. When Carter left, she had picked up the pieces and built a new life, a good life. But her feelings then were nothing compared to what she was feeling now. Loving this man would be far too easy.

"Claire?"

"I want you."

There was a couch against the far wall, and she took his hand and led him there. Holding his eyes with hers, she lifted the ends of her sweater and pulled the garment over her head. For years she'd been buying dull, uninteresting clothes, subduing her vibrant hair and coloring with earth tones and sensible styles. But her lingerie was different. There she had indulged her hunger for pretty things.

And it was worth it just to bring that look to John's face.

Her own pulse fluttered, but she meant to go the whole nine yards. She meant to erase Carter from her memory and replace him with the one man she felt she could have loved and been happy with forever... if only fate had not paired her first with his brother.

Pushing the filmy skirt down past her hips, she stepped out of it, still keeping her eyes on Mack. Watching her, his blue eyes were intense, his breath rapid and obvious in the deep rise and fall of his chest. Suddenly, she wanted his touch. She wanted to touch him. Her palms fairly itched to explore all of him. She wanted to feel the rasp of his beard and the texture of his skin against her own.

He must have sensed her need. His fingers were already working at the buttons on his shirt. With one forceful tug, he had it free of his pants and tossed aside, then he got out of his jeans and briefs and reached for her.

He held her tightly at first, burying his face in her hair. Then he let her go just long enough to strip her bra away and dispense with her bikini. She heard the sharp intake of his breath and her eyes flew to his. It felt incredibly powerful to know his desire matched her own. It was there in the fierce blue of his eyes, in the taut line of his jaw. And then his hands were moving, urgent and strong, as if he couldn't quite manage to curb his impatience. Sweeping down to her hips, he sank his fingers into the softness of her bottom and held her hard against him.

His urgency fired her own need. Her body felt hot and achy. She curled into the heat of him, luxuriating in the sensation of being so close that their bodies were almost fused.

With a sound deep in his throat, he took a handful of
her hair and brought her mouth to meet his. She loved
kissing John, loved the taste and smell and essence of
him, loved the way he took charge, claiming her whole
body by just sealing his mouth to hers.

Her insides were trembling and her knees were weak
when he urged her onto the couch. Coming down over
her, he found his place between her legs. He was hot and
hard, his shoulders quivering with the effort of holding
off.

"I wish we were in a real bed," he said, tangling a
hand in her hair. "I wish there were flowers and soft
music and champagne."

She smiled, tracing his lips with one finger. "No
champagne."

"I don't want to hurt you."

"It's not the first time, John. How can you hurt me?"

Oh, but he could. He could break her heart, but she
didn't want to think of that now. With a hand behind his
neck, she pulled him down for a kiss. Instinctively, her
hips arched and his response was just as instinctive. With
a groan, he thrust into her, deep and true, and then they
found a natural rhythm as if they'd done this a thousand times before. Next came that blank stretch of time
where both were lost in sensation. And finally the moment when together they spun out into ecstasy.

Oh, yes, he could break her heart.

CHAPTER ELEVEN

THE SERVICES for Tim Landry were being held the next day, and Mack planned to go. The last time he'd attended a funeral, it had been his brother's. Tim's could hardly match that one, but, like Carter, he was too young to die, and Mack was filled with sadness and a sense of waste.

His father had announced the night before that he intended to pay his respects. Mack had objected, but had been ignored. He'd noticed that Angus seemed to be losing ground lately, but the old man claimed he wasn't so bad off that he couldn't do the proper thing, seeing as how Tim had been Carter's childhood friend. It was his duty, he'd stated flatly. Tim's parents would expect to see him there. Thankfully, Wyona had elected to stay home.

Scanning the crowd after the church service, Mack wasn't sure what he hoped to discover—whether there was anything to discover—but he was feeling more and more anxious to have the mystery of Landry's death cleared up.

"Are you doing all right, Dad?" There was still the graveside ceremony to go. Holding Angus's cane, he waited while his father managed to seat himself in the town car. "It'll be hot at the cemetery. Pretty wet, too, considering all the rain we've had lately. Maybe I should drop you back at the house."

"My feet have been wet before."

"Hot as blazes out there, too. You know how it is after all the rain we've had. It's like a sauna."

"I'm going. That's it." Folding his hands on the top of his cane, Angus stared straight ahead.

"Right." He closed the car door, torn between amusement and exasperation. Heading around to get in the car, he decided Angus and Claire Woodson had a lot in common.

Claire.

The stakes had suddenly turned personal. Until last night, he had been able to tell himself that his responsibility to his brother's small son—and consequently the boy's mother—was not unlike the long list of other responsibilities he shouldered at Sugarland. Making love with Claire had changed all that. Desire pooled instantly in him and he shifted in his seat to get comfortable. When she'd taken off her clothes, he had nearly lost it. She was usually so demure, so hung up on propriety. She *worked* at being untouchable. It was as though in letting down her hair, her inhibitions had gone, too. And when it was over, he had been satisfied in a way he'd never been with any woman. *Fulfilled* was a better word, but it was one he had never used in terms of sex. But it wasn't sex with Claire, he knew that now. He was in love with her.

Which made finding out who killed Tim Landry so urgent.

"Looks like most folks turned out," Angus said minutes later at the cemetery. Although Mack was around to open the door, Angus refused his help in getting out of the car. Squinting in the sun, Angus looked the crowd over for familiar faces. "There's Wayne Pagett," he observed, shading his eyes with one hand. "I guess he's looking to size up the mourners on the chance that the killer's here paying his respects. Hah!'' He shook his head. "I think I'll have a word or two with Martin. I see him and his boy Glenn over there near the family." Leaning on his cane, he started off.

Mack waited, watching Angus thread a path around aged tombs, heading for Martin Thibodaux. As he approached his old friend, Mack thought he saw a flicker of concern, or maybe wariness, in Martin's eyes. It was brief, almost too fast for Mack to be certain he'd seen anything. And then the two men were shaking hands. Martin, who'd been Angus's attorney for the past thirty years, murmured something. His voice was low, in keeping with the solemn occasion. Beside him, Glenn looked over at Mack with a brief nod, and then the priest signaled to the gathering and the final farewell to Tim Landry began.

Wayne stepped close to Mack a few minutes after the burial. "See anything interesting?"

Mack let out a long breath, scanning the crowd. "Nobody here looks like a killer."

"That's the problem with crime-solving, most killers look like everybody else." Wayne's gaze fell on the group of Landry's family and friends drifting toward the pathway leading out of the cemetery. "Getting anything here would've been a major stroke of luck."

Mack fiddled with the end of his tie. "Yeah, but I wanted to see who showed up."

"Or who didn't."

"Which tells us exactly nothing." He felt a surge of frustration. The killer had to be found. Until that happened, Claire couldn't get on with her life. Now that he'd had a taste of her, he wanted her free of the worry about some goon with a gun waiting for a chance to hurt her and her son. Once the gunman was flushed out, Claire and Mack could get on with sorting out the future.

He knew what he wanted, but he hadn't spoken the words last night. For one thing, he sensed Claire wasn't ready to hear them. Maybe she wouldn't have believed them. The other problem was that he needed to erase Carter's shadow before they talked about a future together.

"The devil's in the details, as they say," Wayne remarked, pulling out his sunglasses. He put them on, and without making it obvious, surveyed the crowd. "I've spent the best part of two days digging around in Tim Landry's background, talking to people, sifting through files, newspaper clippings, doing computer searches. It's time-consuming and tedious, but it's the only way to solve a crime."

He watched some of Tim's buddies from high school. "I started with the present, then began working my way backward in Tim's life. You know something interesting? Almost every time I found his name, Carter was mentioned, too. And Glenn Thibodaux. Those three were practically joined at the hip when they were in high school and college."

Mack focused on a large magnolia tree in the center of the graveyard. He had spent many hours since Carter's death regretting that they'd had so little in common. That they'd barely known each other. "I wasn't paying much attention to Carter then. I'd been in Vietnam, and then there was college . . . Liz . . . Sugarland. You know how it is. I guess I was too occupied with my own problems."

"You didn't live at the big house until after your divorce, as I recall."

"Liz and I had our own place in Lafayette." He laughed shortly. "To her that was bad enough, she wanted to live in New Orleans. And Carter was married to Renee by that time. Now that I think about it, I don't remember seeing much of Carter at all."

After a minute, his gaze settled on Angus sitting on an iron bench talking with Martin Thibodaux. He felt regret, not guilt. Carter hadn't exactly suffered from a lack of attention . . . ever. Angus and Wyona had seen to that from the day he was born, six years after Mack. He knew they'd worried that they would have only one child, so maybe it was natural to carry on over the second son when he finally did show up. Mack didn't like to think about it, but he remembered feeling bewildered about his parents' open partiality to Carter. Maybe that explained why Mack had distanced himself from his brother as soon as he could. The only times he remembered seeing much of Carter back then was when he taught him to fly.

Wayne followed Mack's gaze to the two older men. "Of the three musketeers, Glenn was the popular one in school. Class president, most likely to succeed, all that stuff. He was a politician in training even then. Seems odd that he turned out to be more of a loner than either Tim or Carter."

Wayne fumbled around in his breast pocket for a cigar. "Either that, or considering his political ambitions, he's very careful about what gets to the media. Seems once he set his sights on Baton Rouge, his name doesn't turn up at all in his hometown."

Mack nodded absently, his gaze still on Angus and Martin.

Wayne was watching them, too. He clicked his lighter shut after working up a cloud of blue smoke. "Angus and Martin seem to be going at it over something."

"I was just thinking that," Mack murmured.

"Could be about Claire," Wayne observed, "seeing as how Martin was instrumental in getting her here."

"I don't think so. Claire's turning out to be nothing like any of us expected. She's everything and more that any grandparent could wish for."

"No kidding."

So what was the problem? Mack thought, not picking up on Wayne's wry tone. His father had been almost obsessive about keeping his personal business to himself, discussing it only with his lawyer. Mack hadn't worried about it, because Martin was a trusted friend. They didn't look friendly now; they looked tense, at odds with each other. Maybe something about Angus's affairs was worrying him. Perhaps something that Martin was counseling against?

"How are you, Mack?"

He turned to find Glenn Thibodaux behind him. "Hey, okay, Glenn. It's been a long time." They shook hands.

"You're a busy man."

"Well, what is it they say about raisin' cane?"

"We both know that old saying doesn't suit you. In fact, the way Carter always told it, you were the straight arrow in the family. He was the one most likely to raise Cain."

Mack didn't reply. Now that he was face-to-face with Glenn Thibodaux, he remembered that he'd never particularly liked him. The guy was just too smooth, too glib. Maybe because he was working on a political career. There were only a few politicians Mack genuinely respected.

Thibodaux looked at Wayne. "Hello again, Sheriff."

"Glenn."

"How's the investigation going?"

"Well enough, I'd say."

Thibodaux's eyes narrowed. "There's new evidence?"

Wayne took his cigar out of his mouth. "I think you know I can't comment on an ongoing investigation."

Thibodaux laughed incredulously. "That sounds like a line from a TV show, Sheriff. I think as Tim's friend— one of his oldest friends—I have a right to ask what's being done to find his murderer."

Wayne nodded agreeably. "And I have a right to say no comment."

There was a look of frustration on Thibodaux's face— Why was the guy frustrated? Mack wondered— and then Thibodaux turned on his heel and walked off.

"I think he's pissed," Mack drawled, watching Thibodaux stalk down the pathway. At the wrought-iron gate, he directed a few curt words to his father, then shoved the gate open with more strength than was required. Only the fact that it was old and the hinges a little rusty kept it from banging back against the fence.

A few curious glances followed Thibodaux's progress to Martin's big Lexus, but Mack noticed few of those faces were friendly. Glenn Thibodaux wasn't most popular anymore. Why?

Wayne carefully tapped the ashes from his cigar. "Our golden boy's not going to be much of a politician if he doesn't work on his temper."

Mack nodded. "It definitely needs some adjustment."

"Wonder why he's so curious about Tim?"

"I don't know. I suppose it's logical he'd be interested." Mack scanned the crowd again, forgetting Glenn. His gaze was narrowed in thought. "It's funny, but I can't help thinking the killer's somebody we know, Wayne. Somebody who's walking among us, maybe even secretly laughing at us."

Wayne stopped puffing at his cigar and looked at him. "What makes you say that?"

"Beats me," Mack said. "I guess I'm making about as much sense as my mama now."

Wayne squinted at the crowd through a blue cloud, his face thoughtful. "I don't know, Mack. Stranger things have happened."

CLAIRE WAS on the porch when Mack and Angus got back from the funeral. The sight of her hit him like a kick in the chest. Had she been waiting for him? God, he hoped so. When she hadn't come down for breakfast, he hadn't known what to think. He didn't want her to regret last night. He needed her to feel as good about what had happened between them as he did.

Her hair was loose. It was the first thing he noticed as he got out of the car. That had to be a good sign. Their eyes met over the top of the Lincoln and for a split second, he almost lost his breath. Her smile was soft, shy, vulnerable. She was so damn beautiful. She looked away immediately, fixing her attention on Angus.

"Let me give you a hand, Angus." The older man seemed to actually welcome her help. She slipped a palm beneath his elbow and together they went cautiously up the steps where Wyona waited, wringing her hands. Mack watched, thinking what a change from a week ago when the sound of Claire's name had been enough to set Angus off on a tirade.

By the time they were at the door, Wyona had it open. Angus was winded and a little pale and for once he didn't resist when his wife began clucking and coaxing him inside.

"Did you see Martin?" she asked anxiously.

"Didn't I say I would?" Testy with fatigue, Angus handed her his cane while he took off his jacket.

"How did he look, Angus?"

"Who, Tim? He looked like any young man dead before his time."

"Like Carter?" she whispered, her mouth trembling. Quick tears sprang to her eyes.

"Now, don't start, Mama."

Wyona handed him his cane, then clasped her hands together, prayer-like, beneath her chin. "Did he look . . . peaceful, Angus?"

"I suppose."

"Good. He's happy now."

"He's dead, is what he is." Angus shuffled past her, heading for the living room. Halfway there, he stopped and looked back at Mack. "I'm helping myself to a shot of that brandy, Mack. You gonna join me?"

"It's a little early for me, Dad."

"Hmmph, suit yourself. Come on, Mama. Get me a glass, if you will. Funerals take a lot out of a man."

"All right, Angus."

Claire looked at Mack. "Your father's exhausted. Was the funeral so difficult?"

"I think so. I tried to talk him out of going, but he wouldn't have it any other way."

"You look tired, too."

A wicked glint appeared in his eyes. "I didn't get a lot of sleep last night." Her eyes fell, but he used his finger to lift her chin. "Regrets, Claire?"

"Isn't it a little late for that?"

He studied her silently for a minute. "Claire, there's one question I didn't ask you last night that I should have. Are you involved with anyone?"

"No!" she said, startled. "Do you think I would have...that I'm..." She struggled to clear her thoughts. "You misunderstood. The truth is..." She sucked in a long, deep breath. "The truth is, I don't regret what happened at all. But in the light of day—" she waved her fingers vaguely "—things like that take on a certain, ah, context that makes you wonder—" her voice went a little higher "—makes you wonder what in the world came over you." She cleared her throat slightly. "I mean, me. What came over me."

He was studying her thoughtfully. "How long has it been?"

"Excuse me?"

"How many lovers have there been?"

"I don't feel comfortable talking about this."

"Not very many, right?"

"John..."

"One, two...?"

She sighed. "Why are you asking this?"

His voice lowered. "Not to make you uncomfortable or because I'm curious about you—although I am...curious as hell, if you want to know. Any man in my shoes would be. I don't want you to worry about what happened last night. It was natural and right. It was so good that I'm still not sure I didn't dream the whole thing. But I can see you're having second thoughts. I'm not going to try and coax you back into my bed, although it's almost more than I can bear not to."

He reached out and touched her cheek. "I just want us to get to know each other, Claire. Maybe rock along as we've been doing for a while, if that's what's most comfortable for you. See where it takes us."

He bent his knees a little to get a good look at her face. "How does that sound to you?"

She closed her eyes, then looked at him. "It sounds good."

"Okay." He straightened, releasing an unsteady breath, and glanced around. "I'd kiss you if I didn't know that half a dozen people are probably watching us."

"John . . ." There was protest and an air of endearing embarrassment about her. Her skin was flushed and she wouldn't look at him. He took a handful of her hair, marveling at the silky softness of it. "I only have one request."

"Oh?" She smiled and he knew she guessed what it was.

"Throw away those combs. Please."

"I'll think about it."

Michelle suddenly appeared in the doorway. "Oh, you guys are still out here. Claire, did you tell Dad about that call from Lafayette? It's to remind you of a meeting at four o'clock this afternoon, Dad."

He swore beneath his breath. "What time was that?"

"Not long after you left to go to the funeral."

He touched Claire at the waist, urging her inside. "I told Harvey to fill in for me on that. Or at least I meant to." He swept up a stack of mail on the table just inside the door. "I'm bogged down in paperwork right now. I have to clear my desk. I don't have time to go to Lafayette."

Claire had taken two calls for him herself. "How about Houston?" she said. "You're supposed to be there tomorrow, something about offshore oil leases. A man named Wilson called. Also there's a message from the sugar co-op. Oh, and your mother said she took a call for you, as well."

Michelle bit into an apple. "Dad, you need a secre-, tary."

"Tell me about it," Mack muttered, sifting through the mail.

"How about me?" Claire suggested.

"What?" Mack stopped in the act of scanning a letter.

She shrugged. "You need help and I'm just hanging around consuming hospitality and doing nothing. Why not?"

"Hey, cool," Michelle said. "She's computer literate, too, Dad."

"You are?" The letter in his hand was forgotten.

"Da-a-ad...almost everybody is. Especially somebody who works in a library." She met Claire's eyes. "Overlook him, Claire. He spends too much time in cane fields and boardrooms."

"Michelle!"

She subsided with a shrug and he turned back to Claire. "You think you might be familiar with *my* computer?"

Claire laughed, pushing her hair away from her face. "I'm not promising anything, but I'm familiar with DOS and Windows 95."

"I'm using Windows 95."

Michelle studied her apple. "A match made in heaven," she murmured.

Mack was studying Claire intently. "Are you sure about this?"

"I have a computer at home, John."

Michelle looked startled at Claire's use of her father's given name, then interested.

He shook his head. "No, I mean, are you sure it wouldn't be an imposition?"

With fingers pressed to her temple, Claire pretended to consider that. "Well, let me see, I had planned to go to New Orleans and shop, or maybe pop in at the country club for lunch." Before he could reply, she huffed with exasperation. "I'm bored to distraction here. The extent of my chores is to make my bed and Danny's. It'll be refreshing to do something useful."

"My desk is a war zone."

"I promise not to freak out." She was actually enjoying herself now.

"It sort of got away from me in the last day or so." He pressed a hand to the back of his neck.

"We librarians are noted for bringing order to chaos."

"For heaven's sake, Dad!" Michelle looked as if she wanted to give him a good shake. "Are you trying to talk her out of it? You need help. Claire's volunteering. It seems simple to me."

"You can choose your own hours, naturally," he told Claire.

She shrugged. "Right now's good for me."

After an instant of silence, he nodded. "You got it."

He caught Claire's elbow and hurried her down the long hall, leaving his daughter staring after them thoughtfully.

"John," Michelle murmured, a small smile playing on her lips. "Nobody calls Dad John. Very, ver-ry interesting."

A WEEK LATER, Claire was in Mack's office when Michelle came to tell her that Martin Thibodaux was having lunch with her grandparents and they would like Claire to join them.

"Are you sure?"

Michelle found a computer printout on Mack's desk and began idly paging through it. "I'm sure I got the message right. Why? Is lunch with Mr. Thibodaux a big deal?"

Claire was silent, thinking. "I don't know."

"Where's Dad?"

"He flew to Houston early this morning."

"Leaving his trusty second-in-command in charge, huh?" With a teasing grin, the teenager put down her printout. "Wow, he sure lucked out when you volunteered your services. I heard him tell Jake and Shorty that he now knows every piece of Sugarland equipment, when it was bought, where it's presently being used and when it's going to need replacing, thanks to you."

Claire touched a key, then stood up as the computer was closing out. "Not me, it's all in the software program."

"A program they didn't have until you suggested it."

"I did a little research on the Internet."

"You did a little miracle in the office," Michelle said. Perched on the desk, she watched as Claire put some papers in order, slipped them into a folder, then dropped the folder into a drawer. "It's amazing, you know?"

"Why is it amazing?" Claire asked, smiling faintly.

Michelle spread her hands. "Isn't it obvious? Until you started working together, you two were always arguing. The first week you were here, I don't think a day went by when you weren't squabbling over something."

"I was tense. It wasn't exactly a vacation that brought me to Sugarland."

Michelle waved that away as irrelevant. "Then suddenly you're together in an office all day long and it's like blue skies and rainbows."

"You exaggerate."

"Uh-uh. I notice these things."

Claire knew that tone. She headed for the door, hoping somehow to escape being blindsided.

Michelle followed at a slower pace. "Guess what else I noticed?"

"Where's lunch?" Claire asked brightly. "On the patio or the dining room?"

"The dining room." Not missing a beat, Michelle held up a finger. "I noticed you call my dad John, not Mack like everyone else. Why is that, I wonder?"

"It's his name, Michelle."

"Mack's his name. Nobody, but nobody, calls him John." Up went another finger. "Second thing—I noticed he looks at you. A lot."

"You're imagining that."

"Uh-uh. He *likes* looking at you."

"Michelle . . ."

"It's great. I think it's cool. Really cool." She fell happily into step beside Claire. "My dad's always been a little uptight, all tense and overworked and kinda grim. You know, pulled at from all sides. I don't remember him ever being relaxed and kicked-back like some dads."

They were now passing the kitchen area. Michelle waved absently to Cleo. "But lately he's different. His responsibilities are the same, maybe even worse since he has to look out for you and Danny on top of everything else."

"I would relieve him of that worry if I could," Claire said dryly.

"You know what I mean."

"I'm starving, how about you?"

"I think he's got the hots for you, Claire."

Thank God, Wyona appeared at that moment. "Oh, here you are, Claire. I was just coming to see what was keeping you. Michelle, you did tell her we wanted her for lunch, didn't you?" Wyona fluttered a hand in the direction of the dining room. "Cleo will be serving the salad any minute now."

Inside, Angus stood beside a tall, distinguished-looking man with a shock of white hair. This must be Martin Thibodaux, Claire thought. Although they were the same age, the lawyer looked ten years younger than Angus. And whatever the conversation was about, it had increased the tension around Angus's mouth. His color was off again, too. Had Martin brought bad news? She felt a surge of irritation at the lawyer. Surely he could see that Angus wasn't well enough for business as usual. Why hadn't the man waited until Mack was here?

Angus held out his hand. "Claire."

Martin Thibodaux watched her intently as she crossed the dining room, an odd smile playing on his lips. Angus made the introductions. Although she hadn't met the lawyer, she had spoken with him on the telephone during the negotiations for this visit. Always when they were finished, she'd hung up feeling unsettled. Threatened. She'd put down her reaction to a natural fear of the legal representative of the powerful McMolleres. Now she wondered if she would have felt comfortable dealing with Martin Thibodaux under any conditions. She didn't think so.

"I've been looking forward to meeting you, Ms. Woodson." The lawyer shook out a snowy napkin and put it on his lap. "I was just telling Angus what an excellent job you've done in rearing young Daniel."

"You've met Danny?" She was puzzled.

"A few minutes ago," Angus explained. "We strolled out to the barn where he was playing."

"A fine boy," Martin said, starting in on his shrimp salad.

"Thank you."

"As you've discovered—" he waved a hand "—your little boy has a wonderful heritage waiting here."

Claire wasn't sure whether he meant the dining room, the grandparents or Sugarland. "Everything at Sugarland is certainly impressive," she murmured.

"Impressive, yes." He exchanged a satisfied look with Angus. "And much of it rightfully belongs to Daniel."

She speared a shrimp. If the man had a mission, she'd just as soon he got on with it.

He must have read her expression. With a smile, he shook his head. "Forgive me. I'm not here for business today, although it must sound as if I am. When I learned you were extending your visit with Angus and Wyona, naturally I recalled how fierce you were in stating the conditions for that visit. It was to be brief." He smiled, showing a lot of teeth. "You changed your mind."

"A woman's prerogative." She smiled, baring an equal number of teeth.

"This is the best place for Danny and Claire right now," Angus stated. "Safe as houses, Sugarland is."

"Yes, what with all the trouble..." Wyona's worried gaze was fixed on a tall Waterford goblet.

Claire was alarmed. Surely no one had revealed the reason she'd extended her visit. Until the killer was known, the fewer people who knew that Danny was an eyewitness, the better.

"Trouble comes in sets of three," Wyona continued, the fork in her hand forgotten. "For the longest time, I worried about that." She stared blindly at the food on her plate. "But when so many years passed..." Again her words dribbled to a standstill.

Angus snorted with impatience. "You talk a lot of nonsense nowadays, Mama."

"Tim's death was the second tragedy," she said as though Angus hadn't spoken. "There's another one to go, wait and see."

Claire couldn't quite suppress a little shiver. There was something about Wyona when she started talking like that. She glanced at Martin Thibodaux and found him watching Wyona, too. There was no compassion or concern in his look, just disgust. Her dislike of him rose. Didn't he see that Wyona wasn't well? He was supposed to be an old friend.

"Everyone's agreed that Tim's death was a tragedy, Mama," Angus said, helping himself to a second glass of wine.

Martin looked at Claire. "Tim and Carter were boyhood friends, were you aware of that?"

"Yes. Wyona has a right to feel terribly upset."

"Indeed." He carefully applied butter to a slice of crusty French bread. "My boy Glenn was close to Tim, as well."

"That's what I hear."

"Did you know him?"

"Who, Tim Landry?"

"Ah, actually, I meant Glenn, my son."

"No."

"But you knew Tim?"

"No."

"Carter never mentioned him?"

"No."

"Or Glenn?"

"No, Mr. Thibodaux, he never mentioned either of them."

"Hmm. Odd."

"What is this all about, Mr. Thibodaux?"

"Forgive me, Claire...I may call you Claire, hmm?" Taking her agreement for granted, the lawyer attacked his salad again. "I suppose I was just trying to find some hint of Carter's frame of mind when he was, ah, with you. Naturally we'd like to know what he planned for his child. We've always been a close-knit group here in LaRue. The McMolleres and my family, for example, go back many years."

He reflected for a moment or two, then added thoughtfully, "To tell the truth, I wasn't too surprised when I learned that Carter had arranged his will to include Daniel." He gave a wry chuckle. "I admit to being somewhat chagrined that he'd chosen an attorney in Baton Rouge to handle it."

Her appetite gone, Claire sipped raspberry iced tea. "I'm afraid I can't help you there. I wasn't aware of what he planned, either. I've told Angus and Wyona as much."

Martin touched his mouth with his napkin. It was a meticulous gesture, Claire noted. He was a meticulous man.

"Well, it worked out very well in spite of everything, didn't it? There's only one other detail that I'm sure Carter would have wanted and that's the matter of his name. Daniel is a McMollere, after all. Angus and Wyona would very much like to see that done legally." He looked straight at her. "Have you given that any thought?"

Claire stared, then set her glass down carefully. "I thought you weren't here on business today, Mr. Thibodaux."

"Handling a delicate matter for old friends isn't business, Claire."

She pushed her chair back and stood up. "Well, you weren't quite delicate enough." She smiled tightly at Wyona, who was looking extremely anxious, then at Angus. Neither were quite able to meet her eyes.

"A moment, please, Claire." Martin was on his feet, as politeness demanded. "Just so you'll know, it was Mack, not Angus and Wyona, who asked me to look into the matter of Daniel's name."

Claire stared at him, shaken. "If you'll excuse me, I have a ton of work waiting."

CHAPTER TWELVE

THE HOUSE WAS QUIET. At the bar, Mack unscrewed the cap on a bottle of scotch as the old clock on the mantel tolled the midnight hour. He poured himself a good stiff drink and took a healthy gulp. It went down smooth as silk and he sighed in satisfaction at the rich, smoky bite on his tongue. He had been looking forward to getting home ever since he'd climbed into the Cessna in Houston to make the trip back to Louisiana.

It had been a hell of a trip with appointments stacked back-to-back and one snarl after the other to be untangled. He'd been determined to wrap everything up in a single day. And he had, with the exception of the dispute at the board meeting over offshore oil leases. That, too, he could probably have put to bed if he'd wanted to stay on a couple of days longer, but he hadn't.

It was a new experience for him. Usually when business took him away, he accepted it as part of his responsibility as head of the family. He stayed as long as it took to get the job done and he got home when he could. This time had been different. He had taken care of business in a minimum of time. Flying back, he had felt a heightened sense of eagerness to be at Sugarland.

To see Claire.

His gaze strayed to the stairs. She would be sleeping at this hour. He imagined the look of her in bed, soft and vulnerable, her hair like flame on the pillow. Was she naked? No, not his prim little librarian, but he bet she slept in something pretty and sexy. He'd noticed her underthings the night they'd made love. They were not plain white cotton.

"Dad, you're home."

He turned sharply, splashing scotch on himself and the floor. Michelle stood in the arched entrance. She was barefoot, wearing an oversize T-shirt. Sometimes he forgot how young his daughter actually was.

"Shelly." The old nickname slipped out. He set his glass down and pulled his handkerchief out of his pocket to wipe the liquor off his fingers. "What are you doing creeping around the house at this hour, baby?"

"I heard the Jeep." She went behind the bar and found a roll of paper towels. "When you didn't come upstairs, I decided to check out why."

"I was having a drink."

"You shouldn't drink alone." She bent down and wiped up the spill.

He smiled. "You're too young for whiskey, little girl."

"I know, Dad," she said dryly. "I thought Claire might be with you."

His eyes narrowed. "Why would you think that?"

"Well, she's not in her room. I thought she might have waited up for you."

He was instantly on alert. Did Michelle know they'd slept together? He didn't want her guessing how he felt about Claire, not yet. Not until they'd worked it out themselves. He gazed into his daughter's blue eyes. She looked so damn *smart*. That was the trouble with teenagers today. They knew too much too soon.

"Hard day, huh, Dad?"

"What? Oh. Yeah, I guess. Put it this way, it was a long one."

"It wasn't exactly a picnic around here." She wadded up the paper towel and tossed it in a trash basket behind the bar.

"Why? What happened?"

"Lunch. That's what happened. Something was said while they were all in there that upset Claire. Since she's not in her room, she must be waiting to talk to you about it."

"She's not in her room?"

"Dad, I already said that. She hasn't been around most of the day. I looked everywhere for her trying to find out what was bothering her, but she sort of disappeared."

Alarm made his voice sharp. "What do you mean, disappeared? She hasn't left Sugarland, has she? She knows it's not safe to leave until we find the man who shot Tim. The killer knows her, damn it."

"Dad, chill out. I didn't mean she left, as in getting in a car and driving off. Besides, she hasn't even got a car. I mean, she has one, but she told me—"

"Michelle!"

"Right. She just sort of made herself scarce, Dad, like she needed some private time."

"What about Danny?"

"She kept him with her all day long. He usually hangs out with me or with Shorty and Jake in the workshop— when you're not around, I mean. I finally spotted Claire and him out at the gazebo. She's real friendly most of the time, but something about her was different today. She was, oh, I don't know, closed off, sort of."

He rubbed a hand over his mouth. His reaction wasn't lost on Michelle. "I guess you like her a lot, don't you?"

"Why wouldn't I like her? She's a nice woman."

Michelle rolled her eyes. "Oh, puh-leeze, Dad."

He gave her a fierce look. "You have a problem with that?"

"She's more than nice, Dad. She's a very attractive woman, she's a good mother, she's thoughtful to Grandpa and Mama Wyona, and that takes some doing. Until they got to know her, they weren't exactly her biggest fans, if you know what I mean." She studied her bare toes. "And in spite of the way I talked to her that first day, she's been a good friend to me."

He spoke after a moment. "What do you think upset her, Michelle?"

"I'm not sure because I didn't have lunch with them. Mama Wyona sent me to get her, and the invitation was strictly for her alone."

He was silent, thinking. His parents had mellowed considerably toward Claire, so he wasn't worried that they would pick a time when he was gone to browbeat her about Danny. In fact, he was convinced that when all this was over, Danny and Claire would be a part of their lives. So, what could have transpired at lunch?

"They had a guest, Dad. Grandpa's lawyer was here."

He frowned. "Martin Thibodaux?"

"Uh-huh. I heard Mama Wyona tell Claire that he wanted to meet her."

"It was just the three of them?"

"That's right. And something happened that caused Claire to get up and walk out before they finished eating."

"How do you know all this if you weren't there?"

"Cleo told me." She shrugged, looking a little sheepish.

"Where is she now?"

Michelle's blue eyes gleamed. "I guess you don't mean Cleo?" When he shot her a fierce frown, she grimaced.

"C'mon, Dad, where does Claire spend most of her time nowadays? If she's not out at the gazebo, I mean."

"Michelle . . ."

"In your office, Dad. Working."

"Work . . ." Muttering an oath, he turned away, running his hand over his hair. "Why the *hell* is she working at this hour?" The question wasn't for Michelle. He grabbed his drink, finishing it off in one swallow, then set the glass down with a thump. "Okay, now outta here. It's time you were back in bed."

"You're irritated, Dad. I wouldn't jump on her right now if I were you."

He dropped his head back, staring at the ceiling. "I'm not going to jump on her." *Not the way you mean, anyway.*

"Good. Try to get her to tell you what happened at that lunch meeting. But do it subtly, Dad."

"Anything else?" His mouth quirked in a half smile.

"Good luck."

At his look, she turned to scoot away, barely missing the fatherly swat he aimed at her backside.

HE WAS HOME.

It had been about ten minutes since Claire had seen the sweep of the Jeep's headlights coming up the driveway. A cup of coffee was sitting alongside the computer where she'd been working for the past two hours. She reached for it, her hand slightly unsteady. Her stomach fluttered and she closed her eyes, taking in a mouthful of the strong, chicory-flavored brew. He had that effect on her. She turned back to the monitor, preferring to be busy when he appeared.

"What the hell do you think you're doing?"

Startled, she turned and almost upset the coffee. She'd forgotten how he could move with the silence of a cat. In spite of the words he'd used, he didn't look aggravated. He looked . . . big, rumpled, tired and stunningly male. She forced herself to face the computer again. "What does it look like? I'm entering the numbers from the sugarcane co-op that came in this morning."

He came over, glancing at the monitor. "It'll soon be 1:00 a.m., Claire."

His gaze moved to the couch where Danny was sleeping. "Why isn't Danny in his bed, where he belongs?"

"The bed where he *belongs* is in our condo in Houston. And I wish to God we were both there!" She stood up, pushed her chair back and turned away, locking her arms around herself.

"What's wrong, Claire?"

"I just need to get out of here." She went to the window and looked out. "This situation is enough to drive anybody a little stir-crazy. Danny and I need to go home!"

Suddenly he was behind her. She drew a quick, tense breath feeling his arms go around her, enveloping her in his strength. In all the sensual markers familiar to her now—his smell, the sound of his voice, his breathing, his hard body length so compatible with hers. She fought the urge to lean into him. How could she even *want* to turn to him after what he'd done?

"What is it, sweetheart? What's happened?"

Sweetheart. She closed her eyes, wishing things were different.

He gave her an insistent little squeeze. "Michelle said Martin Thibodaux came to lunch. Tell me about it."

"Shrimp salad and French bread. Raspberry ice tea."

"Not the menu, sugar. The agenda. Michelle said they sent for you. I'm asking why."

She pulled out of his embrace. "Stop playing games, for heaven's sake," she said wearily. "Mr. Thibodaux's courtly manner was impressive, but even he couldn't pretty up the real purpose for coming to see me."

He was frowning. "Fill me in, Claire. What purpose?"

"Oh, come on. What is the point in this? You know what they wanted. Mr. Thibodaux told me that it was your idea to begin with, that he was acting on your authority." She moved behind a chair, needing a barrier between them. "It just caught me by surprise, that's all. What I find hard to accept is that you didn't come straight to me. How could you think that it would be easier having your lawyer help you do this?"

Mack shook his head with impatience. "To do what, Claire?"

"Steal my son! That's what."

He stared, uncomprehending.

"Don't give me that look. The whole purpose of your stuffy lawyer's visit today was to get me to agree to have Danny's name changed to McMollere. He rattled on about the wonderful heritage Danny has here at Sugarland, about how as Carter's son it's rightfully his and that all I have to do is sign on the dotted line and *presto!* Danny's a McMollere and everything's just peachy-keen."

Mack was shaking his head long before she was finished. "That idiot!" he muttered.

Claire barely heard him. "And where would it end, if you don't mind my asking? Make Danny a McMollere legally, then entice him to Sugarland for frequent visits, ply him with gifts and ponies and tractor rides, and who knows what else? The sky's the limit when you have wealth and power. Then what? Adoption? Well, it's not going to happen, do you hear me? He has a parent, thank you. I'm going to be out of here as soon as it's humanly possible and I'm taking my son with me." She touched her chest. "My son, Daniel *Woodson*. And you can take that back to Mr. Martin Thibodaux, your precious lawyer, and see what he says about it!"

"He was out of line, Claire. He had no business—"

"Are you saying you didn't instruct him to draw up the papers to have my son's name changed?"

He drove his hand through his hair. "No. Actually—"

"He was acting without your approval?"

"No, I did tell him that I . . . that we wanted Danny to have Carter's name. But it was—"

"You had no right! Don't you see that? How dare you!"

"It was before I met you, Claire!" He swung away in frustration, shoving his hands into his pockets. "It was early on, when we were trying to get you to agree to a visitation."

"Nothing was ever said about changing Danny's name," she murmured, thinking how right she'd been that Carter's family was ruthless when they wanted something.

"Not then, no!" Mack's tone became conciliatory. "But he is a McMollere, whether you want to acknowledge that or not, Claire. He should have his father's name. It's a way to right a wrong."

"I don't believe you were thinking of righting any wrongs when you told Mr. Thibodaux to draw up the papers," she said bitterly.

"No, but it wasn't as cold-blooded as you make it sound. We hoped that after your visit, you would see we weren't the kind of people who would take advantage of you. It might sound old-fashioned, but my parents believed that removing the stigma of illegitimacy would be something you'd welcome."

She didn't look at him until he moved close and tipped her chin up. He looked deeply into her eyes. "Has it been so terrible living here? Are the McMolleres so awful that you don't want Danny to have his father's name?"

She turned away, forcing herself not to cave in just because he'd touched her. "You don't understand, do you? It's beside the point that you now know Danny and me. What matters is that you would have rammed this through the courts. You have the power. Whether or not Danny should have the McMollere name is something that we should work out together. You should have consulted me, even if the relationship between us was less than friendly."

"Is that the reason you wouldn't let him out of your sight today?" he asked after a moment. "You were afraid that somebody here would grab him, take him away and you'd never see your son again? Is that what you really think we'd do?"

"No, of course not."

He glanced at the sleeping boy. "Then what?"

"You wouldn't understand."

"Try me."

She shook her head, turning away. "It's just that I felt so . . . betrayed. I'd allowed myself to be lulled into feeling safe here, even with a killer out there looking for my son." She sighed, looking over her shoulder at Mack.

"It really shook me to discover that there was another threat to Danny, one that I hadn't fully realized."

"There's no threat to Danny here. As soon as Martin opens his office tomorrow morning, he will be told to tear up those papers. I should have instructed him to do that before now, but it wasn't important anymore."

She gave a bewildered cry. "Wasn't important? How can you say that? You know your parents are not going to give up until Danny is legally a McMollere."

He said nothing, but there was a flash of something in his eyes and she saw it before he could suppress it.

"What is it?"

"This is probably not a good time."

"A good time for what?"

He drew in a breath, coming to a decision. "The problem with Danny's name was going to resolve itself," he said. "Or at least that's what I was hoping."

"How was that going to happen?"

His gaze cut away, then came back to her. "I was thinking that you'd change Danny's name to McMollere if that was your name, too."

"My name?"

"Yeah, your name."

Her heart was suddenly in her throat.

"I'm talking marriage, Claire."

She was so astonished that she could only stare.

He managed a wry smile. "You can't be that surprised."

"But I am," she murmured.

"Not a good time," he repeated. "I should have gone with my instincts."

Her head was spinning. "I just can't deal with this on top of everything else, John."

"We've been to bed together, Claire. It was mind-blowing, don't even try to deny that. We've both been hot to try it again, you know it and I know it. We have to deal with that fact sooner or later."

She looked away. "Later, then."

She couldn't afford to open that Pandora's box. The last thing she wanted right now was a reminder of that night. With the house quiet and sleeping around them and his incredible proposal still swirling in her head, it would take very little for her to fall in his arms again. He was right. She had been hot to try it again. For a minute, the desire was so strong that she almost moaned. She swallowed hard, pushing the craving away.

"I wanted to talk to you about something else," she said. Her tone began huskily, but she firmed it up by clearing her throat. "It's about your mother."

"What about her?"

Claire moved away to gather her thoughts and stopped at the desk. "Angus is the sick person in this house, but everybody treats Wyona as though *she* is the invalid. And yet no attempt is made to get any treatment for her. Why is that?"

"She doesn't need treatment."

"Do you really believe that?"

"I know she's . . . fragile. She was always a dependent sort of woman, nothing like you are. She had Dad to take care of her, to pamper her. That changed with his stroke."

"Are you saying your mother wasn't always so easily agitated?"

"What do you mean, 'easily agitated'?" he asked.

"She acted very peculiar over Danny seeing somebody get shot. I put down her reaction to a grandmother's natural horror that a young child should have witnessed something so terrible. And then when the victim turned out to be Tim Landry, somebody she actually knew, she was even more...agitated." Claire toyed with a paperweight for a moment, then replaced it. "Again, her reaction was natural, but Wyona kept trying to link Tim's death to Carter's. Didn't you notice that?"

Mack grunted with impatience. "There is no link between the two. Carter's plane crash was an accident. Pure and simple."

Claire was unconvinced. "She seems so determined about the connection."

"She's wrong. Carter's death just...well, she just hasn't been the same since it happened."

"I thought you said her problems began with Angus's stroke."

"I said Dad's stroke was tough for her."

"Well, let's talk about Angus then."

"What about him?"

"You remember the day Sheriff Pagett came to tell us about Tim?" Mack nodded, just one curt bob of his head. "When you went out as the sheriff was leaving, Angus wanted to know if I'd had any calls or visitors at the hotel."

Mack frowned. "Did he say why he was asking?"

"Not really. He wanted to know if Tim had called me at the hotel that day."

"What?"

"You heard me. Angus told me Tim and Carter were best friends. He implied Tim might have called or visited me. He also wanted to know if Carter had talked freely about his friends to me."

He was shaking his head. "What was he getting at?"

"He mentioned the coincidence of Carter's son witnessing Tim's death."

He stood there in silence for a minute, his gaze fixed on a point beyond Claire. "And one more thing," she said. "At lunch today, I was interrogated by Mr. Thibodaux."

He snorted a laugh. "Interrogated?"

"Yes, interrogated," she repeated stubbornly.

"I thought you said his purpose in coming here today was to coerce you into changing Danny's name."

"This was before he mentioned that."

"Oh. Okay, what did he want to know?"

"The same things Angus wanted to know. He mentioned his own son, Glenn, I think he said his name was."

"Glenn?"

"He asked if Carter had ever mentioned him."

"Mentioned *Glenn?*"

"Yes, Glenn. And Tim. Like everyone else around here, he seems convinced that Carter shared oodles of confidences with me."

Mack walked to the window and stood gazing out over the cane fields, washed to a cool blue-green in the moonlight.

"Now, what I want to know," Claire said, leaning against the desk, "is this. Do they think Carter told me something that he wasn't supposed to reveal? Maybe it's something they don't want known. Are they trying to find out if he told me something that'll embarrass them?"

Mack turned, chuckling. He raised his eyebrows in mock alarm. "Ah, I get it. They want to know if you know something that you don't know you know?"

She gave him an offended look. "Go ahead, laugh. But why are they all pussyfooting around whatever it is they think I know? Carter's dead. Tim's dead. What can it matter now?" She moved from the desk and began pacing. "And why does your mother keep saying that stuff about tragedies happening three in a row?"

"I wouldn't put a lot of stock in the stuff Mama says," he said dryly.

"I thought you said she wasn't in need of treatment."

"She doesn't need treatment in the medical sense. But she's . . . imaginative."

"So we can discount most of what she says?"

"When she begins talking like that, I'm afraid so."

"Then you're going to dismiss everything I've just said as being a product of *my* overactive imagination, too. Is that it?"

He sighed. "That's not it. I understand where you're coming from on this, Claire. "You've got some guy out there who's a threat to the safety of your son. And to yours, as well. You're stuck at Sugarland against your will. If you could make some sense out of what's happened and possibly come up with something to flush this guy out, then you can pick up and carry on with your life the way you want it."

"I'm grasping at straws. That's what you're saying."

He shrugged, obviously thinking exactly that. "You're not the kind of woman who's content to sit back and wait."

"Nothing I've said comes across as sounding logical or reasonable to you? You're not the least bit tempted to say there could be something here?"

He looked at her in exasperation. "The ramblings of two old people and a chance remark or two from a lawyer? Not really, Claire."

"Fine. Okay with me." She straightened away from the desk. "I'll know to pursue these things on my own then."

"Claire." He caught her by the shoulders. "We're going round and round here and getting nowhere. Let's give it a rest. Let me carry Danny upstairs and put him to bed and then you can invite me into *your* bed and we can be together tonight."

His words stole the breath from her body. She felt intense need and then a wave of sensual heat moved through her, weakening her limbs and her will. After the argument they'd just had, she was amazed at how much she longed to do just what he said.

He bent his head and kissed her. It was deliberate and unhurried, a wet, thorough blending of his mouth with hers. For a minute—a long minute—she was caught in the dark sweetness of his kiss, then she pushed at his arms.

"John, you agreed."

He pulled her back to him, burying his face in her hair. "I'm trying. It's driving me crazy having you here, working in the same room with you, watching you move, smelling your perfume, not touching you. That's the hardest part, keeping my hands off you." As he spoke, his hands were everywhere, down her back to her waist, then up to cup her breasts, then back down again to sink into her buttocks. He groaned as he held her there, pushing into the soft cleft between her legs.

She turned her head to avoid another kiss, but he followed, nibbling and cajoling, eating away at her resolve.

"No..." She pushed at his chest, breathing as hard as he was, feeling the same needs. "We can't do this now, John. It was a mistake the first time. Please, don't push me."

With a frustrated sound, he pressed his mouth to her temple. For a long time, he simply held her. She felt the heat of him, sensed the turmoil within him. Then he breathed out and the tension eased. "Okay. Not tonight."

He let her go and when she looked into his eyes, she caught her breath at the naked passion and need. "But soon, Claire, soon. And that's a promise, too."

CHAPTER THIRTEEN

CLAIRE WAITED until everybody was out of the house the next morning to have a talk with Wyona. She was determined to find out if there was any basis to Wyona's insistence that Tim's death and Carter's were connected.

Claire had spent a restless night. Keeping John McMollere out of her bed was proving to be a monumental task. Not so much because of his efforts to coax her back into his arms, but because of her own desire. He had touched her heart with that one night of love. But she knew she was right to wait until her life was on an even keel before trying to sort out their relationship. Clearing up the mystery of Tim Landry's death would go a long way toward doing exactly that.

Angus had finished breakfast and was dozing in front of the television in the sun room, but Wyona was nowhere to be found. Claire finally located her in the library.

Standing at the door, Claire watched her arranging roses in a crystal vase. Obviously just in from the rose garden, she still wore a wide-brim straw hat banded with pink grosgrain ribbon and a long dress with tiny pink flowers to match. Claire was reminded of a Victorian lady, that is, until she saw Wyona's shoes. She smiled. They were chunky Reebok running shoes.

"What beautiful roses, Wyona." She had dropped the formal, "Mrs. McMollere," days ago at Wyona's insistence.

"Oh, it's you, Claire. Come and look at this really lovely yellow bloom. It smells heavenly." Wyona stripped a few leaves from the stem and handed over the flower. "So many of the new varieties today don't have any fragrance."

"Mmm, thank you." Claire closed her eyes. The rose gave off a heavenly fragrance.

"That particular yellow is very becoming to someone with your complexion and striking hair color," she said.

A compliment, no less! "I'm definitely a redhead."

"Carter's hair was brown."

"I know," Claire said dryly. "Thank goodness that Danny's is coal black."

"Like Mack's." Wyona snapped off a faded bloom. "Yes, he's a McMollere, all the way."

Claire gritted her teeth. Did these people never think of anything else? With the rose beneath her nose, she looked around the paneled walls of the room. "Do you know, this is the first house I've ever been in that actually has a bona fide library? Most people have their books parked here and there all over the place."

"Angus likes it this way."

Claire stopped at a section of bookcase where several framed pictures were arranged, mostly of Carter. Carter in kindergarten. Carter in middle school. Carter with his boyhood buddies. Ah, one of Carter and Angus. Would Carter have turned out as stiff-necked as his father? she wondered. No one would ever know.

She moved to another picture. It was Carter in a football uniform. She studied the photograph with interest. He looked handsome and carefree. Slanting across his mouth was a wicked grin.

"He was such a handful, that boy," Wyona said softly.

Claire hadn't realized that Wyona had come to stand beside her. "Hmm, I gather that he was very high-spirited." Selfish and irresponsible, too, as she recalled, but she doubted that Wyona wanted to hear that assessment. Spotting a picture of Carter and Mack, she smiled at Mack's expression. "I must show this to Danny," she murmured. "He gets this same look on his face when he's angry."

"He's smiling in that picture," Wyona said, taking the photograph from Claire. Her eyes were on Carter.

Claire quickly realized her gaff. "I meant Mack, not Carter," she said gently.

"I suppose there is a resemblance," Wyona admitted, but it was clearly a reluctant admission.

"Mostly Danny is just Danny, at least to me," Claire said in an attempt to soothe Wyona's feathers. But whether Wyona wanted to see it or not, in coloring and facial expressions, the boy was far more like his uncle Mack, Claire thought. She stepped back and looked at Wyona. "You should bring Danny in here sometime and show him these pictures of his father. He's very curious about Carter, you know."

"You're right," Wyona murmured, her gaze fixed on the two boys in the picture. "I should do that while there's still time."

Still time?

"Wyona, may I ask you something?" she asked after a moment.

"About Carter?"

"Carter and Tim Landry."

A flicker of something came and went in her pale eyes. Moving slowly, she replaced the picture, then reached up to take off the straw hat. "They're both gone now. Two tragedies."

"Yes. I've been wondering about their friendship."

She twisted the brim of the hat. "They were very close as boys, but not so much when they got older. Things tend to pull people in different directions, careers, changing interests, marriage."

"You mentioned Carter was high-spirited, but everyone says Tim Landry was very quiet, even shy. It doesn't sound as if they had much in common."

"Oh, but when the three of them were together, well, you know how it is. Boys will be boys."

"The three of them?"

Wyona nodded. "Carter, Tim and Glenn Thibodaux."

"Glenn Thibodaux."

Wyona's mouth thinned as if tasting something sour. "He's in politics now, you know."

"In Baton Rouge, yes," Claire murmured. "I believe somebody mentioned that."

"He'll be good at that."

Claire tucked her hands beneath her arms, deciding to try another tack. "You know, as the mother of a little boy myself, I find that it's so difficult trying to raise him right. He makes friends with people whose values might be different. When he's away from home, he's exposed to good and bad. And peer pressure is a powerful force. An unsuspecting boy can be led astray. As a mother yourself, did you find that to be the case?"

"Not with Mack. He always knew just who he was and he wouldn't be influenced no matter what." She touched her forehead with fingers that were not quite steady. "Carter, now, he didn't have that innate strength."

"He was led astray?"

"Once or twice."

"With Tim Landry?"

"And Glenn, don't forget him." Wyona's tone hardened on his name. Then she drew a shaky breath. "Now he's here and they're gone. There's no justice. Absolutely no justice in this world anymore." Her eyes were bright with tears.

Claire sighed, suddenly not liking what she was doing. She probably could keep at it and eventually all of Carter's skeletons would be out of the closet, but Wyona was so pitiful. There had to be another way to get at the truth. She'd make a poor detective, she decided.

To distract Wyona, she glanced at a lower shelf where several high-school yearbooks were stacked. "Oh, look at this." She pulled a yearbook out marked 1972 and opened it. "It's the year Mack graduated from high school, isn't it?" Curious to see what he'd been like at eighteen, she paged through it looking for his picture. Where John McMollere was concerned, she wanted to know everything.

"Oops!" A newspaper clipping fell to the floor. Claire bent down and scooped it up, then frowned as she scanned it. "'Girl drowned in bayou,'" she read, frowning. "'The body of eighteen-year-old Kimberly Ledet was discovered early Wednesday morning by two trappers in Bayou LeBlanc. According to a spokesman for the coroner, other evidence is being withheld pending a hearing. She was reported missing by her parents on December twenty-first.'"

Claire shook her head. "Oh, those poor people. To lose a child..." She shook her head. "And at Christmastime, too. How sad." She raised her eyes to Wyona's. "Was she a classmate of Mack's?"

"Mack's? No."

Claire checked the cover, wondering why the article had been clipped and saved in his yearbook if he didn't know her. "She wasn't a friend?"

"No one knew her. She was from Lafayette." Wyona took the clipping and could barely read it her hands were shaking so much. "This doesn't belong in that book. I don't know how it came to be there."

"Obviously someone clipped the article and slipped it inside this yearbook to save. What is the date? Could it have been Carter?"

"No! He's the last person it could be."

"What's wrong, Wyona? Who is Kimberly Ledet?"

But Wyona was already drifting into that shadowy state. "Fate, that's what it is." With a frightened look, she turned away. "We were meant to find this clipping this morning. *You* were meant to find this."

Claire touched the older woman's shoulder gently. "Why, Wyona? Why me?"

"Why? Because that's why you came. The minute they said it was Tim Landry, that's when I knew."

She moved toward the chair and sank down slowly, still clinging to the straw hat. To Claire, she seemed more fragile than ever.

"Wyona, are you all right?" Alarmed by the stark paleness of her face, Claire urged her to rest against the back of the chair. "Don't move while I run and get you some brandy."

She dashed out, heading for the sun room where brandy and glasses were kept for Angus. Grabbing the decanter and a single glass, she ran out and nearly collided with Angus in the hall.

"Here now, girl! What's the rush?"

Great. Absolutely the last person she needed to cope with right now was Angus.

Using his cane, he pointed at the decanter. "Where're you going with that brandy at this hour? It's not even lunchtime."

She hurried past him. "The library," she called over her shoulder, then promptly forgot him in her worry over Wyona. If she was having some kind of terrible attack, it would be Claire's fault. She should never have initiated the conversation about Carter and his friends.

Rushing to Wyona, she poured a splash of brandy into the glass and set down the decanter with a thump. Wyona's eyes were closed and her head rested against the back of the chair. She looked limp and lifeless, like one of her faded roses. Claire leaned close, anxiously searching her face. She was breathing. Claire sighed with relief as the lace on the bodice of the flower-sprigged dress rose and fell ... barely.

"Wyona." Claire spoke softly. In one hand, she held the brandy. With the other, she picked up a wrist and rubbed her thumb over the delicate tendons. The woman's lashes fluttered the tiniest bit. Claire put the glass to her lips. "Take a little taste if you can, Wyona."

To Claire's relief, she managed to get her to swallow some of the brandy.

"Here, now, what's going on?" Angus made his way straight to his wife. "What is it, Mama? Are you sick?"

Already a little color was in Wyona's cheeks. She looked anxiously at her husband, then fumbled for his hand. "She found it, Angus. I knew she would. I told you she would." Her voice was weak, but there was no mistaking its urgency. "It was just a matter of time and now that time has come."

"What the devil are you blabbing about, woman?" He pulled away and turned to Claire with a suspicious frown. "What's she talking about?"

Claire found the old man's attitude appalling. Didn't he see that his wife was barely conscious? And distressed over something. Claire felt a stab of guilt. She was the one responsible for upsetting Wyona. The last thing she wanted was to chance upsetting Angus, too. *He* was the seriously ill one, after all. "We were talking about Carter and Tim, when she—"

"What in blazes is there to say about Carter and Tim? They're both gone. Let 'em rest in peace, for God's sake!"

Claire drew a patient breath. "Wyona seems to think there's some connection between Carter's death and Tim's. She is so insistent about it that I thought someone should hear her out. That way, we might find that she does indeed know something."

"Damn it!" The old man was livid. "My boy Carter died in a plane crash. There's no more to be learned about his death than that. Go get the accident report from the police, if you don't believe it."

"I believe it, Angus, but—"

"But nothing! And as for Tim Landry, what in the name of Jehoshaphat can Wyona tell you about that? She hasn't left Sugarland property in months except to go to the doctor."

Without waiting for a reply, Angus turned to Wyona. "I told you not to be carrying on about this, woman. What d'you mean by goin' behind my back?"

"I'm sorry, Angus." It was barely a whisper. Tears welled up and she held her shaking fingers to her mouth. "But there's no use in trying to run away from it any longer. She found—"

"Not another word!" he thundered. "I mean it, Wyona."

"Angus, please." Claire said. "You're making things worse." It was an effort, but she kept her tone calm and reasonable. The man seemed blind to everything except his need to dominate. "She's not well. She needs to go to her bedroom and rest."

"Not before I know exactly what you two have been yammering on about," Angus blustered.

She sighed. "I told you, Angus. It was about Danny and Carter and yes, Tim, and the challenges of raising children." No need to tell him how far afield the conversation had strayed.

"Hah! No woman-talk like that would have sent her into a swoon." He turned to his wife. "What've you been saying, Wyona?"

Wyona clutched the hat to her chest and looked at him with pure misery in her eyes. "She found the clipping about Kimberly."

He shot Claire a fierce look. "So what if she did? There's nothing to be made from an old newspaper clipping. Ancient history, that's what it is."

"Yes, but—"

"No buts, Wyona!"

Claire moved closer to Wyona, pressing her shoulder reassuringly. "Angus, I'm going to help her upstairs now. The two of you can discuss all this later, okay?"

He gave Claire a pugnacious glare. "I'm holding you to that, missy. See if I don't. You and I are having a conversation with some real straight talk." He shuffled toward a tall wingback chair, grumbling, "I don't know what you think you're about, coming to Sugarland and turning things upside down this way. Got Wyona all dithered up about that old case. Ancient history, I say.

What's done is done.'' He sank into the chair as though suddenly running out of steam. Claire noticed that his hands on his cane were trembling and his color was not good.

"Are you all right, Angus?'' Bully or not, he was a sick man.

"I'm fine. Never been better.'' He waved a surly hand toward a small table. "Just hand me that phone before you leave. Won't matter much, the cat's out of the bag, but—'' He stopped, appearing startled that the two women were still there. "Well, go on, you two. You've done all the damage down here you can, at least for now.''

After a minute, Claire turned back to Wyona and took the straw hat from her. With some help, the older woman managed to stand. Claire had walked her halfway to the library door, when Mack strode into the room. "What's going on here? Mama, what's wrong?''

First Angus, now Mack. Claire sighed wearily. "We thought you were going to be out all day.''

"Cleo called me. Said there was a ruckus going on in the library.''

"Your mother had a little spell and I'm helping her upstairs to get some rest.''

His frown was as fierce as Angus's. "What kind of spell? Mama?'' He searched her face. "What happened?''

"Not now, please, John.'' Claire gave him a beseeching look.

He looked as though he wanted to argue, but instead he moved closer to his mother and gently picked her up. "I'll carry her. You go get her bed ready. Please, Claire.'' After another worried look at Wyona, Claire hurried out.

Mack reached the library door, then turned to look at Angus. "I'll be down in a minute, Dad, okay?"

Angus replied with another impatient wave of his hand. As soon as everyone was gone, he reached for the phone.

MACK'S THOUGHTS were in turmoil when he came back downstairs a few minutes later. He could no longer dismiss everything his mother said as the imaginings of an old lady. Something had happened in the past. If he could get to the bottom of it, maybe his mother could find some peace. It might even shed some light on the situation that had Claire boxed in at Sugarland.

But first, he'd deal with Angus, Mack decided, rounding the newel at the bottom of the stairs. He'd heard enough of the exchange in the library to convince him that his mother wasn't the only one in the house who was losing it. Angus had been so furious with Claire that he'd been insulting. His father obviously considered Claire's curiosity out of line, but she had a right to be interested in anything that might shed light on the situation forcing her to stay at Sugarland. Considering that her son's life was threatened because of Tim's murder, who had a better right?

Angus wouldn't like it, not the straight talk or any intrusive questions about what in hell was going on. His father obviously had some secrets. What were they? Mack wondered as he walked into the library. What did it have to do with the three men—Carter and Tim and Glenn? Was Martin Thibodaux involved? And what about the clipping Claire said his mother was so upset about? He couldn't remember hearing about a sixteen-year-old girl drowning.

At the library door, he hesitated. There was no sign of Angus, but he heard the faint pulsing of an electronic tone. After a second, he identified it as the signal that came from a telephone when the receiver had been left off the hook. It was when he rounded the tall leather chair that he saw Angus.

"Dad!"

His father was on the floor in front of the chair. Hunkering down beside him, Mack saw that the elderly man was conscious. He must have staggered into the bookshelves as he fell, as several articles were scattered on and around him—an old yearbook and some framed pictures. He cleared them away. "What happened, Dad?"

A second look told him Angus was beyond speech. He lay with his head at an unnatural angle against the chair leg. Looking into Mack's eyes, his mouth worked soundlessly. Something inside Mack tore apart. A deep, dark dread filled him. Angus's one hand flailed out, feebly grasping for the still-beeping handset. Mack shoved it aside and grabbed for a chair cushion to place beneath the sick man's head. Angus protested, still groping for the phone. Mack fumbled for the receiver and slammed it into its cradle, then turned back to his father. "It's okay, Dad, we're gonna get you to the hospital. You'll be okay."

Angus tried to speak, but produced only a garbled syllable or two. Mack murmured more reassurance, then rose and lunged for the telephone. There was no 911 in this remote corner of the parish, but a sticker on every phone in the house had the emergency number of the ambulance service. Shaking with fear, he managed to punch out the number and tell the dispatcher to send an ambulance.

That done, he slammed down the receiver and turned to Angus, but stopped short of touching him until he'd breathed in a few calming breaths. Now was not the time to fall apart. Angus was still now, making no sounds. His eyes were fixed, Mack saw with a flash of terror. Reaching for his father's hand, he tried to find a pulse, but to no avail. He quickly shifted to the carotid in Angus's neck. There! Thin and uneven, but it was beating. He studied the still mask of Angus's face fearfully. His skin was the color of paste and one side of his mouth was drawn down.

"Claire!" Mack yelled, hoping she could tell him what to do until the ambulance arrived. But even if she couldn't, he wanted her with him. Needed her.

His heart hammering, he leaned over his father. "Hang on, Dad. Help is on the way. You're gonna be okay."

But there was a knot in his stomach even as he said the words. He knew they were not true.

THE NEXT TWELVE HOURS were like a nightmare in slow motion. The ambulance arrived after what seemed an eternity, but in reality was only about twenty minutes. Until then, Mack and Claire together had desperately performed CPR when it appeared that Angus had stopped breathing all together. But both had known that with each minute that ticked by, the elderly man was slipping farther and farther away.

Grim-faced, Mack watched the two emergency medical technicians working intensely over Angus. He heard one of them say it looked like a stroke, not a heart attack. From their demeanor, he knew Angus's chances were slim.

"I'm coming with you," Claire said moments later as Angus was being lifted from the library floor onto a stretcher.

Mack's car keys were already in his hand. He gave her a stern look. "You can't. It's not safe for you to leave Sugarland."

But she was already tucking in her shirt and smoothing her hair. "We don't have time to argue. You need someone with you while you wait."

"You can't go, Claire."

"Whoever is threatening Danny and me has made me a prisoner here. How long must I be his victim? I want to be the one to call the shots in my life, not him." She slipped her purse strap onto her shoulder. "I'm coming with you."

"What about Danny?"

"Michelle is going to watch him and Cleo's with your mother. Thanks to that brandy, Wyona is still sleeping."

"Everything's fine, Dad." Michelle looked scared, but she was hiding it bravely. She stood near the door with an arm around Danny's shoulders. The little boy's eyes were big as he watched the EMTs wheel Angus through the foyer and out the front door.

"I've already called Jake," Michelle said. "He has two little brothers, so he's used to taking care of kids. He'll help me with Danny so y'all won't have to worry about a thing. Even if you're there all night." She hurried on before he could object, "We'll be good, Dad. Promise."

"That's perfect," Claire said, believing it. Jake was so eager to prove to Mack that he valued his job that she had no hesitation in trusting Danny with him. And he wasn't about to mess up where Michelle was concerned.

"Just be sure if Danny's out of the house that you're with him, Michelle. Don't let him out of your sight for a single minute."

"I won't, honest. I know what's at stake."

"Is Grandpa Angus gonna die like my real daddy?" Danny asked anxiously.

Claire went to him. "He's very sick, Danny. But no one knows the answer to your question. The doctors will try to help him at the hospital."

"Like they fixed my broken arm?" He held up his cast.

"Just like that." She kissed him and went with Mack down the front steps.

As they were climbing into the Jeep, Jake came hurrying around the corner, wiping greasy hands on a shop rag. Mack stopped and motioned him over. "Michelle says you'll be able to stay, is that right?"

"Yes, sir." He stuck the rag in his back pocket.

"You see anything suspicious, you call Sheriff Pagett. You got that?"

"Yes, sir," the teenager said. "Between me and Shorty, nobody'll get near here, you can count on that."

In front of them, the ambulance was pulling out. Mack started the Jeep. Claire rolled down the window on her side and called out to Michelle, "Tell Wyona we'll call as soon as we know anything."

NOW THERE WAS only the waiting. Mack was incapable of just sitting and doing nothing. He moved back and forth from the closed double doors of the Intensive Care Unit to the chairs designated for family members. He drank black coffee and watched the clock. Several times, Dr. Guillot, Angus's physician for over twenty years, came out to talk to them. Each time, the news was grimmer. Finally, Mack sat down beside Claire. With his arms resting on his knees, he stared at his feet.

"I can't believe he's dying, Claire."

She touched his arm, giving it a little squeeze. "You don't know that. Don't assume the worst. He may survive this."

"I don't think so." He got up and went to the window. Pulling the drape aside, he looked out. It was after ten. Visiting hours were over. People were streaming out of the hospital, heading for their cars. For the most part, the people they loved were getting well in this place.

Claire rose and went to stand beside him.

"I used to wish my father was like Wayne Pagett," he said. "He was so different from Angus. He actually talked to his son. And to the rest of us kids. He went to all our ball games. He cautioned us about sex. He taught us to fish. He taught us to shoot. He took us to the hunting camp the first day of deer season every year. Duck season, too. He showed us how to clean everything we shot and not to shoot if we didn't plan to use it. It'd be four o'clock in the morning and so cold that you didn't give a damn if you never saw a duck fly by. Next thing, you'd hear 'em first, then there they'd be and we'd shoot, blindly at first, Wayne cussing us 'cause we'd jumped the gun, but laughing his butt off..."

He dropped his head, gazing a long time at his boots. "And I'd wish he was my father."

She leaned her head against his arm wordlessly.

He shifted, staring again into the night. "Danny needs a father."

Her breath caught. "All children need a father and a mother," she said quietly.

"Maybe Carter was so late to step up to the plate because he didn't have much of a role model in Angus. Or in me."

"You were only six years older. Hardly a father figure." She rubbed his arm. "Michelle is a terrific kid, John."

"I used to vow I'd be a better father than my own." His tone was low and bitter. "Is that a terrible thing to say when he's probably in there dying right now?" He jerked his head in the direction of the ICU.

"It's honest."

He rested his forehead against the glass. "But I loved him, Claire." His tone wavered hoarsely. "I swear to God I did."

She slipped an arm around his waist, longing to give him the comfort he craved. "I know," she whispered.

He turned and pulled her close. They stood rocking slightly, absorbing warmth and closeness.

God help her, she loved him so much.

Someone appeared at the door. "Mack?"

It was Dr. Guillot. For a heartbeat, Mack didn't move. Drawing a deep breath, he turned and faced him.

The physician shook his head. "I'm sorry, Mack. The stroke was massive, but he hung in there. Then his heart gave out. We did everything we could. He's gone."

IT WAS DARK by the time they left the hospital. Mack walked with her to the car without a word. He insisted on driving, but once he got behind the wheel, he fumbled inserting the key. And then when he started the Jeep to pull out of the parking lot, he seemed disoriented for a few seconds.

"Do you want me to drive?" Claire asked with concern.

"No, I'm okay." But instead of leaving, he sat with his hands on the wheel without moving for several minutes. "Will you help me tell Mama?"

"Yes, if you want me to."

"And Michelle?"

"Of course."

He nodded, and then turned into the street. For the first few miles he seemed lost in thought. Which was perfectly normal, Claire knew. She remembered the hours just after her mother had died. She had been the sole caretaker and with her mother gone she was suddenly free. Like Angus, her mother had been a difficult person, self-absorbed and demanding. But Claire hadn't relished her freedom, not at that moment. What she'd felt was a sense of being cast afloat suddenly. Of having no connection to anything or anyone. Of being completely alone in the world. It was a desolate feeling. At least Mack had a family. He'd be comforted and grounded by them.

Still, Claire had no intention of leaving him alone that night.

Everyone in the house was finally settled when she went to his bedroom. It was empty and dark, but she heard sounds in the bathroom. The shower was a good place to grieve. Much as she longed to step into the stall, wrap her arms around him and share his pain, she knew he probably needed this time alone.

He had not turned on the lights. It was dark except for the bar of light coming from the bathroom door, slightly ajar. She guessed that he'd come in and walked straight to the bathroom. That he'd preferred the darkness. Sinking into a chair beneath the window, she tucked her feet under her and waited for him to finish.

Overhead, a ceiling fan revolved, stirring the air in lazy circles. August nights were hot and humid, but a death in the house was a chilling thing. She folded her arms around herself and the shower stopped. She heard the glass door slide, she heard him moving, probably drying off.

The door opened and he stopped when he saw her. He was wearing plain white briefs. He'd half dried his hair, separating it into wet strands. All she could see of his face was the ruggedly defined angle of his chin. Watching him, she felt an overwhelming need to touch him, to come to him with compassion and...she admitted it readily...love.

Uncurling from the chair, she stood up and went to him.

He let out a low, mournful sound and put his arms around her. Burying his face in her hair, he murmured her name. His hands on her back were restless and seeking. He held her so close that there was no way to separate his body from hers. His breathing from hers. He took handfuls of her hair and held himself rigid while he shuddered with grief and pain. She stroked his back and neck, slipped her fingers into his hair and whispered words of reassurance and compassion. She knew what he was about. He'd suffered a loss and he was seeking a way to fill that emptiness. And out of her love, Claire wanted to give him what he needed.

His mouth found hers then in a kiss that was hungry and desperate and carnal, all at once. His tongue plunged deep, swirling to mate with hers. With his hand, he held her pressed to his lower body. There was no mistaking his erection. After sharing the dark, somber reality of death that night, he was driven to reaffirm life in the most elemental way. Something elemental and fierce rose in her in answer to his need.

"I want you," he told her hoarsely. "I want to be with you tonight. Don't say no, Claire."

There was passion in his voice, yes, but mostly need. It reached deep, combining with her own. To be held close, to feel the solid warmth of his body, to know the closeness that a few hours could bring, she could give him all this. She wanted to give him all this.

She took his hand and led him to the bed.

CHAPTER FOURTEEN

IN THE FIRST FEW DAYS after Angus died, Claire worried that Wyona might drift into a complete breakdown. She had listened quietly to Mack as he broke the news that Angus was gone. With her hands clasped beneath her chin, she had blinked back tears. Angus had never been the same after his stroke, she told them. Perhaps it was meant to be. And then she had assured Mack and Claire that she was all right and had retreated to the room she'd shared with Angus for more than forty-five years. Watching her throughout the ordeal of the wake and funeral, Claire wondered about the woman she'd been before... when? Before what?

Mack was no help. He could barely remember when his mother hadn't been fragile and almost helplessly dependent upon Angus. However, now that the funeral was behind them, Claire's own situation was preying on her mind again. She needed to talk to Wyona. The woman knew something, but it was destined to remain a secret forever if everybody treated her like glass for the rest of her life.

She said as much to Mack one night as they were sorting through Angus's papers.

"Do you think she's strong enough for me to bring up the subject of Carter and Tim again?"

Mack closed a file and looked at her. "I used to think my father was the most stubborn human being on the planet. Now that he's gone, you're ready to assume that role, huh?''

"There's something there, I know it," she insisted. "And you know it, too. Don't deny it. What about that clipping that upset her so much?"

He tossed the file aside. "Let it be, Claire."

Her hands went to her waist. "Is this some more of your 'don't worry your pretty little head and your sugar daddy will take care of everything' routine, Mc-Mollere?"

"Sugar daddy?" His eyebrows went up and his mouth twitched. "Hmm, sounds interesting."

"This is serious, darn it. You know what I mean."

He shrugged with a wry expression.

She stood up and began pacing. "I can't just sit around here and wait for something to happen. Even if that clipping turns out to have nothing to do with my situation, it's worth asking a few questions." She stopped. "If you don't think we should chance mentioning it to your mother, then I'm going to ask Sheriff Pagett about the drowning of that girl."

He sighed and leaned back, pinching the bridge of his nose. "There's no need. I've already mentioned it to Wayne."

"You did? When? What did he say? Did he remember it?"

"Whoa, take a breath. He remembered it, but said the incident happened in this parish, not Abadie. So it was out of his jurisdiction."

She looked frustrated. "But what about her? Who was she?"

"A girl from Lafayette, he remembered that."

She made a sound. "I know that much. Wyona told me."

"He also recalled there was some question about where she'd been on the night she apparently drowned. Nobody ever came forward with any answers. Officially, it's still an unsolved mystery."

"Does he think it was murder?"

"He thinks it was a suspicious death, which doesn't necessarily mean foul play."

"But he's making inquiries?"

"Very quietly. Which is why you and I aren't going to start combing back issues of the newspaper in LaRue or visiting the dead girl's parents or interviewing the coroner. So put any thoughts of that kind out of your mind."

She gave him a warning look. "You know how I feel when you start issuing ultimatums, John."

He grinned. "Oh, I'm John again, am I?" Then before she could dart away, he lunged forward in the chair and grabbed her. With a squeak, she found herself tumbled into his lap. He caught her chin in his hand and held her so close that his mouth almost touched hers as he spoke. "Forget Kimberly Ledet. We may be barking up the wrong tree, anyway. Let Wayne do his job." He put his arms around her and rested his forehead against hers. "When he finds out anything, we'll be the first to know."

"You're sure?"

"Trust me."

She did. Utterly. Since the night that Angus died, she had given up even pretending that she wasn't crazy about this man. She had not been back in his bed, not because she didn't want to be, but because it was awkward with Michelle and Danny in the house, and in the aftermath of his father's death, there had been so many other demands on Mack. Added to that, there was her own situation. It was getting harder and harder to just sit and wait.

"Mommy, Mommy, where are you?"

They broke apart at the sound of Danny's voice. Mack muttered an oath as Claire tried to scramble off his lap. She just made it before Danny dashed into the room waving a framed picture.

"Mommy, it's him! It's him! Uncle Mack, look, look, here he is!"

Claire took the picture, giving it only a quick glance. "Calm down, Danny. I've told you not to run in the house. You might hurt your arm again."

He was trembling with excitement. "It's the bad policeman, Mommy! That's him." He snatched the picture away from Claire and shoved it at Mack. "Look, Uncle Mack, look, he's with my daddy."

"What?" Mack took the photograph, frowning.

Claire leaned over, trying to get a good look. It was one of the photos she'd noticed that day in the library with Wyona. In it, Carter was standing next to a small private plane. The photo had been taken soon after he'd acquired his license, according to Wyona. Beside him stood Tim Landry and another man Claire did not recognize. She glanced at Mack. "Who is it? Do you know him?"

She could see that he did. He looked stunned. "It's Glenn Thibodaux."

"What—"

"Martin Thibodaux's son."

"That awful man who came to lunch? The family lawyer?"

"Yeah." He squatted before Danny. "Are you sure, Danny?"

The boy nodded earnestly. "It's him, Uncle Mack."

Mack raised his eyes to Claire. "What do you think?"

Shaking her head helplessly, she sat down, reaching for Danny and pulling him close. "Danny, how can you be so sure? I know you saw the man from the balcony and later at Star-Mart, but think hard. This picture was taken a while ago and people change. It could be someone who looks like this man."

Danny's bottom lip came out and he dropped his chin to his chest. "You never believe me."

Claire slipped an arm around his shoulder. "We believe you, honey. We just want to make sure that this is the right man. It's very important."

He knuckled away the tears in his eyes and sniffed.

"Did you find this picture in the library, Danny?"

"Uh-huh. Mama Wyona promised to show me pictures and stuff about my daddy and she said they were in there, but she never would. So I asked Michelle if it was okay for me to look on my own and she said yes, so I went in by myself and there was a lot of them. And that's how I found that one."

Claire glanced at Mack. "I guess I'm responsible. I told Danny that his grandmother had a lot of pictures of Carter. I suppose we shouldn't be surprised that he ran out of patience." She gave Danny's shoulder a squeeze. "Where is Michelle now?"

"She's talking on the phone to her mother."

Mack frowned. "Did Liz call?"

Danny shrugged. "I don't know." He looked from Mack to Claire. "What about the bad policeman? Are you gonna catch him? I'm telling the truth, honest I am."

Mack pulled his chair over and sat down close to the boy. "Hey, hotshot, we're not saying you're wrong. We know you wouldn't make up a story like this. We just need to be sure this is the guy that you saw from that hotel balcony. You're sure he's the one who had a gun and shot Tim Landry?" He paused, holding the picture so Danny had to look at it.

The boy nodded, but a little less emphatically. Mack waited, giving him plenty of time. Then Danny lifted his eyes to Mack's. "Do you know him, Uncle Mack?"

"If this is the man, then yes, I know him."

"Is he real bad?"

"Well, now, that's hard to say. I haven't been around him much in the last few years."

"Do you know where he lives?"

Mack ruffled his hair with affection. "Not exactly, son, but I know someone who does."

Danny brightened. "Then how about we go and look at his hand and see if he has that mark, and if he does then he's the one."

"THE SCAR." Claire clapped a hand to her forehead. "I can't believe we forgot about that. If it's there, Danny's right. He's never met Glenn Thibodaux, so he couldn't make up an identifying mark. Who's going to argue with that? Then again, if Glenn has no scar on his hand I'm betting that Wayne Pagett will say we don't have a case."

Mack grunted and draped his wrist over the steering wheel.

Claire continued her monologue. "Hmm, I just can't see how Kimberly Ledet figures in all of this." She frowned, chewing at her bottom lip as she gazed at the roadside.

They were in the Jeep heading for Wayne Pagett's office. Mack had put in a call to Wayne, but he was out. The dispatcher who talked to them refused to give any details on the sheriff's whereabouts, so they'd had no choice but to go to his office and wait for him.

Mack, of course, had tried to persuade Claire to stay safely at Sugarland until they found out where Glenn Thibodaux was, but now that there was light at the end of the tunnel, she couldn't just sit and wait. She'd left Danny with Michelle.

She finally noticed his silence. "Are you going to brood all the way to Wayne's office?" He didn't reply. "Did you honestly expect me to wait at Sugarland when we've finally got a glimmer of a clue as to who we've been hiding from all this time?"

"It's safer for you to stay out of sight, Claire."

"I don't see how you figure that. The bad cop has a name now. We know it's Glenn Thibodaux."

"We don't know that at all. Glenn's not a cop."

She sighed, knowing he was right. She crossed her arms over her chest. "I realize we only have Danny's word, but I believe him."

"He's just a kid, Claire. A young kid. You may believe him, but the rest of the world is going to be very skeptical."

"It's not only Danny." She was shaking her head. "It was the look on your mother's face when we told her. I can't describe it. She looked scared, did you notice? And...and...oh, I don't know...resigned. She didn't look surprised that the person Danny saw was Glenn. It was like she expected it."

"That's a lot to read in a look."

"Go ahead. Be a skeptic. But wait and see."

He pulled into a parking slot at the sheriff's office and cut the engine. "That's what I plan to do." As he got out of the Jeep, he spotted Wayne's vehicle in the reserved space. "Looks like the sheriff's back. C'mon, let's dump this in his lap where it belongs."

Wayne was standing in the doorway of his office when they reached the dispatcher's desk. "Hey, I was just about to call you. Come on inside."

"What's up?" Mack asked as soon as the door closed.

Wayne rubbed his hand over his wiry gray hair. "Helluva thing, Mack. Glenn Thibodaux is dead."

"What!"

He was shaking his head. "Seems he and two other guys went deep-sea fishing in the gulf. Left before daybreak in Glenn's boat. According to the Coast Guard, they got caught in a squall. They rode out the storm, thinking they might make it, after all. Then the damnedest thing—a fire broke out in the galley. There was an explosion and all three wound up in the drink. The Coast Guard found two of 'em, but Glenn was never spotted."

"You're sure he's dead?"

Wayne shrugged, scratching his head. "Presumed dead. They found his life jacket, empty and scorched. No sign of Glenn."

Claire gave Mack a stunned look. "This is incredible."

"Did you know him, Claire?" Wayne asked.

"No, no... I just... we just..."

"She's trying to say that Glenn's the reason we came over to talk to you tonight," Mack said. "Danny claims it was Glenn Thibodaux he saw shoot Tim Landry."

"Come on." Wayne leaned back, his gaze going from one to the other.

"It's the truth. Danny found an old picture of the threesome. Carter, Tim and Glenn. One look and the boy fingered Glenn."

"Is he sure? He's what, five years old?"

Mack shrugged. "He seemed pretty certain, Wayne."

The sheriff sat thinking. "Glenn Thibodaux," he murmured finally.

Claire spoke softly. "And now he's dead."

With a contemplative look, Wayne took out a cigar. "I keep gettin' surprised in this business."

Claire watched him peel away the cellophane. "If Wyona were here, she'd say that makes the third tragedy. First Carter, then Tim, now Glenn."

Wayne grunted. "Last time I was at Sugarland, she mentioned that old saw about tragedy coming in sets of three. You don't think she counted Angus's passing that way?"

Claire shook her head. "No, I don't. She told me so at the funeral. Angus was old and sick, she said. He'd had a good, long life."

"Well, this sure is one for the books." Idly, Wayne played with the cigar.

"Yeah, a strange coincidence," Mack murmured.

All three lapsed into silence. "I never believed much in coincidence," Wayne said.

"Me, neither."

Claire frowned, studying them both. "What? What're you saying?"

Wayne straightened, pulling himself up closer to his desk. "Not much to say at this point, but you can believe I'm going to be digging into Glenn Thibodaux's life looking for anything that'll connect him to Tim Landry."

Mack asked, "How about Kimberly Ledet? Did you turn up anything there?"

"Well, yes and no. The girl was a freshman in college in Lafayette. The police department's investigation was conducted by Leon Monroe. I remember him, but he's retired now and living with his daughter somewhere in Texas, they tell me. Anyway, the girl told her roommate she was going home for the weekend. She told her folks that she was visiting her roommate's family. So it looks like she was setting herself up for some kind of clandestine date. Her roommate claims she wasn't a party to any of this.

"No one saw her after four in the afternoon on Friday. Her body was found early Sunday morning. She'd been dead about eighteen hours. Here's the odd thing." He picked up his cigar again.

"A woman who was on her way out of town for a two-week vacation—it was Christmas, remember?—said she saw a girl who fit Kimberly's description at a fast-food restaurant Friday evening. Kimberly got in the car with several young men—could have been college students, she said—and they drove off. She couldn't recall what a single one of them looked like, but she remembered the girl. She thought at the time that young women didn't worry about their reputations like they used to."

"What about the car?" Claire asked. "Did she describe it?"

"Only in general terms. Claims she wasn't good with cars."

Claire made an impatient sound. "What about the girl's attitude? Her demeanor? Did she look scared? Nervous?"

"Happy and smiling. No reluctance whatsoever."

"How many boys in the car?"

"The witness wasn't sure. It was dark."

"Where was this fast-food restaurant?" Mack asked.

"LaRue."

Claire was frowning. "So what conclusion did the police draw from all that?"

Wayne shrugged. "That whoever the boys were, they hadn't coerced her. That somehow, something had gone wrong. The case file went into the inactive drawer after a few months when they didn't turn up a single clue. I can understand and even sympathize with them. The crime scene was a swampy area of Bayou LeBlanc. They dragged the shallows for about a hundred-yard radius, but all they turned up was sunken litter."

Again the three were silent, thinking their own thoughts.

"Well, is there anything that could remotely link Carter, Tim or Glenn to Kimberly?" Claire finally asked.

"Not that I can see," Mack said.

"Unless they were the unidentified boys in the car," she said.

"Uh-huh," Wayne said.

"And now that Glenn is dead and his body lost in the gulf, we will never know for sure whether he was the man that Danny saw in the hotel," Claire murmured.

Mack drew a deep breath. "It appears so, yes."

Claire looked at them both. "There is the scar on his hand. Danny was so sure about that. Does Glenn have a scar?"

Wayne straightened. "I can sure find out."

"Better for you to ask than me," Mack said, getting to his feet. "We need to get back, Wayne." He leaned over and shook the sheriff's hand.

"Anything turns up, I'll keep you posted," Wayne said. "And I'll let you know about the scar."

"Thanks," they both said.

TEN MINUTES LATER, they were back in the Jeep. Claire gazed moodily through the window as the miles flashed by. After a while, she realized they were on McMollere land. Lush fields of sugarcane grew densely on both sides of the highway. Soon it would be cutting season. She was sorry suddenly that she would miss that. She should be happy that it was finally safe for her and Danny to leave Sugarland.

"Danny and I can go back to Houston now."

"Yeah, I thought you'd say that." Mack kept his eyes on the road. "I think you should stay put for the time being."

"Why? With Glenn dead, we can resume a normal life."

"*If* he's dead."

"What do you know? You think it's a little too convenient that Glenn Thibodaux should suddenly drown at sea?"

"I'm almost as suspicious about convenient drownings as I am about coincidences."

"It is very convenient. I have the feeling that Sheriff Pagett wasn't convinced, either."

"Think about it. Glenn murders Tim Landry in broad daylight in a hotel. Next, he tries to kidnap a five-year-old boy in a busy store. These are the actions of a desperate man."

"Or a deranged one."

"Yeah, well. I keep asking myself why." He braked, approaching a four-way stop and waited for a sport vehicle to cross.

"Maybe we'll never know the answer to that."

"Maybe. We'll see." He pulled away from the intersection.

She looked at him. "What are you planning to do?"

"What I'm *not* planning to do is assume that it's safe for you and Danny to be your own again. The guy's *presumed* drowned. That's not quite good enough for me."

She felt the stirrings of impatience. "And if his body never turns up? What then, John?"

"Then I guess you can never go back to Houston."

She rolled her eyes. "Be serious. Houston is where Danny and I live—job, house, friends, real life. Remember all that? Well, for us it's in Houston."

"It doesn't have to be."

"What?"

He propped an arm on the window and rubbed his temple with exasperation. Then abruptly he whipped into an unpaved side road, stopping with a screech, and flung off his seat belt.

"Wait! What're you doing?" Claire looked around in confusion. "Where are we?"

"We're on McMollere land."

"I guessed that," she said dryly.

"Don't worry, we're safe here."

For a heartbeat, she was silent. Then she said softly, "I'm not worried and I always feel safe when I'm with you, John."

He cocked his head, looking at her. "Then maybe this is a good time. Better than the last time I tried."

"Tried what?"

"To propose to you."

"Propose?"

"Yeah, propose. As in marriage. Will you marry me, Claire Woodson? . . . Well?"

"I'm thinking about it."

He faced her in his seat, left elbow on the steering wheel. With his right hand, he reached over and popped the clasp on her seat belt. "Come here."

She backed against the window on her side, her eyes sparkling with mischief. There could be a killer still stalking her and her son, two days ago they'd attended her son's grandfather's funeral and she'd just learned about a violent death. Why was her heart singing?

She smiled. "Come and get me."

With a surprised laugh, he threw a leg over the console, reaching for her at the same time. He swore as he bumped his head on the rearview mirror, but Claire was giggling, not helping at all. Somehow he managed to get his hands on her, but the console was a big problem. His mouth swooped down to take hers. She drew in a quick breath, expecting explosive passion. And she was right. His mouth claimed hers fiercely, fusing them with an intimacy that made her heart turn over. As his hands plunged into her disheveled hair, pleasure bloomed deep inside and spread all the way to her toes.

She was all nerve endings and blind desire when he tore his mouth from hers. "This is the dumbest thing I've done lately," he complained, shifting so that the gearshift wasn't gouging his thigh. He had her sprawled over his lap. With one hand, he stroked her hair. Against his heat and hardness, she felt the frantic beat of his heart.

Claire looked up at him. "What, you want to take it back?"

"The proposal?" From the muted light of the dash, she saw his eyes were blazing blue. His voice went deep as his gaze dropped to her mouth. "Not on your life, babe."

She touched his lips with one finger and spoke softly, "There you go again, John McMollere, calling me names."

He kissed the finger, then bit it gently. "Yeah, and I've got a lot more. How about sweetheart, angel, sugar, love of my life?"

"I like the last one."

"I do love you, Claire."

She closed her eyes, feeling her heart turn over. "I love you, too, John McMollere."

"Will you marry me and stay at Sugarland with me?"

"Yes." She leaned closer and touched her lips to his.

It was a sweet kiss, tender and loving. She put her hands on both sides of his face and leaned in to deepen it.

"Wait." With his hands on her waist, he lifted her and deposited her back in her seat. "Stay there."

He got out of the Jeep and slammed the door. She watched with a puzzled little smile as he walked around to her side. "Jump out," he said after he opened the door.

"What—"

Reaching in, he lifted her and set her on the ground, then he got back in, fumbled at the edge of the seat for the lever that positioned it and shoved it as far back as he could. "Now we can do this right," he said, reaching for her.

She was suddenly on his lap again. "John! What're you doing?" She looked around frantically. "Somebody might see us."

"Nobody's gonna see us. We passed one car in the last ten miles." He managed to get her astride him and when he moved she gave a surprised little groan.

"Oh, dear."

"Uh-huh."

She sighed as he began nuzzling her throat. She felt a flush of heat and intense pleasure. With his hand pressed to the small of her back, he held her against the thick warmth of his arousal. "Good, huh?" The words came from deep in his throat, husky and low.

"Yes."

Beneath her denim skirt, his hands glided over her bare thighs, coaxing her open for him. When he touched her there, she gasped. "Kiss me, sweetheart," he told her.

Blindly, she sought his mouth. This time when they kissed, it was like spontaneous combustion. Desire exploded. Lips and tongues blended in an erotic dance. Hands fought for new territory. He disposed of her blouse and bra and groaned when her breasts spilled into his hands. Claire fumbled at his waist, trying to pull his shirttails free so that she could touch him, too, and when she finally managed it, she sighed with the pleasure of stroking sleek flesh over hard muscle and bone.

His mouth was all over—at her throat, her ear, the curve of her shoulder, then he found her breasts and the white-hot heat when he closed over her nipple drew a frenzied cry from her soul.

She threw her head back, caressing his face and neck and shoulders with frantic hands as his tongue lashed roughly, lustfully, carnally over now-sensitized areolas. She wriggled restlessly, pressing closer. He gave a satisfied grunt and she realized that he was fumbling with his jeans, freeing himself. Shuddering, she felt a dark desire that was primitive and elemental and a fierce need to know the fullness of him now.

"John . . ."

"Soon, baby, just let me—" He slipped his hands beneath her skirt and found her. Murmuring erotic words and disjointed phrases of passion and need, he stripped her of her underpants while they maneuvered for a workable position. Their lips met again in a devouring kiss. He squeezed the softness of her derriere and held her tight against his arousal.

With a whimper of want and need, she helped him lift her above his erection and then she was impaled. Her wild cry blended with his growl of satisfaction. Shuddering, he gasped her name, burying his face in the softness of her breasts.

Claire felt vulnerable and utterly possessed by the strength and power of him. Seconds passed while he let her body adjust to his invasion. Trust and love and pure joy gave her confidence. And then she began to move... tentatively. Using her knees for leverage, she gently rocked into him.

He managed a smile of sheer male delight and let her set a slow rhythm. With her arms wound around his neck, Claire grew more bold. It was a torch to his tinder. With his face pressed to her throat, he was suddenly out of control. She felt his hands tense on her waist, his body growing more urgent, his thrusts came quicker, harder, deeper. Her breath grew choppy and uneven, blending with the great gusts of his passion. She sensed he was straining to withhold his climax. Her head fell to his shoulder as a deep yearning need beckoned somewhere beyond her...so close...so close. And then in a shower of light it was there.

She came in a bright consuming storm of desire. Her sharp cry was muffled against his neck just as he found his own deep, hard, long release.

They were both too weak to move for a long—a very long—minute. Claire's body was limp and trembling. Mack held her close. Beneath her ear, his heartbeat thundered. She smiled, thinking how they must look. If anybody happened along to see them now, her reputation would be ruined.

"What?" he asked, cutting his eyes to hers. He didn't seem capable of moving.

"Just thinking that I don't act very much like a librarian anymore, do I?"

His chuckle was a low rumble beneath her ear. "You don't think librarians do it in a Jeep?"

"No."

"Not even to celebrate an engagement?"

"Not even then."

He moved a speck so that he could kiss her ear. "Then they don't know what they're missing."

A moment later, she gave a regretful sigh. "I guess we can't stay here all night, huh?"

He smiled into her hair. "Sorry, sugar."

"Okay." She eased herself back and leaned down to find her bra and shirt. Mack wouldn't let her off his lap and he was no help while she tried to put her things back on. He kept kissing her and touching her and saying ridiculously romantic, crazily erotic things to her. Then when she started to climb off, he stopped her. The light from the dash was dim, but she could see he had an unholy grin on his face.

"So, *now* is it okay to change Danny's name?"

CHAPTER FIFTEEN

THEY WERE STILL chuckling when they turned into the driveway at Sugarland. It was past ten and the house was quiet. But as Mack drove around to the garage, he saw that the barn was ablaze with light. The door was wide open and a vehicle was parked nearby. A pickup. In the blink of an eye, his good humor vanished.

"Damn it, that's Jake's pickup! And there he is with Michelle." He downshifted, turning away from the garage to head in the direction of the barn. He was there in a quarter of a minute, almost fishtailing the Jeep when he slammed on his brakes.

"The minute my back's turned, she sets up a midnight rendezvous," he grumbled, fumbling for the latch.

He already had the door open, when Claire grabbed his arm. "It's not midnight and they're hardly hidden," she said, holding him back. "Michelle's baby-sitting Danny and she knew we were expected back any minute. I'm sure there's an explanation."

"There'd better be an explanation." But Claire's words had been enough to make him stop and think. "C'mon, let's see what they have to say."

The two kids were waiting beside Jake's pickup. Jake stood staunchly by Michelle's side, clearly expecting the worst. He was a nice boy, Claire thought, but they were both going to have some explaining to do. Mack was steaming. Meeting alone at this hour was definitely a no-no.

And then she saw Michelle's tears.

Her first thought was for Danny. "What's wrong?" she asked, her heart taking off in fright. "Is Danny okay?"

Using both hands, Michelle wiped her cheeks. "He's fine. He's in the tack room playing with the kittens."

Mack's face was stern. "Two hours past his bedtime? This had better be good, Michelle."

Michelle sniffed and glanced apologetically at Jake. "Before you jump on Jake, this wasn't his idea. I called him because I just needed a shoulder to cry on. He told me you wouldn't like it."

"He was right about that. Is it your grandmother?"

She shook her head, her eyes filling again. "It's worse than that. It's *Mom!*"

"Liz?" He hesitated only a second, glancing at Claire. Some of the sternness left him. "What happened? Is she all right?"

Michelle's mouth twisted bitterly. "Of course, she's all right. She's *always* all right. It's the people in her life that aren't all right." A new gush of tears came. "What's the matter with her, Dad? Why does she do this? Does she just try to think up ways to make us miserable?"

"Whoa, honey. What are you trying to tell us?" He went to her and slipped an arm around her waist. Michelle instantly turned her face into his shirt and dissolved into stormy tears.

"Oh, D-Daddy, she's making me go b-back th-there!" she wailed.

Over her head, Mack gave Claire a bewildered look. She turned to Jake, who looked almost as miserable as Michelle. "Can you fill us in, Jake?"

"Yes, ma'am. Michelle got a call from her mother a couple of hours ago telling her to pack her things, that she had to come home. She told Michelle she'd been punished long enough and now that she and Mr. De-Bartolo were back from the cruise, they wanted Michelle in Washington where she belonged, before school starts."

"It's not fair!" Michelle cried, hanging on to Mack's shirtfront. "I don't belong there. She's only doing it to be mean."

"Wait a minute, Shelly." Mack tipped her face up. "You want to stay here? With me?"

Michelle nodded miserably. "I didn't want to at first, but now it seems like home. Danny's sweet and you're gonna be marrying Claire and she's nice. And Jake's here." She lifted a shoulder despondently. "I was starting to feel like I belonged somewhere."

Mack tucked her beneath his shoulder. "You always belonged here, Shelly. Never doubt that." Then his voice changed. "But tell me more about Liz changing her mind. You say that she decided out of the blue that it was time for you to go back to Washington?"

"Uh-huh, and I know why. It's my own fault!" She was tearing up again.

"Why is it your fault, Michelle?" Claire asked, watching the girl start to pace.

"Because I told her about you and Daddy. We talked on the phone after she got back from the cruise. Before she left, I begged her to let me come home, but that was before I knew you and Danny, Claire." She sniffed again, holding her hair away from her face before letting it fall. She looked quickly at Mack, then away. "We were always fighting then, Daddy, you remember how it was. But somehow after Claire got here, things between us were better. I guess she made both of us stop and think a little.''

"I guess she did, honey," Mack said, smiling faintly.

Michelle's expression changed. "It took me a little while to see what Mom has been doing all these years. It's like she loves to get a rise out of you, Daddy. She likes sticking it to you any way she can, even if it means everybody gets hurt, including me. Well, that day when I told her on the phone that Claire was here with Danny and I liked them both a lot and so did you, she hung up so fast.''

She gave them all a knowing look and her voice was bitter. "She only called so I'd be sure and tell you what a good time she and Victor had and how much money the trip cost and who they saw there—as if anybody here at Sugarland cares about that stupid Washington political stuff! Anyway, she called again a little while ago. I don't think she could stand sitting by knowing you might be happy, Daddy." More tears sprang to her eyes, eyes as blue as her father's. And she was looking at him with her heart in her eyes. "B-but it's so d-different now. I love you now, D-daddy!" She threw her arms around his neck, sobbing.

"I love you, too, baby."

"And I d-don't want to go back there."

"You won't have to," he said huskily. "It's okay, don't cry." Over his daughter's dark head, Mack met Claire's eyes and her heart turned over. He had such a look on his face. He held Michelle close while she sobbed piteously. "You don't have to go and live with her if you don't want to, Shelly baby. Not anymore."

She went still, then looked up at him. "I don't?"

"No, you don't." He tucked a damp curl behind her ear. "All I need to know is that you want to stay here."

"Oh, Daddy! Do you really mean it? You'd really stand up for me against Mom after I've been such a brat?"

"I really would." He ruffled her hair as if she were no older than Danny. "Just answer me this one thing. How did you guess I was going to marry Claire?"

"Oh, Daddy." Michelle laughed and wiped the last of her tears away. "It was so obvious. You two couldn't spend three minutes together without sparks flying. Anybody could see it was love at first sight."

Mack shot Claire a helpless glance.

"It's true, isn't it?" Michelle looked at them both, her smile still a little teary.

He caught Claire's hand and pulled her over, tucking his arm around her. For a second, they were lost in the look they shared. "Yeah, it's true," he said softly.

Michelle bumped Jake's arm with a knowing look. But there was some anxiety in her voice when she asked Claire, "Is it gonna be okay with you if I live here? I mean, after you're married?"

Claire looked astonished. "It's your home, Michelle. John is your father. It wouldn't be the same if you weren't here."

"Oh, Claire." Her face began to crumple again.

"Oh, no, you don't," Mack said, giving the teenager's hair a tug. "Any more tears tonight and you'll dehydrate."

She made another lightning-quick recovery. "Okay. C'mon, Jake. Let's go get Danny from the tack room. I know, I know," she said, seeing the gathering frown on Mack's face. "Jake's gotta go home now. And he will, but Danny'll want to tell him bye. He's crazy about Jake."

With a helpless shrug, Jake let her tug him away toward the rear of the barn. Claire's and Mack's eyes met. "I'm surrounded by high-powered women," he grumbled.

"She's definitely a force to be reckoned with, even now," Claire said. She gave him an affectionate hug, then teased, "But relax, Dad. In about ten years, she can take over the management of Sugarland and you can retire."

"Smart aleck." He was ready to kiss her, when Michelle and Jake came hurrying from the tack room. One look at their faces and Claire's hand went to her throat.

"What is it? Where's Danny?"

"Oh, Claire..." Michelle's face was white.

Mack turned to Jake.

"We couldn't find him, Mr. McMollere," Jake said, his young features grave. He glanced once at Claire, then held out a single small tennis shoe. "It looks like he's gone."

LATER, when Claire tried to recall the hours that followed Danny's disappearance, there was only a blank, black void. In the first frantic moments, her mind refused to accept that something so devastating could happen. Mack sent Jake and Michelle running to the house to check that Danny had not decided to go there. But deep inside, Claire knew he would never walk anywhere alone in the dark. He would never walk anywhere when he was missing a shoe.

That was when the crushing reality nearly overwhelmed her—that single, grubby little Reebok. With everything in her, she resisted the obvious. Her baby, her son, her very reason for being for over five years, could not be gone.

It's all my fault," Michelle said, her face tortured with guilt. "When Jake drove up, I left Danny in the tack room playing with the kittens. I was upset over what Mom said. I didn't even think about Danny not being safe with Jake and me standing nearby." She looked imploringly at Claire, her face tear-stained. "I'm so sorry, Claire. I wish it were me instead."

Claire covered her face with her hands, unable to reply. Mack put his arms around her. "We'll find him, sweetheart. I swear it."

Resting her head on his chest, Claire looked dumbly toward the cane fields, at their peak growth now, thick, tall, almost impenetrable. Dark green and ominous, they stretched in all directions. Her little boy was out there somewhere.

It was nearly midnight. Even if Danny were on the premises, the chances of spotting him were next to nothing. She shuddered thinking of the hazards: snakes—cane fields were overrun with snakes. And wild animals. Raccoons and possums roamed freely and they were known to carry rabies. Most chilling of all—alligators. With the abundance of water surrounding the area, alligators were frequently spotted.

Please, God, keep him safe.

Even in her prayers, she couldn't bring herself to speak the unspeakable.

Because deep in her soul, she knew Danny hadn't decided on his own to leave the barn, not with a litter of kittens to play with and Jake and Michelle nearby to entertain him. He wasn't even on Sugarland, not anymore. Claire knew as surely as she knew her own name that Glenn Thibodaux had taken her son.

"He wasn't drowned," she said in a dead voice. "I don't know how I ever believed that for a minute. He murdered Tim Landry, and because Danny saw him do it, he intends to get rid of him.''

"Thibodaux." Mack knew without asking who she was talking about. "To do that, he had to have a car. It's tough to get a strange vehicle on Sugarland property without somebody noticing."

Jake had been quiet, standing apart with his hands in his back pockets. Now he stepped forward. "It can be done, Mr. McMollere. I know a place. It's pretty deserted, too."

"I won't ask how," Mack said, shooting a glance at Michelle. "Just tell us where."

"It's where that old cypress logging road crosses the bayou. The bridge is condemned, but I've driven over it lately. It'll hold. Then you could just pull your car into some of the tall cane that begins right at the bank of the bayou and nobody'd ever know it was there. It's not a ten-minute walk from the barn."

"I remember it." Mack rubbed his cheek thoughtfully. "Glenn spent a lot of time at Sugarland when he and Carter were kids. It's logical he'd remember the spot, too."

Renewed terror filled Claire's mind. A deserted stretch of road, an old bridge crossing a deep bayou. Why would Thibodaux even hesitate? She began to tremble uncontrollably.

"There wasn't much traffic as I was driving out here tonight," Jake said, screwing up his face reflectively. "After I turned off Brewster Road, I only saw a couple of cars. I recognized two of them. But there was a Ford Explorer I didn't know. I remember because he was going pretty slow, so I passed him."

Mack was frowning. "The same vehicle was at the four-way stop when Claire and I were about five miles from Sugarland." He raised his eyebrows at Jake. "Dark, loaded, right?"

Jake nodded. "Top-of-the-line."

"I'm guessing you didn't get a look at the driver's face."

"No, sir. It was too dark."

"Yeah, same here."

Jake was still thinking. "There was a political sticker on the bumper."

"Glenn's active in politics." With his hand clamped on the back of his neck, Mack studied the ground at his feet. If Glenn Thibodaux was the one who'd murdered Tim, kidnapping the boy who was the only witness wasn't much of a stretch.

Michelle made a small sound. "Remember what Danny said the day he broke his arm? He said he saw the bad cop and the man was driving something that looked like your Jeep Cherokee, Dad. It could have been an Explorer."

"Is Glenn Thibodaux a cop?" Jake asked, looking confused.

"No."

"We're wasting time!" Claire cried, pulling away from Mack in desperation. "Danny saw a badge of some kind and assumed it meant the man was a lawman. Or he could have assumed it because of the gun. He's only five years old. As for his car, wouldn't Wayne Pagett know?" She looked at Mack. "Let's call him and tell him to put out a bulletin."

"I'll call him on my car phone. He's on his way. He'll issue an APB for the vehicle, count on it. But what we need is probable cause to pick up Glenn."

"Then shouldn't we get on it? He could be on his way to God-knows-where by now." She began to cry. "We have to do something. Now!"

Refusing to panic, Mack rousted the men who worked the sugarcane to cover the fields and grounds surrounding the house and compound. Searching the bayou would require lights and equipment not on hand at Sugarland. That was Wayne's department. He hoped to God they wouldn't need it.

WYONA WAS WAITING for them when they got to the house, awakened by the commotion. She wanted to know what was going on. Even in her despair, Claire noticed something different about the older woman. Her whole demeanor was less fragile. The look in her eye demanded honesty.

"It's Danny, Mama." Even Mack seemed to see the change. He made no attempt to keep the bad news from her. "He's missing."

"You mean he's run away?"

"We don't think so. We've got the men out searching, just in case, but there's a possibility that somebody may have taken him."

Wyona sat down. "Glenn."

With a quick glance at Claire, Mack went over and sat down beside her. "What makes you think it's Glenn, Mama?"

"Because he's evil," she said, gazing at a spot beyond Mack. For a moment, she seemed to drift back into a hazy comfort zone, but then she blinked and her eyes returned to him and Claire, clear and lucid. "With Tim gone and now Angus, I hoped that Glenn would let it be. That should have assured him and Martin that their secret was safe. They've never considered me a threat," she added as a bitter aside. "But no. When once a web of deceit is woven, the threads are ever tangling."

"What web of deceit, Mama? What secret?" Mack looked as if he wanted to shake her.

She stared momentarily at her hands in her lap. "Kimberly Ledet, of course."

"The girl in the clipping?" Claire asked.

"Yes. Glenn is responsible for her death."

Mack looked stunned. "Mama."

She removed her glasses and held them in her lap. "You're shocked." The diamond on her finger winked brilliantly as she rubbed her eyes. "Of course, it's understandable. How would I know anything about the death of a young college girl all those years ago? Well, I know about it because my son was involved and it ruined his life."

"Carter," Claire said softly.

"Yes, Carter. Of course, Carter."

Claire had been standing, unable to sit still with the terror of Danny's disappearance consuming her. Now, with a rush of compassion for Wyona, she went to the couch and sat down beside her. "What did Carter have to do with Kimberly's death, Wyona?" she asked gently. "And why does that have anything to do with Danny's disappearance?"

Wyona sighed. "It's such a long story. But I don't think there's time to spare. If Glenn has taken Danny, he's capable of heartless violence. Look at Tim."

"You know that he killed Tim?"

"I suspected it. And then when Danny recognized him, of course, I knew." She smoothed a hand over the soft material of her robe and looked again at Mack. "Pick up the phone, Mack. Call Martin. Tell him Danny's missing and that if he knows anything of Glenn's whereabouts, then he must do the right thing. If he doesn't cooperate, then I will speak to him.''

Mack stared at his mother as though he were looking at a stranger. Which wasn't far off the mark, Claire thought. He didn't move.

"John, for God's sake!" Claire cried.

He stood up. "I'm calling Wayne. He'll handle Martin." Without another word, he headed for the telephone.

Claire touched Wyona's hand. "Thank you."

The woman's eyes were bright with tears. "Don't thank me yet. I should have spoken up before Danny was dragged into danger. Keeping Carter's secrets means nothing now." Her voice was filled with pain. "I just couldn't believe that it would go this far!"

At the telephone, Mack was speaking to Wayne Pagett, but he was looking at his mother. After relating what Wyona suspected, he nodded once or twice, spoke again tersely, answered a question and then told Wayne that he would wait to hear from him. He hung up and went back to the women.

"They patched me through to Wayne in a patrol car on his way here. He's not too far from Martin Thibodaux's house now. He'll swing by there and see what the man has to say to all this, then get back to me here. Now, Mama..." He sat down again beside Wyona. "What did Carter have to do with Kimberly's death?"

"In a sense, nothing. At least, not directly."

"Mama—"

She closed her eyes. "I hoped I'd never have to tell this, Mack."

"There's Danny to think of now, Mama. He's five years old. Wherever he is, he's scared. You have to tell us everything."

"Yes, I know. And I love Danny, I do."

"So what about Carter?"

"He was at the hunting camp that weekend with Glenn and Tim Landry."

"Hunting camp." Mack pushed a hand through his hair. "Would that be Martin's camp, the cabin where he and Dad went every chance they got?"

"Yes," she said bitterly. "After it happened, I would have died before ever stepping foot in that place again, but Angus continued to go when Martin invited him. I think it was a way of reminding us that we were just as involved in that black deed as Martin and Glenn."

"Glenn murdered Kimberly Ledet?" Mack asked incredulously.

"Not exactly murder. He made a secret date with her that night, but he didn't tell the girl that two of his friends were going to be at the hunting camp, too. Later, Carter said Kimberly was a little nervous at finding herself alone with three young men. Then they all got a little drunk—you know how it can be with college kids. Kimberly got scared and ran to the dock and got in the boat. She must have thought she'd be safe in a boat on the water." Wyona rubbed her forehead wearily. "At least, she'd be safer there than she would be at the mercy of three young men who were drunk.

"She managed to get the boat launched, but not before Glenn jumped in with her. He laughed in the face of her tears, so Carter told us later. While Glenn was trying to force her to have sex, the boat turned over."

"Trying to rape her, you mean," Mack said evenly.

"Oh, yes. Dear God, yes," Wyona whispered in a voice that still revealed horror. The hand at her throat was trembling now. But they weren't the aimless tremors that Claire had seen since she'd known her. It was the sick despair of a woman who has carried a dark burden for too many years.

"Then he drowned her to keep her from telling," Mack guessed.

"No. Carter swears that he and Tim watched from the dock as Glenn struggled with her and the boat turned over."

"It was nighttime," Claire whispered, imagining the girl's horror.

"Yes, and they couldn't find her. They searched and searched. They dived into the water, but it was cold."

"December, a few days before Christmas." Claire recalled the date from the clipping.

"And they just walked away?" Mack asked with anger and disgust. "They decided it was no use, so what the hell, is that the way it was?"

Now his mother was weeping, pitiful sobs of guilt and regret. Claire put her arms around her. "It's all right, Wyona. It's in the past. There's nothing you could have done."

Wyona was shaking her head. "I could have said something. That girl's poor parents. It was Christmas. When Angus told me, I never enjoyed another Christmas and I never deserved to. It was my punishment!"

As well as becoming neurotic and turning into a pathetic wreck, Claire thought sadly. By losing interest in everything and obsessing over Carter—spoiled, selfish, unworthy Carter. What a price to pay for keeping secrets.

"So what did you do about it, Mama?"

Claire had never seen Mack so stern.

"Martin fixed everything." Wyona wiped her eyes with a tissue and put her glasses back on. "The boys called him, of course. Or rather Glenn did. Carter wasn't about to call Angus. He said he knew Angus would pitch a fit. He'd launch into their same old quarrel. Why couldn't Carter be more like his brother? Mack would never have gotten involved in anything so shoddy. So reprehensible. And, of course, that was true.''

"This wasn't just shoddy, Mama,'' Mack said. "It was criminal.''

"Well, of course, we knew that. All of us. And that's why Martin got busy trying to fix it. He sent the boys back to school, that minute. Right then and there. He removed every trace of evidence that anybody had been there that weekend.'' She looked sadly at her hands. "Nature was on our side, as well. The girl's body was found two days later a long way from Martin's camp.''

Mack was staring with astonishment at his mother. "You knew this all along, Mama, and you said nothing?''

"No, not then. Angus didn't tell me until I overheard him berating Carter for having the affair. Angus reminded him of that tragedy and asked him how many times would he mess up before he would straighten up and be a man?''

"Is that when Carter came to see me and wanted custody of Danny?'' Claire asked.

Wyona nodded, shamefaced. "I think so.'' The look she gave Claire was imploring. "He was finally doing something he thought was right, I know it.'' Wyona wiped her eyes again.

Mack stood up suddenly, storming away from them and winding up at the window. He turned to his mother. "Do you realize what you've done, Mama? Glenn's not going to leave something like this up to chance, hoping you won't talk. Eventually, everybody who had a hand in Kimberly Ledet's death will have to go. The miracle is that he waited this long."

"Why would he kill Tim in broad daylight?" Claire asked.

"Who the hell knows?" Weary impatience made Mack sound abrupt.

"Angus and Martin talked about that." Wyona looked at Claire apologetically. "The day of the luncheon. They thought the two of them—Tim and Glenn—must have decided to go and see Claire at the hotel. Martin admitted Glenn could have found out that Claire was coming to see us, Martin being our attorney, you see. They must have wondered whether Claire knew, whether Carter had told her about Kimberly. As long as she was in Houston, she wasn't much of a threat, but if she knew, she would have to be silenced. At least that's the way Glenn would have looked at it."

Claire was shaking her head. "Carter never breathed a word of this to me."

"It's hardly the kind of secret you tell anybody under any circumstances," Mack said, and his voice had an underlying hardness. He was reeling from what he'd learned about his family. "What we've got to do now is to make sure Glenn doesn't have a chance to do anything else."

Before he'd finished talking, he was reaching for the phone and punching in a number. "Patch me in to the sheriff," he snapped to whoever answered. "Yeah . . . right . . . okay." He paused. "It's me, Wayne. What've you got?" Holding Claire's gaze from across the room, he listened for half a minute, then nodded. "Yeah, I'll meet you there. I'm closer than you. I know where it's at." He hung up.

"We're going to the camp."

Claire jumped up. "Is Danny there?"

"Wayne seems to think the odds are good that he is. Martin's pretty shaken, but Wayne said he didn't seem too surprised. Claims he's been concerned about his son lately. That ever since Tim's funeral, Glenn's been strange." He glanced at his mother. "Martin seems to think that Glenn could have taken Danny out to the hunting camp."

Wyona gave a helpless gasp. "Oh, no."

"I'm meeting them out there."

"I'm going, too," Claire told him.

"One more thing." Mack touched Claire's arm. "Martin told Wayne that Glenn had an accident last year when he went skiing. Broke his wrist and two fingers. He was left with a scar on the back of his hand."

Claire gave a wordless sound.

"We're wasting time." Mack caught her arm and gently urged her toward the door. Wyona was weeping softly as it closed behind them.

CHAPTER SIXTEEN

IT TOOK THIRTY-FIVE grueling minutes to drive to Martin Thibodaux's cabin on the bayou. With every mile, Claire's mind teemed with unspeakable pictures: Danny begging for his mommy, Danny abandoned in a boggy swamp, Danny held hostage by a psychopath—

But her mind stopped there. She couldn't complete a picture so horrible. She felt such devastating fear that the world narrowed down to the night, the centerline in the blacktop rushing toward them in the glare of the headlights and Mack beside her, stern and silent, lost in his own thoughts. She could only imagine how he must feel learning that his parents had harbored such a secret about Carter for so many years.

"We'll find Danny," he said suddenly. "He'll be okay, Claire."

He didn't know that. He couldn't. But her heart ached with anguish and the desperate hope that he might be right. Some part of her realized that Mack needed to end the chain of wrongdoing that was begun all those years ago when Kimberly Ledet died.

So many people gone. Please God, no more.

"That's it, just ahead," Mack said, slowing down.

The road was not marked except for one small red reflector mounted on a wooden stake to prevent overshooting the turn. Mack braked to take it, then accelerated again, spewing gravel as the tires gained traction. He'd driven with single-minded intensity, more than once drawing a muted gasp from Claire when it had seemed the Jeep would surely spin out of control. She guessed the trip would have taken much longer if he hadn't driven like a man possessed.

Every second that ticked by was a gamble on Danny's life.

A few yards along and the road narrowed, overhung with tall, dense trees. Even on a sunny day, there would be little light along here, Claire thought. And what a good place to hide. Nobody could find it unless they knew it was there. She shivered at what Kimberly Ledet must have felt all those years ago.

She couldn't let herself think of Danny's fear when forced to make this trip with a stranger he'd witnessed shoot and kill a man.

Dear God, don't let us be too late.

Suddenly, Mack shut off the headlights and slowed the Jeep to a crawl. "The camp is another quarter of a mile ahead. Wayne should be waiting around this bend," he said.

Another fifty yards and they stopped. Claire saw movement in the darkness ahead and realized that several police cruisers were parked in the middle of the road.

Except for the din of nature at night, there was absolute silence—no radio noise or human sounds. Two men stood behind one of the cruisers. No one else could be seen.

"That's Martin Thibodaux with the sheriff," she murmured, wrapping her arms around herself.

"Yeah. I assume he's here to try and reason with Glenn."

If he's in there and *if* Danny's with him and *if* it's not too late. But she forced the negative thoughts down. Danny must be in there and it couldn't be too late.

The sound of Mack's door opening seemed magnified in the total silence although he'd done it with care. He closed it enough to douse the dome light. Her heart pounding, Claire got out, doing the same with the passenger-side door, then caught up with him as he went toward the two men.

"Wayne." Mack greeted the sheriff quietly. To Martin Thibodaux, he gave only a stony look.

Martin did not miss the slight. He had a handkerchief in his hand, which looked eerily white in the darkness. As he mopped his forehead, Claire could see, even in the dark, that he was shaken. Sensing her scrutiny, the lawyer looked at her. "I'm terribly sorry about this, Ms. Woodson. I never dreamed Glenn would go this far. I'm sure your little boy is okay. I don't think Glenn would—"

"Can it, Martin," Mack snapped. "Just get your butt up to that cabin and tell that psychopath son of yours that if Danny's not out of there in about ten seconds, it won't be Wayne here he'll have to answer to. It'll be me."

Wayne touched his arm. "Hold on, Mack. Save your outrage for later. Right now, we need to get the lay of the land. Could be Glenn's not even here. Martin's going up to the cabin to check."

"We're not staying back here, are we, Sheriff?" Claire asked anxiously. "If Danny's in there, I want to be close by."

Wayne sighed. "I guess it's useless asking you to let me and my men handle this, Claire. Come on." He signaled to men who were apparently fanned out in the woods, then they started walking.

It seemed only a few minutes until the cabin materialized in the darkness. It was in a clearing with no other dwellings in sight. A classic Creole design of weathered cypress, it had a high-pitched roof and a deep front wraparound porch with a railing. One whole side was overgrown with ancient wisteria. It was almost picturesque in its simplicity. The front door was in the center, with windows on either side. No light was visible anywhere. It appeared empty. Claire's heart sank. She made a small, anguished sound and Mack's arm came around her waist.

"He's in there, sweetheart," he whispered, his lips against her ear as he spoke. "He can't afford to have any light showing."

Wayne nodded at Martin Thibodaux. "You take it from here, Martin. I don't have to remind you what's at stake. Your son has burned his bridges. If I believed in fate, I'd say that Danny being Carter's son has some significance here. Go in there and do what you can to see that no other tragedy happens."

After a brief hesitation, Martin gave a curt nod and started toward the cabin. His footsteps were slow, almost wary. Was he afraid of his own son? Claire wondered with horror. At that moment, the cloud bank obscuring the moon parted and the house was suddenly bathed in silvery light.

Straining to see better, Claire held her breath. Then her heart jumped. Through the window, there was movement of some kind. She reached out blindly to tell Mack and found only empty space.

Spinning around, she realized he was gone. He'd simply melted into the darkness. She was left standing with Wayne, who looked at her and put his finger to his lips, shaking his head.

What was going on?

She forced herself to concentrate as Martin stepped up onto the wooden porch, making no effort now to keep his approach quiet. The door was shoved open abruptly and in a flurry of movement Glenn appeared.

"Daddy, Daddy, it's me. Help me!"

Claire blinked in confusion. The voice was not Danny's, but Michelle's. Glenn Thibodaux had an arm clamped across her throat, holding her against his body as a shield. He had a gun.

"Michelle." Claire breathed the girl's name. Her thoughts whirled questioningly. How? When? Michelle was supposed to be at Sugarland waiting for them, wasn't she? And where was Danny? Dear God, where was Danny? She looked around, searching desperately for Mack.

"I've got her, Pagett!" It was Glenn Thibodaux. "You try to get me, she gets it. I'm serious here, man."

Keeping close to the door, not risking edging farther onto the porch, Thibodaux held the gun briefly aloft, then shoved it roughly against Michelle's temple. She whimpered in pain.

"Take it easy, Glenn." Wayne's voice was calm.

"I'm fresh out of options, Sheriff, so don't do anything stupid. I need to get out of here and this little bitch is gonna be my ticket to do it."

Martin seemed to come to life. He put out a hand. "Glenn, you've got to give this up, son. It's too late."

"Shut up, Dad!" Thibodaux said savagely. "I should have guessed you'd wimp out. Another ten minutes and I'd have been out of here."

"Where's the boy, Thibodaux?" Wayne called out. Behind him, Claire had both hands pressed to her mouth.

"The brat got away, climbed out of the window with the help of Miss Teenage Twit here, then disappeared. Dark as it was, I had to let him go." He laughed harshly. "But what the hell, one hostage is as good as another. Right, baby?" He stroked the gun barrel down Michelle's cheek. "What I need's a ticket out of here and the McMollere princess is just as good as Carter's bastard, huh, Sheriff?"

"Maybe. Then again, maybe not, Thibodaux." Appearing relaxed, his weapon still holstered, Wayne slipped a cigar from his shirt pocket and casually stuck it in his mouth. "Seems to me you still need the boy. It was his testimony that was gonna put you in Angola."

Beside him, Claire was horrified. Why was he reminding Glenn of Angola? It was one of the toughest, vilest prisons in America.

"I'm not going to Angola!"

"Well, with that little girl as a hostage, you're hardly headed for the Bahamas," Wayne drawled.

"Glenn, give it up," Martin begged.

"Shut up, old man!"

"Dad—dee—ee—" Michelle's cry was abruptly shut off when Thibodaux jerked his arm tight against her throat.

"I'm warning you! Where's McMollere?" Thibodaux looked around wildly as though expecting Mack to emerge. "Show yourself, damn it! Otherwise your little girl is liable to get hurt. I am flat out of patience, big guy."

"I'm over here, Thibodaux." Mack stepped from the deep shadows by the side of the porch.

"Good. Smart." Thibodaux turned slightly toward him, keeping Michelle close. "I don't have the patience to play these little games. I'm outta here as soon as you folks clear a path for me and my new girlfriend."

"Glenn, son, it's too late." Martin took a step closer, his hand out in appeal. "Let the girl go."

Thibodaux laughed. "And then what, Dad? Give myself up? You don't get it, do you? I'd spend the next decade in Angola for shooting that pansy, Tim. So...no, I don't think so."

"Why did you shoot Tim?" Mack asked in a conversational tone.

"The idiot was gonna blab everything. Said he couldn't live with the secret any longer." He hissed with disgust. "Dumb jerk."

"Everything about what? The rape of Kimberly Ledet?" Mack asked.

"I didn't rape her and I didn't kill her, either. It was an accident, one of those things." Thibodaux rubbed his cheek momentarily against Michelle's hair. "Tim knew I was at the hotel to find out if Carter had said anything to Claire. Be just like Carter to do something stupid like that. He always did talk too much. Can you believe Tim was gonna go see Pagett, tell him everything, whether Claire knew anything or not? His conscience was hurting," Glenn sneered. "Is that stupid, or what?"

"You thought Carter might have told Claire what happened at the camp?" Mack asked.

Glenn made an impatient sound. "Hell, I didn't know whether he did or not. I was there to find out, but I could see that Tim was gonna blab to the sheriff, anyway." His mouth twisted with disgust. "I had to kill him. It was his own dumb fault."

For a few seconds, nobody moved. Thibodaux seemed to realize how much he'd revealed. His father was staring at him in total shock. For the first time, his laugh was less cocky.

"Let the girl go, Glenn," Wayne said quietly. "Give me a statement about Kimberly's...accident and it'll go easier on you."

"Go to hell."

"Daddy, I think I'm gonna be sick," Michelle said weakly. Then, before Thibodaux could react, she began to make little coughing sounds as she went limp, dead weight in his arms.

"Now, Jake!" Mack yelled.

Behind Thibodaux, a dark form hurtled through the open door, hitting him at the knees. With a startled bellow, he went down in a tangle of arms and legs. Martin recoiled, stumbling back on the steps. Watching in horror, Claire saw the gun fly across the porch floor as Mack vaulted over the waist-high railing. He kicked it out into the tangled wisteria, then bent and plucked his daughter from the melee. He set her on her feet and she threw her arms around him, burying her face in his shirtfront.

He pressed her head into his chest. "Shelly, Shelly..."

"I'm okay, Daddy. I'm not really sick."

Trembling, shaken, scared within an inch of his life, Mack stood with his arms around her and thanked God. "You can tell me later how you got here, young lady," he growled, "but right now, go out there where Claire is standing and see if you can stay out of trouble."

"Okay, Daddy." Uncharacteristically meek, Michelle did as she was told.

Jake was astride Thibodaux, who was facedown on the floor, his arm forced up behind him at a painful angle. Sternly, Mack told Jake he could let go as half a dozen uniformed men exploded onto the porch. When

Thibodaux went down, they'd charged from the woods and raced for the porch, their weapons ready to fire. One of the deputies grabbed a handful of shirt and hauled Thibodaux to his feet. Mack faced him, his expression so forbidding that Thibodaux instinctively tried to step backward.

"Where's the boy?"

Thibodaux stared stonily into the woods. "I told you. He took off in the dark when the girl boosted him out through the window."

"Where's my son?" Claire screamed, flying up the porch steps. With her nails bared, she was intent on scratching the eyes out of the man who'd taken him. He would tell her where Danny was or she would personally—

Mack put out a hand to stop her.

"He's okay, Claire," Jake said quickly. He put his two fingers in his mouth and whistled shrilly. "Come on down, Danny!"

"Okay," came the faint response.

As one, the crowd looked up. The sound of scrabbling feet on roof shingles gave way to the short grunts and pantings of a small boy. Two short legs appeared, scuttling over the rain gutters to dangle in midair in a search for something to get his feet on. In his jeans and only one Reebok, Danny hung suspended for a second before Mack jerked forward and grabbed him around his knees. "Whoa, hotshot, I've gotcha."

"Oh, Danny, Danny..." Claire reached for him, snatching him away from Mack, hugging him as if she'd never let him go. Tearfully, she kissed his face and ear and hair and then his face again, then hugged him some more. Until finally, from his wiggling and squirming and the dire embarrassment on his face, she realized she would have to let him go. "Are you okay?" she asked anxiously. "Did you hurt your arm?"

"I'm okay, Mommy, you don't have to cry. My arm's fine. Jake and Michelle got me away from the bad cop."

"I'm crying because I'm happy," she told him, taking a handkerchief from Mack.

Michelle ruffled his hair. "You were very brave up there, Danny-boy. You did just what Jake told you."

"That bad cop didn't know I was up there all that time!" Danny cried, grinning. He watched while Wayne's deputies cuffed and hauled a sullen Thibodaux toward one of the cruisers, now pulsing its bright blue flashers.

"How did you get up there?" Mack asked.

Michelle and Jake exchanged a sheepish look. As usual, it was Jake who was first to step up to the plate. "The truth is, we screwed up, sir. It came out all right, but we were real lucky." He glanced at Michelle. "I made the mistake of saying I knew how to get to the Thibodaux camp by the bayou. We decided to try and get there fast, just in case."

"That's not how it was." Michelle was shaking her head. "Jake's trying to keep me out of trouble."

"As usual," Mack said dryly.

Michelle gave her dad an apologetic shrug. "It was my fault Danny got snatched. I figured I owed it to him and Claire to try and rescue him. Jake said flat no. But I was going whether he went with me or not. Then I started the boat from the dock at Sugarland and Jake had to go or stand by while I went alone."

"We got here before anybody else," Jake said, picking up the story. "We snuck up to the back bedroom window, but it was too high to crawl into and too small."

"For Jake, not me. *If* I stood on Jake's shoulders," Michelle said, her blue eyes bright.

Jake slipped his hands into his back pockets. "I boosted her up and she crawled into the room, then passed Danny out to me. He'd been left in the bedroom by himself while Thibodaux was making phone calls from his cellular trying to get a plane ride to Mexico."

"How do you know that?"

"We could hear him, plain as day," Michelle said.

"And then what?"

"I passed Danny through the window to Jake and I guess we must have made some noise, because that's when Glenn burst in and saw me." She looked toward the cruiser where Thibodaux sat. "Fortunately, he thought I was alone." She was shaking her head. "He didn't know Jake was with me, and when he looked out the bedroom window, there was no sign of Danny. Remember, it was pitch dark!"

"How'd you get Danny on the roof?"

"It was brilliant!" Michelle crowed.

Jake gave her a severe look. "It was pure panic. Thibodaux was gonna be out looking for Danny any minute. So I boosted him up onto the roof fast, and climbed up there myself. There was that big, thick vine growing against the side of the building." He gestured and they all looked.

"Wisteria," Claire murmured, her hands on Danny's chest, holding him against her thighs. She couldn't bring herself to turn him loose now that she had him safe again.

"Thibodaux was out looking all over, but he never checked the roof. So I figured Danny'd be safe there until y'all got here, because my next problem was to try and rescue Michelle."

"Like I said, the bedroom window was too small for Jake to squeeze into," Michelle explained.

"I had no chance but to come in from the back door. What took so long was waiting for Thibodaux to get distracted."

"It really distracted him when his dad appeared," Michelle said. "Boy, was he ticked off! He just knew Mr. Thibodaux had led the cops to him. He said some words I've never even heard in the movies!"

"He cussed a lot before I got rescued," Danny said, wanting to get into the conversation. "I bit him when he kidnapped me from the tack room. That made him mad. I told him I hoped it made a scar to match the one on his other hand."

Everybody laughed.

"Then I told him I saw that picture with him and my daddy in it and that's how we knew he was the one who shot that man at the hotel."

Mack and Claire exchanged an alarmed look.

"If you ever get kidnapped again, maybe you shouldn't do so much talking," Michelle advised him.

"But if I do, you and Jake could rescue me again," Danny said.

"Michelle could have gotten hurt, too, Danny," Claire said, quietly admonishing.

"Your mom's right, Danny. We were lucky." Michelle looked at Claire. "Now that it's all over, I realize it could all have ended in disaster, big-time. But I was so upset because I felt responsible for Danny's being kidnapped that I had to do something."

Claire gave her a warm hug. "It's okay. Everything did turn out all right and we were all lucky. Let's just be thankful it's all over." She looked up and smiled into Mack's blue, blue eyes.

Danny tugged on her hand. "C'mon, Mommy, I gotta check on the kittens and my pony. Let's go home."

Mack winked at her. "I don't think he means Houston."

"You're right." Leaning her head against his arm, she sighed with happiness. "Thank goodness."

EVERYONE WAS SETTLED and the house was finally quiet when Claire slipped out. It was nearly dawn. Beyond the gently waving tops of the sugarcane, a rose-pink sky gave a soft glow to the fresh, new day. She drew a deep breath and smiled as Mack materialized out of the shadows.

He held out his arms and without a word, she stepped into them and was enfolded next to his heart.

"It's been a long night," he said, kissing the top of her head. "You must be dead on your feet."

She didn't reply for a second, listening to the even, heavy thud of his heartbeat beneath her ear. "Uh-huh. But first, I wanted to watch the sunrise and count my blessings."

"I had the same thought."

For a few moments, they stood, swaying and thinking, enjoying the beauty of the new morning and the joy of being together alone...touching.

"We were so lucky," she whispered.

"God, yes."

Although she was gazing at Wyona's rose garden, Claire was seeing the dark, forbidding waters of a bayou. "It's sad...so many tragedies stemming from that one night all those years ago."

"Yeah. I'm still trying to take it in."

"The girl's death, your mother's mental health, Tim's spiral into alcoholism, his murder, your father's fatal stroke, Glenn's brutality—what a price paid by everyone in keeping that ugly secret."

"Martin told me tonight that he was the person Dad was talking to on the phone when he had the stroke. Dad called to tell him that their secret wasn't secret anymore. That you knew about Kimberly."

Claire frowned. "I didn't, not really, but I was getting close. If Angus hadn't died, I probably would have put it all together very soon using what Wyona said."

"It was only a matter of time, and Martin realized that. He called Glenn and Glenn went ballistic. He knew he would have to get Danny."

"But it was already too late."

Mack was shaking his head. "I think by that time, he'd lost it. Killing Tim was really stupid."

"One thing puzzles me. Remember the badge that Danny saw, making us assume the shooter was a cop? Where did Glenn get a badge?"

"He sometimes served on an honorary security detail for the governor. Maybe he planned to use it that day to intimidate you or something. Who knows?" He was thoughtful, his gaze fixed on a point in the brightening sky. "Carter seems to be the only one who escaped."

"I don't think he escaped." Claire rubbed her hand over his heart. "I think that by escaping the consequences that night, a pattern was established in Carter's life that eventually ruined everything—his marriage, his role as a good son, his chance at being a father, even his career. From what I've learned about him, Carter never distinguished himself in anything."

"Unlike Thibodaux. If you hadn't come to town and he hadn't gotten spooked over what you knew or didn't know, he probably would have gone on to a very successful career in politics."

Claire turned her nose into his chest and happily breathed in the scent of him. "But I did and I'm glad."

Mack leaned back, searching her face. "Can we put this behind us, sweetheart?"

She knew he meant Carter and the affair that had cost her so much personally. And Danny's close call, which circled back to Carter again. Could she come into a family with that kind of history? She smiled. How could she not if she wanted John McMollere?

"Yes."

There was a second when his hands on her waist tightened almost painfully. Then his arms went fully around her and he swung her about, kissing her soundly.

Birds were chirping now. A blue jay chattered noisily nearby. A mockingbird trilled a sweet song from the pear tree somewhere behind the vegetable garden. In the distance, a crop duster's airplane took off, its engine revving powerfully over the cane fields. The day's early rose freshness was already threatened by the heat and mugginess of late summer. It would be another hot one.

Sugarland.

Home, now and always.

EPILOGUE

SOMEBODY WAS PLAYING music, but Mack barely noticed. It was background just as everything else at that moment in the church was background—the crowd, the flowers, the candles, the softly beautiful colors shining through stain-glass windows in bright December sunshine.

He swallowed, resisting the urge to pull at the stiff collar of his shirt to ease the constriction in his throat. It had been a long time since he'd worn a tuxedo and it was no more comfortable now as then. Looking straight ahead, he flexed his shoulders in the perfectly tailored jacket and recrossed his hands just below the cummerbund, but he couldn't get a glimpse of his watch. Shouldn't the ceremony be starting? Was something wrong? Had she changed her mind? He fixed his gaze on that one spot in the back of the church and willed her to appear.

"Relax, you gotta few minutes yet." Wayne, the very picture of a relaxed best man, spoke from the side of his mouth. He bumped Mack's elbow with his own. "Nobody said this would be easy."

Mack swore to get his own back. And it wouldn't be long. Wayne's own nuptials to Jake's mother were coming up in February. See how relaxed he'd feel when the shoe was on the other foot.

At last there was some movement in the back, but it was his mother, not his bride. Wyona came down the aisle on Jake's arm. The boy looked almost as uncomfortable in his tux as Mack felt in his. Wyona met Mack's eyes and smiled. No need to ask how she felt about his marriage to Claire.

Then beside him, Wayne chuckled fondly. "Would you look at this—two little angels."

Mack felt a rush of pride and joy. His children began the slow walk down the aisle—Michelle in a wine-dark dress and Danny in a miniature black tuxedo just like Mack's. Catching his eye, his daughter gave him an impudent wink, while Danny grinned. The boy's adoption was not final, but it would be soon. And Michelle was now a permanent part of his life. It had taken a trip to Washington, but Liz had finally given grudging permission.

"Hey, now *there's* a beautiful redhead."

But Wayne's taunt went unheard as the music swelled into the traditional song and Mack's gaze locked on his bride. She was radiant in candlelight satin and lace. Sunshine from the high arched window struck her hair and turned it into dark fire. It was caught on top of her head, but little curls dangled at her nape. The style was sexy and slightly old-fashioned and it suited her, he decided. Sometimes. Desire stirred at the thought of how her hair felt. How it looked fanned out on his pillow. She looked right at him and smiled softly, her mouth parting as if waiting for his kiss. Everything about her pleased him. He had never loved a woman as he loved Claire.

And after today she would be his.

Now she was only a step or two away and his heart seemed too big for his chest. He reached for her hand and together they faced forward. Then the beautiful words were spoken that would join them forever.

"Dearly beloved . . ."

Merry Christmas, Baby!

A romantic collection filled with the magic
of Christmas and the joy of children.

SUSAN WIGGS, Karen Young and
Bobby Hutchinson bring you Christmas wishes,
weddings and romance, in a charming
trio of stories that will warm up your
holiday season.

MERRY CHRISTMAS, BABY! also contains
Harlequin's special gift to you—a set of
FREE GIFT TAGS included in every book.

Brighten up your holiday season with
MERRY CHRISTMAS, BABY!

Available in November at
your favorite retail store.

Look us up on-line at: http://www.romance.net

MCB

The collection of the year!
NEW YORK TIMES BESTSELLING AUTHORS

Linda Lael Miller
Wild About Harry

Janet Dailey
Sweet Promise

Elizabeth Lowell
Reckless Love

Penny Jordan
Love's Choices

and featuring
Nora Roberts
The Calhoun Women

This special trade-size edition features four of the wildly
popular titles in the Calhoun miniseries together in
one volume—a true collector's item!

Pick up these great authors and a chance to win
a weekend for two in New York City at the
Marriott Marquis Hotel on Broadway! We'll pay
for your flight, your hotel—even a Broadway show!

Available in December at your favorite retail outlet.

NEW YORK
MARQUIS

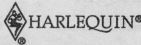 

NYT1296-R

You are cordially invited to a

HOMETOWN REUNION

September 1996—August 1997

Bad boys, cowboys, babies. Feuding families,
arson, mistaken identity, a mom on the run...
Where can you find romance and adventure?
Tyler, Wisconsin, that's where!

So join us in this not-so-sleepy little town and
experience the love, the laughter and the
tears of those who call it home.

WELCOME TO A
HOMETOWN REUNION

The Murphys and the Stirlings have been
feuding for fifty years—ever since Magdalena
left Clarence at the altar, or vice versa.
Two generations later, Sandy Murphy and
Drew Stirling are unwilling partners in an
advertising campaign, and sparks fly. Everyone
in Tyler is wondering if history will repeat itself.

***Love and War* by Peg Sutherland,**
Available in November 1996
at your favorite retail store.

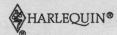

HARLEQUIN®

Look us up on-line at: http://www.romance.net   HTR3

HARLEQUIN ®

Scandals

A passionate story of romance, where bold, daring characters set out to defy their world of propriety and strict social codes.

"Scandals—a story that will make your heart race and your pulse pound. Spectacular!"
—Suzanne Forster

"Devon is daring, dangerous and altogether delicious."
—Amanda Quick

Don't miss this wonderful full-length novel from Regency favorite Georgina Devon.

Available in December, wherever Harlequin books are sold.

REBECCA

43 LIGHT STREET

YORK

FACE TO FACE

Bestselling author Rebecca York returns to "43 Light Street"
for an original story of past secrets, deadly deceptions—and
the most intimate betrayal.

She woke in a hospital—with amnesia...and with child.
According to her rescuer, whose striking face is the last
image she remembers, she's Justine Hollingsworth. But
nothing about her life seems to fit, except for the baby
inside her and Mike Lancer's arms around her. Consumed
by forbidden passion and racked by nameless fear, she
must discover if she is Justine...or the victim of some mind
game. Her life—and her unborn child's—depends on it....

Don't miss *Face To Face*—Available in October, wherever
Harlequin books are sold.

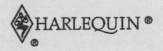

HARLEQUIN ®

®

43FTF

Look us up on-line at: http://www.romance.net

1997
Reader's Engagement Book
A calendar of important dates
and anniversaries for readers to use!

Informative and entertaining—with notable
dates and trivia highlighted throughout the year.

Handy, convenient, pocketbook size to help you
keep track of your own personal important dates.

Added bonus—contains $5.00 worth of coupons
for upcoming Harlequin and Silhouette books.
This calendar more than pays for itself!

Available beginning in November at
your favorite retail outlet.

HARLEQUIN ®   Silhouette®